Highest Praise for
John Lutz

"John Lutz knows how to make you shiver."
—Harlan Coben

"Lutz offers up a heart-pounding roller coaster of a tale."
—Jeffery Deaver

"John Lutz is one of the masters of the police novel."
—Ridley Pearson

"John Lutz is a major talent."
—John Lescroart

"I've been a fan for years."
—T. Jefferson Parker

"John Lutz just keeps getting better and better."
—Tony Hillerman

"Lutz ranks with such vintage masters of big-city murder as Lawrence Block and Ed McBain."
—St. Louis Post-Dispatch

"Lutz is among the best."
—San Diego Union

"Lutz knows how to seize and hold the reader's imagination."
—Cleveland Plain Dealer

"It's easy to see why he's won an Edgar and two Shamuses."
—Publishers Weekly

ALSO BY JOHN LUTZ

Slaughter

Frenzy

Carnage: The Prequel to "Frenzy" (e-short)

Twist

Pulse

Switch (e-short)

Serial

Mister X

Urge to Kill

Night Kills

In for the Kill

Chill of Night

Fear the Night

Darker Than Night

Night Victims

The Night Watcher

The Night Caller

Final Seconds (with David August)

The Ex

Single White Female

Available from Kensington Publishing Corp. and Pinnacle Books

JOHN LUTZ

THE HONORABLE TRAITORS

A THOMAS LAKER THRILLER

PINNACLE BOOKS
Kensington Publishing Corp.
www.kensingtonbooks.com

PINNACLE BOOKS are published by

Kensington Publishing Corp.
119 West 40th Street
New York, NY 10018

All Kensington titles, imprints, and distributed lines are available at special quantity discounts for bulk purchases for sales promotions, premiums, fund-raising, educational, or institutional use. Special book excerpts or customized printings can also be created to fit specific needs. For details, write or phone the office of the Kensington sales manager: Kensington Publishing Corp., 119 West 40th Street, New York, NY 10018, attn: Sales Department; phone 1-800-221-2647.

ISBN-13: 978-0-7860-4093-3
ISBN-10: 0-7860-4093-9

First printing: February 2018

10 9 8 7 6 5 4 3 2 1

Printed in the United States of America

First electronic edition: February 2018

ISBN-13: 978-0-7860-4094-0
ISBN-10: 0-7860-4094-7

For Barbara

1

Try to look into the NSA, and you see only yourself.

The thought struck Laker as he drove up to the headquarters of the National Security Agency, a big cube of black glass. In it he saw the reflection of the row of flags in front of the building and the cars in the parking lot, including the one he was driving, a white van from the motor pool.

The mirror effect would seem ironic to members of the public, especially those who valued their constitutional right to privacy, and thought the NSA didn't. But members of the public couldn't get this far, couldn't even get through the gate.

Laker had only driven over from another building in the complex. He was one of the NSA's own. The agency's possible abuse of its considerable powers didn't worry him.

Shouldn't worry him, anyway.

She was waiting at the curb in front of the main doors, right where he'd been told she would be: a slender woman of thirty, in the sort of dark pantsuit favored by federal employees. Her auburn hair was gathered in a knot at the nape of her neck. Rather casually gathered, for tendrils were floating in the breeze. She was a classic beauty, as he'd also been told. Oval face, long, straight nose, wide-set dark eyes. She looked at the approaching van and didn't recognize it. Looked at the tall man getting out, in a blue suit, with dark hair and neatly trimmed beard, and didn't recognize him, either.

"Ava North?" he asked.

As he stepped onto the curb in front of her, she unconsciously fell back a little. People often did. Laker had played college football and still looked as if he were wearing shoulder pads. He tended to loom. Then there was the way he turned his head a bit to the left and looked at people askance, as if listening hard to what they said and not believing any of it.

In fact, he was only favoring his good ear. He was mostly deaf in the other one, the result of the IED blast that had flipped his Humvee in Baghdad.

"Bill couldn't make it," he explained to Ava. "Something came up at the last minute. He asked me to drive you. I'm Tom."

Her eyes narrowed. "I'll need more than Tom."

"Thomas F. Laker. I work in the Saltonsall Building." He pointed at it across the parking lot. "Just down the hall from Bill. Want to call him? See my creds?"

He proffered his cell phone in one hand, his wallet in the other, and smiled at her. She didn't return the smile. Only said, "So you're Laker. Well." Then she stepped off the curb and opened the van's front passenger door.

As he got in beside her, she said, "What are you expecting to happen this afternoon, Laker?"

He started up and headed for the gate. "We're going to the Cheltenham Long Term Care Community in Towson, where we'll pick up your grandmother. Then we go to the old family house in Chevy Chase. There's something your grandmother wants you to have. Bill said you just need someone to drive, fetch, and carry."

"Right. That's it. Aren't you a bit overqualified?"

"I'm just a colleague of Bill's who had nothing much on his schedule this afternoon."

She gave an impatient sigh. "Do you really think I don't know who you are?"

Laker stroked his beard uneasily. Ava North was a very junior cryptographer, if a promising one. She had joined the NSA only two years ago, after completing advanced degrees in math and linguistics at MIT. Someone at her level of security clearance wasn't supposed to know who he was. But there was as much shop talk, as many internal leaks, in the NSA as in any other agency.

"Thomas Laker," she said. "One of the best running backs Notre Dame ever had. Expected to turn pro. But you said no to the NFL recruiters in favor of the one from CIA. Served with distinction in Pakistan, Afghanistan, Iraq. Returned to Langley as one of the most talked-about candidates for deputy director. That didn't happen. Instead you are officially just some sort of consultant for NSA. Which I think is totally bogus."

Laker was relieved. She knew only the old stuff. Nothing about his current status. He said, "You're right. My consultant's retainer is practically a pension. I'm semi-retired."

"You're kind of young for that."

"Had a feeling I'd used up my luck."

"I doubt it. And you're in the Gray Outfit."

She definitely wasn't supposed to know that.

"Also," she said, "you have a sometimes nickname. *Lucky*. Lucky Laker."

"I like the alliteration," he said.

They had reached the gate. Laker was grateful for the distraction, for the opportunity to turn his face away from Ava's keen brown eyes. He lowered the window, handed over his creds, chatted with the guards about the weather as they logged his and Ava's departure on their computer. Then he turned onto the busy suburban street, pressing the button to run the window back up, sealing them in the cool, quiet interior.

"Well?' she said. "Are you going to deny it? Or do you have to shoot me?"

"Neither will be necessary. You know why people call us the Gray Outfit? Because we're a bunch of dull, middle-aged bureaucrats."

"Who report directly to the Secretary of Homeland Security," she said.

"Mostly on our lack of progress. We try to persuade various agencies to cooperate better. Share information more freely. Important work, but very dull."

"That's not exactly what I've heard. What the CIA won't tell the FBI, what the DEA won't tell the NSA, they will tell you guys. Because as individuals you have reputations. And connections. You end up in possession of the hottest secrets in town. Information you can't just sit on. And you don't. You act on it."

"Your informants have overactive imaginations."

She gave him a long sigh. "Laker, just tell me. My grandmother wants me to have something of hers. Maybe it's her wedding dress. Maybe it's a family photo album, I don't know. Why is the Secretary of Homeland Security interested enough to send you?"

"Because your grandmother is Tillie North."

2

The extended-care facility was as pleasant as such a place could be, a low brick building on a wooded campus. Laker maneuvered the van close to the entrance and stayed with it while Ava went in.

As she usually had during her long career in Washington society, Matilda Brigham North appeared with a retinue. Ava pushed her wheelchair, and orderlies and nurses carried her walker, oxygen tank, bag of medications, purse, umbrella, and overcoat.

Laker got out and opened the passenger door. Ava had told him that Tillie liked to ride in front, a preference that had disconcerted generations of limo drivers. It was a hot July afternoon, but the slight figure in the chair was swathed in sweaters and shawls. Her head was down, and he could see only sparse white hair and spotted scalp. But when Ava introduced him, she looked up. Under the wrinkled skin, it was easy to recognize the bone structure of one of the great beauties of the 1940s and '50s. The blue eyes were keen and bright.

"Ava's told me all about you," she said, in a voice soft but without a quaver.

"Has she?" He suppressed his irritation.

"You're one of Sam Mason's boys." Mason was the head of the Gray Outfit. "Haven't seen him since he was a midshipman at Annapolis. How'd he turn out?"

"Smart and tough," Laker said. He wasn't being loyal, just accurate.

"Nice of him to send his best. May I call you Tom? Or is it Lucky?"

"Tom. Please."

"I'm Tillie." Her right hand emerged from the folds of her shawl, pale and bony and trembling, but her grip was still strong.

Laker slid open the back door to supervise the loading of the wheelchair and other equipment. He hoped there would be room for whatever Tillie was giving Ava. Meanwhile, a nurse and Ava were helping Tillie stand up from the chair, take a step to the van, turn, and settle in the front passenger seat. It took a long time. She was breathing hard when Laker got in beside her.

"How did I get trapped in this old carcass?" she said.

"I'm sorry. It must be hard."

"Well, it's not for much longer." She smiled at him. "Can you help me buckle this belt? Otherwise I'll be fumbling with it for the next five miles, driving you both mad."

"I'll do it, Grandma," said Ava, scooting forward from her seat in the back. They set off across suburban Maryland.

Tillie was quiet for a while. Then she asked, "Has there been a lot of interest in our little errand today?"

The question took Laker by surprise, but then he reflected that Tillie had been making news all her life and was bound to be interested. "Yes. Nothing in the mainstream media but a lot of gossip and speculation, both offline and on. There's even a hashtag, #tillybequest."

"A hashtag is—" Ava began.

"I know, darling. Tom, are there that many people tweeting guesses about what I'm passing on?"

"Four hundred twenty-seven, last time I checked."

"Everybody's guessing but Ava," said Tillie with a smile. "She hasn't asked once. You've always been a great respecter of secrets, darling. When you were six, Ephraim said you were destined for the CIA. He wasn't far wrong."

Ephraim North, Tillie's late husband, had been a partner in one of Washington's top law firms. A skillful fund-raiser and fixer, he'd been a boon to some administrations, a bane to others. He and Tillie had golfed with Ike, played touch football with the Kennedys. But relations with LBJ had been strained after their son was killed in Vietnam, and their house in Chevy Chase had become one of the nerve centers of opposition to Nixon as Watergate festered. For decades Tillie had been the hostess whose invitations no one refused, the confidante of everyone who mattered.

Laker couldn't resist. He asked her if it was true that she was the one who had advised Betty Ford to appear on *The Mary Tyler Moore Show*.

She laughed. "Honestly, Tom, I wish I could remember. But when you're as near the end as I am, it's like you're closing the circle. The recent decades fade away. Your far-off youth seems clearer and clearer."

"The Truman years?"

"Even earlier. The war. I suppose it's only people my age who talk like that. Say 'the war' and expect everyone to know they mean World War II."

"The good war," Laker said.

She laughed again, sadly this time. "Well, it wasn't like the war you were in—*are* in. IEDs. Drone strikes. Hostage executions on YouTube. Going on and on, no end in sight. But I wouldn't exactly call World War II a good war."

"Maybe wars only become good when they've been over for a long time," said Ava.

"And your side won," Laker added.

"You're both right. People have gotten nostalgic about World War II. Silly little things like code names have a cachet. Let me try out a quiz on you, Tom. No jumping in, Ava. You know everything."

Ava rolled her eyes.

"All right," Laker said.

"Fat Man and Little Boy."

"The first nuclear bombs. Fat Man was dropped on Nagasaki, Little Boy on Hiroshima."

"Very good. Overlord."

"The invasion of Normandy."

"Torch."

Laker searched his memory, shrugged.

"Code name for the invasion of North Africa."

"Of course. Sorry."

"East Wind, Rain."

When Laker didn't respond, there was an exhalation of impatience from Ava in the back.

"Tell him, darling," said Tillie.

"Japanese code phrase to launch the attack on Pearl Harbor."

"Bobby Soxer," said Tillie.

No word from the backseat. He looked in the rear-view mirror. Ava was stumped.

"That would be a Sinatra fan," he said.

"You got it," Tillie said with a laugh.

They were arriving. Laker turned off the road and stopped, his way barred by a tall iron gate between granite posts. A video camera atop one of the posts swiveled to cover the van. "The family that's renting the house is away at the shore, but the staff should be expecting us," Ava said.

They were. Laker spoke through the intercom, and the heavy gates swung open. He drove through an allée of tall pin oak trees, and the house came into view. It was a mansion in the Georgian style, built around 1900, with white columns supporting a pediment and red brick wings that stretched a long way in both directions. Gardeners were at work, trimming hedges, weeding the well-kept lawn, raking the oyster-shell drive.

"The scene of some of Washington's most legendary parties," Ava said.

"I could bore you two for hours," Tillie said. "But let's skip it. Take the turning on the left."

The driveway led around the house, past formal gardens with vine-covered walls and fountains throwing spurts of water that glittered in the sun. They drove by outbuildings and more workmen. Tillie was silent. Laker glanced over, to see her gazing through the windshield, wrinkled face set. Her mood had changed. Seeing her house again must depress her.

"That's the storage shed," she said. "Stop here."

They were a hundred feet away from a small wooden building with a flat shingled roof and boarded-up windows. "I can get closer," he said.

"This is fine."

He stopped the van, got out, and came around to open her door. Ava had gotten out, too. White head bent, Tillie was taking a key from her purse with a shaky hand. Ava reached for it. "You can stay here, Grandma. We'll get it. Just tell us what to look for."

"No, I may have to poke around a bit. Bring my walker."

It took both of them to extract her gently from the car. Five minutes of patient effort and she was standing, leaning on the walker. All of them were breathing hard. She said, "I'll be right back."

Laker and Ava exchanged a baffled look. "I'm coming with you," Ava said.

"Wait here, Ava."

"I'll come," he said. "You're going to need me to carry whatever it is, aren't you?"

"No. It's just an old book."

Leaning on the walker, she slid it slowly forward and hobbled after it. After a few steps, she looked at them over her shoulder. The blue eyes were imperious. "Get in the van, you two. Turn on the air-conditioning. This'll take a while."

They obeyed. He was sweating, and the cool draft from the dashboard vents felt good. They watched as Tillie drew slowly nearer to the storage building.

Ava sat hunched with anxiety. She murmured, "If she falls she'll never recover. But she's so stubborn . . ."

"Sure I shouldn't go after her? I hate to think of her trying to move boxes."

"Maybe she just doesn't want to give it—this book, whatever it is—up until she absolutely has to. She's been very discreet. Ever since Granddad's death, people have been after her to write her memoirs. You can't imagine the persuasion agents and ghostwriters have applied. The advances publishers have offered. And of course various professors and archivists have been after her papers. But she's kept her secrets."

Laker gave her a sideways look.

"What?"

"Before, you said you thought it was a family photo album. But now you think it's something a good deal more, don't you?"

"I don't know what to think."

Tillie had reached the door. Leaning over her walker, she unlocked it and pushed it open. Entering, she was lost from view.

Laker glanced at his watch. "I'll give her a minute, then go offer to help."

"She won't welcome—"

A brilliant flash. The roof leapt up from the building like a cork from a champagne bottle. The boom of the explosion and the shock wave hit them, shaking the van on its springs. Flames burst from the doorway.

"Oh God—" Ava had her door open, one foot on the ground.

Laker pulled her back as shingles and planks rained down on the van, bouncing off its hood and windshield. Ava wrenched free and ran toward the building. Laker ran after her and tackled her. She kicked at him but couldn't break his grip.

Raising his head, he squinted at the building. Already the fire was roaring. Soon its heat would be unbearable. He shouted, "Ava, it's no use."

She ceased fighting him. He lifted his weight off her.

After a moment she struggled to her knees, then to her feet, and allowed him to draw her away.

3

There had been eight men working on the estate that afternoon, all employees of Waxman Landscaping, Inc. It was their bad luck to be swept into the maw of a major incident investigation.

Local police questioned them on the spot, then herded them into the shade of a magnolia tree to await the state police. Upon arrival, the state police put them in a van and took them to headquarters, where they were questioned again. Their hands were examined for chemical traces left by handling explosives. Results were negative. Their IDs and records were checked. Again results were negative; the four Mexicans turned out to be legal immigrants. Then they had to wait, in case the FBI wanted to question them. But it turned out the FBI wasn't interested.

The whole landscaping crew was a disappointment to the investigators. None were suspects; none were even useful as witnesses. Earl Richardson, the only one who was working close enough to the storage shed to see the explosion, was subjected to more interrogation than the others. When the transcripts were examined, it was noted that his answers were remarkably consistent, if otherwise uninteresting. He was a meticulous man, or more likely, an unimaginative one.

When the men were released, reporters and cameras were waiting for them in the parking lot. Those who had stamina, or wanted more attention, began to answer questions one more time. Earl Richardson slipped away into the gathering dusk.

His destination was the Rest Ease Motel, a quarter of a mile away. He checked in and paid cash. In his room, he went straight to the bathroom sink and looked at himself in the mirror. It was a long, appraising gaze.

A less-interested observer would have said there was nothing much to see.

Earl Richardson was a slim man of average height. He had thick brown hair under a sweat-stained John Deere cap, brown eyes, a craggy face. His sunken cheeks were stubbly with a few day's growth. His muscular hands had dirt-rimmed nails and an assortment of scars.

He removed his shirt. He had a workingman's seamed, brown face, neck and arms, but a pale torso. He wet and soaped a washcloth and scrubbed vigorously. The tan washed away in the sink. So did the dirt under his nails, and the scars on his hands. Then he opened his mouth, revealing teeth that sprouted unevenly with gaps between. He yanked out the prosthetic. His own teeth were white and even.

Next the cap came off. He turned on the faucets and bent over, and brown hair dye followed the suntan down the drain. His own hair was black. Once he shaved, the craggy, undernourished face looked fine-boned and faintly Asiatic, a long, slightly drooping nose and high cheekbones. Finally, he popped brown contact lenses out of his eyes, which he rubbed with evident relief.

Then he opened his eyes. They were blue.

He used one of them to wink at the image in the mirror.

4

The trouble with the other intelligence agencies, Sam Mason would say, with only minimal provocation, was that they were way the hell out in the suburbs, surrounded by tall fences, so people never saw anybody all day but their fellow spooks. That's what made the CIA and the NSA so *shy.* They preferred to gather intel via satellite. If they needed to get closer, they sent a drone.

The Gray Outfit doesn't do signals intelligence, image intelligence, or measurement and signature intelligence. We do human intelligence, Mason would conclude, heavily saucing the jargon terms with sarcasm. So we're in the city, where the humans are.

So small and well-connected was the Outfit that Mason had been able to find room for its headquarters on Capitol Hill itself, in a Victorian-era townhouse within sight of the great dome. The bronze plaque by the door said, "National Alliance of Auto Parts Distributors, LLC."

His office on the second floor had been a back bedroom. Its only window faced the blank wall of the building across the alley. That helped thwart electronic eavesdropping. Mason wasn't the kind of guy to waste time gazing out a window anyway.

At the moment, he was gazing across his desk at Laker. "The report is in from the Maryland State Police," he said.

There was no report on his desk. Mason hated papers for their tendency to fall into the wrong hands. Computers could be hacked, and don't even talk to him about the Cloud. He kept everything in his head. His highly polished mahogany desktop held only his mountainous reflection. He was a bald, thick-necked man with wide, sloping shoulders. He looked like a professional wrestler when he didn't have his bifocals on.

"Apparently there were paint cans and cleaning solutions stored in the shed, which was unventilated. Nobody goes in there and fumes built up. Tillie's walker must have scraped the concrete floor and caused a spark. A tragic accident."

Laker stroked his beard. "Does anybody believe that?"

Mason didn't answer. He folded his hands behind his head and leaned back in his high-backed leather chair, gazing at a stained-glass panel in the ceiling. He was ascetic about most things, but he liked a comfortable chair.

"It was a bomb and a cover-up," Laker said.

"Easy, Laker. I wouldn't say cover-up. The report is impressive. The state cops did a good job. They just didn't find anything."

"Meaning the killers knew their business."

"If you're right, they took a hell of a chance. Tillie North was a famous lady. With a lot of friends in this town."

"The word was out. About her wanting to pass something on to her granddaughter. Somebody decided it was worth taking a chance to prevent that. I suppose nothing was found at the scene?"

"We're talking about a wooden building, containing a lot of cardboard boxes full of paper. By the time the fire trucks got there it had all burned. Nothing left but shingles and gutters and nails." Mason's lips tightened. "And some teeth. A few bone fragments."

"Anybody have a theory what Tillie meant to pass on?"

"Everybody has a theory. The Norths were the confidants of presidents. Every secret that's been floating around this town for the last five administrations, they figured Tillie was about to spill it."

"A lot of people are relieved, then."

"Nobody is going to say that. But some folks I'm not going to name think an investigation would have major downside risks."

"They're not going to get their way. This isn't over."

"No. The pressure's on. Somebody's going to have an attack of conscience. Or make a stupid mistake. Which in this town often comes to the same thing."

"I keep thinking about how Tillie—Mrs. North—was acting right before she died. Some of the things she said didn't make sense. I have questions."

"I read your report."

"I'd like to have a talk with Ray Hilton. Try to get the FBI into this thing."

"No, Laker. Weren't you listening? Somebody's going to make a stupid mistake, but it won't be us. We can't afford mistakes."

"How about attacks of conscience?"

"Can't afford those, either."

5

That evening, a storm broke the heat wave that had oppressed Washington for weeks. Ava North, standing on Laker's threshold, had damp hair and a streaming raincoat. He wondered, but didn't ask, how she had found out where he lived. It was well off the beaten track, an old building in Anacostia, near the Navy Yard.

Her lower eyelids were puffy and red-rimmed, her face pale. She had been doing a lot of crying and not much sleeping. Ignoring his offer to take her coat, she stepped past him. He went to sit on the sofa while she walked around, looking at the views.

It took a while. Laker had the whole top floor. There were windows all around, and no interior walls except the one that turned one corner into a bathroom. Strong shifting winds shook the old window sashes in their frames and drove the raindrops at one window or another, making a sound as if somebody was throwing fistfuls of pebbles against the glass.

"Somebody told me you lived in a converted loft," she said. "But this is just a loft."

"The neighborhood isn't fashionable enough to attract pro rehabbers. We're all do-it-yourselfers in this building. It used to be a pin factory. If you pass a magnet over the cracks between the floorboards, you can still bring up a pin or two."

She walked on. The lamplight from the sitting area no longer reached her. She was a willowy shadow against the city lights, head down, hands in her pockets.

"You look at people so *hard,* Laker. I can feel your eyes—tracking me, like you used to track a pass you meant to catch back at Notre Dame."

He stroked his beard, wondering what she was doing here. But he didn't say anything. He let her take her time.

She turned away from the windows, stepped into an area demarcated by low bookshelves that he used as an office. She inspected the treadmill with a platform on which rested his computer. "So you're one of those trendy people who works at a walking desk. It keeps you fit, obviously."

"I think best on my feet."

"Doesn't surprise me."

She wandered over to a wooden platform, on which stood a teepee. The ceiling was just high enough to clear the tops of the stakes. "This looks like the real thing."

"It is. Made by a full-blooded Sioux who respected his traditions. He started with deerskins. Terrific guy. Good friend."

"He gave it to you."

"Left it to me." Laker hesitated. "He went back for his fourth tour in Iraq. It was one too many."

"The teepee is your bedroom, I guess. You were one of those kids who were always pestering their parents to let them camp out in the backyard."

"They didn't mind, except when I wanted to do it in January."

"The loft isn't soundproofed. Neighborhood like this, you must get a lot of street noise all night long. Are you a sound sleeper?"

"No. But it isn't noise that keeps me awake."

She was approaching the area where he was sitting. A glass coffee table rested on a Persian rug with an intricate pattern and muted colors. Sofas and armchairs surrounded it.

"I've been busy the last few days," she said. "Dealing with messages of condolence. Hundreds of them. Most of the people didn't know Tillie well. She'd outlived almost all of her generation. They're just taking the opportunity to pump me for information. Hot inside stuff. Or they're angling for an invitation to the funeral. Rumor is, every living ex-president is going to attend. It's become quite a hot ticket."

She stepped into the light and stood looking down on Laker, still with her hands in her pockets. "Your phone message was different. You sounded genuinely sorry. More than that. Guilty. You're thinking you should have saved her."

"I should have been more alert. I used to be, every minute, for years. In the Middle East I wouldn't dream of getting into a vehicle or entering an unfamiliar building without having it swept first."

"For a bomb, you mean?"

He nodded.

"You think my grandmother was murdered. So do I."

She sank down on the sofa opposite him. Sighed heavily. "But, Laker? It wasn't your fault. You were driving an old lady around suburban Maryland. Why would you expect any trouble?"

"A lot of people knew what we were doing. Hashtag tilliebequest. I'm wondering how word got around so widely and so fast."

"This is Washington and she was Tillie North."

"Yes, but it had to start somewhere."

"It started with Tillie," Ava said.

"You mean she let something slip to people at the retirement home?"

"No question of letting it slip. It was deliberate. I've found out that the day before, she made half a dozen phone calls. They were to people who were likely to spread the word that there was something very special from her past that she was going to pass on to her granddaughter."

Laker frowned. "She had decades of experience in feeding or starving the rumor mongers, whichever suited her purposes. Why would Tillie want Washington to know she was making you the heir to her secrets?"

"Washington already knew that. I visited her every week. She'd named me executrix of her estate. When she died, I would go through everything she'd left behind. So you have it backwards, Laker. She arranged this outing so everyone would know she had *not* passed on her most closely guarded secret to me. Not yet. She was about to."

"You're saying, she was offering someone the

chance to prevent it from happening. Destroy the secret. Kill her."

"Yes."

"That's why she insisted on going in the shed alone."

Ava bowed her head. Laker got up and fetched a box of tissues, which he put next to her. But she wasn't sobbing. She just couldn't go on.

He said, "My turn to say it. Don't blame yourself."

"It does me some good to recall how hard these last few years have been on her. Her body getting weaker, more pain-wracked all the time. It didn't help that her mind remained clear, her memory sharp. She'd seen a lot of life. Too much. She was ready to go."

A gust of wind shook the windows and made rain patter against the panes. He thought back to the drive to the house in Chevy Chase. Tillie had known she was going to her death. Had seemed resigned—more than that. Almost cheerful. Quizzing them about World War II code words. What had she been thinking about in her last moments? He said, "Would you like a drink?"

"I'm not much of a drinker. What would you recommend for an occasion like this?"

He went to the tall black safe where the pin company president had kept his cash. It was so heavy that subsequent tenants had just left it where it was. Laker had turned it into a liquor cabinet. He selected a bottle, brought it back, and poured two small glasses.

Ava sniffed hers suspiciously. "It smells like furniture stripper."

"It's Speyside Cardhu, a single-malt scotch. You're supposed to—"

She threw her head back and upended the glass.

"God. It tastes like furniture stripper, too."

"I was about to say, you're supposed to sip it."

"Pour me another. I'll try again."

He did and she lifted her glass. "Matilda Brigham North. Hail and farewell."

They clinked glasses. Laker said, "It was a good death. I'm sure she felt that way. Whatever her secret was, it will never be known. You're safe. It's over."

Ava gave him a long, level look over the rim of the glass. He felt lightness in the pit of his stomach and a ripple down his spine. In a low voice she said, "It's only beginning."

"What?"

"Grandma wasn't trying to keep me safe. She knew no one could keep me safe. She was just giving me a headstart."

Ava put down her glass, reached into her raincoat pocket, and laid a packet on the table between them.

"This came in the mail today."

6

It was a parcel wrapped in heavy brown paper, sealed with thick tape. He recalled Tillie saying that what she was going to give Ava was a book. This was the right size. There was no return address, but the postmark was Cheltenham, Maryland, the date the last day of Tillie's life. It was addressed to Ava's apartment on New Hampshire Avenue.

"Is this your grandmother's handwriting?"

"Tillie couldn't write anymore, with her arthritis. But I recognize the hand. It's Teresa's. Tillie's most loyal nurse. I'm sure she took it to the post office."

"And are you sure that this is—well, that this is it?"

"Tillie's bequest, like the hashtag said? Yes. She kept it with her, of course. It was never in that storage shed. I suppose you're going to ask why I haven't opened it."

"No, I'm not. Your grandmother was an expert on secrets. She kept a lot of them. She judged that somebody would kill to guard this one, and she was right. If I'd received this package I'd be scared shitless."

Ava smiled wanly. "I doubt that. But thanks."

"You want me to open it?"

She nodded. "I guess I must trust you."

Again she gave him that look that hollowed out his stomach and riffled his vertebrae.

He took a penknife from a drawer and carefully slit the tape. Folded back the paper. The book inside was obviously old. It had probably cost someone a few dollars when a dollar was a lot of money. It was bound in vellum with gilt-edged pages. The endpapers were patterned silk, the spine sewn. The pages were thick and cream colored, written on with fountain pen in a blue ink that had faded with the years.

"It looks like a journal of some sort," Laker said. "It's mostly in Japanese."

"My grandmother was fluent."

"Really?"

"She learned it from *her* grandmother. She and her husband were Protestant missionaries in the Pacific, Japan and other places. Their last post was Hawaii, and they settled down there. Tillie grew up in Honolulu. She told me her first job was at the head office of Dole pineapple, as secretary handling the Japanese correspondence."

"The only part I can understand is the headings," Laker said.

"It's a diary?"

"If so, she didn't keep it every day: 6/14/41, then 6/20/41. Only a few months before Pearl Harbor. Does that fit? Was your grandmother in Hawaii in 1941?"

"I think so. After the war broke out, her parents sent her to the mainland. I don't know the exact date. But she spent most of the war years here. I've seen pictures of her wedding. Granddad is wearing an Army uniform."

She extended a hand for the book.

"You read Japanese?" Laker asked. "I guess that's not surprising, for someone with a Ph.D. in linguistics."

"Sounds like you're inviting me to be pedantic." Ava said. "I'm a linguist, which means a scientist who studies how language works. Useful for making and breaking codes, which is what NSA pays me for. A person who can speak a lot of languages is a polyglot."

"And you're that, too."

"Well, I know some Japanese."

She paged through the book. Her dark eyebrows drew together in concentration, and a long crease divided her brow. "This is baffling."

"You can't understand what it says?" Laker asked.

"No, that part is easy enough. 'It's raining, mother, don't go outside.'—'I have been fishing all day and have caught nothing.'—'The fields have been diked and leveled off. We must hurry to plant potatoes and radishes.' It's all bits and snatches. A lot of breaks and repeated words."

"Is it a code of some sort?"

"My first guess would be no. I get no sense of an underlying system. You noticed in the headings, after every date there's an address? 417 Tusitala. 88 Lemon Rd. 519 Uluniu."

"All streets in Honolulu."

"Really? I've never been there." Turning pages, she came to a blank one. The next ones were blank, too. "So that's it. We have fifteen or twenty entries, each a date, an address, and a few lines of doggerel."

"What's the last date?"

"Eleven, two, forty-one."

"Just over a month before Pearl Harbor."

"We shouldn't jump to the conclusion that this has anything to do with the Japanese attack, Laker. Tillie wasn't involved with powerful men and great events at this point in her life. She was barely out of her teens. Just a missionaries' kid, working as a secretary for Dole."

"Okay. But why is this book so important, do you think?"

She flipped back, rereading and shaking her head. "'Lizard so still so quick. Lizard.' I don't know, maybe it *is* a code."

"You can work on it on the plane."

"Plane?"

"To Honolulu."

"What do you expect to find there?"

"I don't know. But you said Tillie gave you a head-start. Let's use it. Before whoever killed Tillie figures out that this book still exists, and that you have it. We'll take the first flight tomorrow morning."

"It'll have to be a later flight. The funeral is tomorrow. You should come. It may be . . . interesting."

He nodded gravely. "Considering what we know."

7

Ava could see nothing but blue ocean from the plane's window, but her ears were telling her that they had begun a gentle descent. She got up. She wanted to talk to Laker before the fasten-seatbelts sign went on. She moved down the wide aisle and opened the curtain. She was in first class, he in tourist. It had been the same on the flight from Washington to Los Angeles, and during the long layover at LAX he had kept his distance. He wasn't much into explanations, she'd noticed, and she was getting more nervous as they neared Hawaii.

He would soothe her. Just being near the big, broad-shouldered man made her feel protected. She liked the way he bent down to listen to her, half-turning his head to bring his good ear to bear. She knew about the IED blast in Baghdad that had partially deafened him.

Now hold on, she told herself. No going soft on Laker. Wariness had been bred into Ava, as the offspring of a prominent Washington family, long before she joined the NSA. People were not what they seemed. If you trusted someone instinctively, better mistrust your instincts.

If she'd needed a reminder of the soundness of that rule, yesterday's funeral would have provided it. The capital's hypocrisy had been on full display. People were texting in church. At the gravesite. Anytime, in fact, that they were sure a camera wasn't pointed at them. In the receiving line there had been phony smiles and crocodile tears.

Then there were the former presidents. They didn't do receiving lines. You were brought to them, after their Secret Service details had treated you to a final pass of the handheld metal detector. It was so confusing, meeting former presidents. The ones you'd voted against turned out to be nice guys, while the ones you'd voted for were jerks.

The worst part was that in church, people spoke at the microphone of Tillie's tragic accident. At the reception, they speculated in whispers about who had murdered her.

Ava had not spoken to Laker, but every time she'd caught sight of him, literally standing head and shoulders above the crowd, she'd felt a little better. Was she looking for a father figure in this tall man with his deliberate movements and soft but authoritative voice? He was older than she was, but she couldn't tell how much. His close-cropped hair was still black, but there were streaks of gray in his neatly trimmed beard.

Just ask the man about his plan, she told herself sternly. Keep emotion out of it.

In the more narrow confines of the tourist cabin, a line of people waiting for the lavatories blocked most of the aisle. As she hesitated, the lavatory door next to her folded open and Laker stepped out. She had to look twice. He'd shaved off his beard. Now he didn't look much over forty.

She stepped close and spoke just loud enough to be heard over the rush of air around the fuselage. "Why the shave?"

"I've been to Honolulu before. Might be useful to look different."

"A naked face is the best disguise? I think so, too. And who would expect you to have a cleft chin, just like Cary Grant?"

Laker gave her a puzzled look. Which was understandable.

God, Ava, pull yourself together.

They squeezed through the crowd to a pair of empty seats. The plane was half-empty. July must be off-season for Hawaii.

"Any luck with the code?" he asked.

"It's not code. Just gibberish. I'm not surprised. How would a twenty-year-old secretary at Dole learn how to write code? Why would she need to?"

He said nothing. Which was a sensible response to questions you didn't know the answer to. She changed the subject. "I didn't see much of you at the funeral."

"You had your hands full with members of Congress. POTUSes and FLOTUSes. I was talking with aides, assistants, and secretaries. Chauffeurs are especially informative. They overhear a lot of conversations in the backseat."

"Conversations about Tillie?"

"And you."

She leaned close and whispered, "Does anybody know about the journal?"

"No."

She sat back. "That's a relief, anyway."

"But it's common knowledge that Tillie grew up in Hawaii. You flying there is going to arouse interest."

"Laker, I wasn't dumb enough to tell anybody."

"The NSA trolls through airline reservation computers regularly."

"Right. I knew that," said Ava, irritated with herself for forgetting. "As do other agencies. Meaning a lot of people know I'm on this plane now."

He nodded. "That's why I've been keeping my distance."

"You've been watching me?"

"To see if anyone else is."

"And so far I'm clean. Or we wouldn't be talking now."

"Yes. But all the agencies have field offices or other assets in Honolulu. We should expect surveillance, maybe even an approach."

"What do you want me to do?"

"It's in our interest to keep them confused. Act like you're on vacation. You needed a few days away from the stress of Washington. Check into a hotel in Waikiki and lounge by the pool."

"And wait for some guy to offer to rub sunblock on my back, then ask too many questions while he's doing it?"

"Exactly. Anything like that happens, call me."

"Uh huh. So why am I the goat? Why don't you loll around at poolside? If they're going through passenger lists, they know you're on this plane, too."

"I'm using alternative ID."

"Oh. You're not Laker. And, since you weren't seated next to me, there's no reason for anyone to connect us. What will you be doing?"

"Seeing what I can find out about your grandmother's life during the time she was keeping the journal."

"Why do I get the feeling you just want to keep me safe?"

He gave her that quizzical look of his. "You're not safe anywhere, Ava. We have to assume that somebody knew about the journal. And murdered your grandmother to prevent it from falling into your hands."

"Then he thinks he succeeded. That the book is ashes."

"We can't count on that. Better give it to me before we land."

"No. I'll do as you say otherwise, but I'm keeping the journal."

8

He followed her through the airport corridors to ground transportation, keeping well back, with plenty of other travelers between them. She passed the security barrier and the small crowd waiting to meet arriving passengers. No one detached from it to follow her.

Still he tagged along as she headed for ground transportation, towing her wheeled carry-on. She was drawing occasional glances. Her dark pantsuit, standard Washington wear, was conspicuous among the arriving vacationers. Her beauty was conspicuous, too.

A few passersby—all male—stopped and turned for a second look at the slender redhead. At the counter, the guy was taking way too long to arrange her ride on the courtesy van to The Royal Hawaiian hotel.

Laker had to smile. What right did hc have to be irritated? He turned and headed for the rental-car counters. Nobody from an intelligence agency was following Ava. Guys trying to hook up with her were none of his business. She could no doubt handle them on her own.

He should have rented a nondescript four-door, but there was a Mustang convertible available and he couldn't resist. Must be the island spirit getting into him. Once on the road with the top down, he was pleased with the choice. The weather was beautiful, of course. The temperature was probably the same as Washington's, but the humidity was much lower.

He took the fastest route to Honolulu, which was not the prettiest. The Nimitz Freeway ran past factories and warehouses, power lines and billboards. It looked like any mainland city. Exiting the freeway, he was among steel-and-glass skyscrapers that could have been downtown anywhere. But between the buildings, he saw sparkling blue ocean in one direction, lush green mountains in the other. Looking *maukashe* and *makaishe* the Hawaiians called it, and the urge was irresistible. He wondered how people got any work done here.

He parked and went into the building that housed the Honolulu *Advertiser*. When beginning an investigation, particularly in a town he didn't know well, Laker made the newspaper his first stop. In his experience, reporters always found out a lot more than they were able to put in the paper, for reasons of space, or for other, more interesting reasons. You could always get them to talk by saying you were a fellow writer working on a book and offering them lunch.

Half an hour later, he was seated at a table by the window at Kakaako Kitchen, across from Joseph Kalapalea, obituaries editor. "I thought it was a career disaster when they sent me to the obit desk," Joe was saying. "And it probably was. But I like the work. You write an essay that sums up a person's whole life. And it's usually the last time that person will appear in the paper. So you get the final word."

Joe had unruly black hair, golden skin, and narrow dark brown eyes. Like many Honolulans, he was a hybrid of Hawaiian, Japanese, and mainland Caucasian. A stocky man in his forties, he was dressed in flip-flops, three-quarter-length pants with cargo pockets, and a blue T-shirt. The Hawaiian version of business casual put the stress on casual.

"You said there was a hang-up with your Tillie North piece."

"It's finished. The editor's holding it, waiting to hear if the Maryland cops change their mind about her death being accidental. You know anything about that?"

"I'm sure I don't know anything you don't already know."

The waiter arrived with their food: *laulau,* assorted meats and fish wrapped in *ti* leaves. Joe insisted that he try *poi*, taro root pounded to a light-brown mush. Laker found it kind of bland. Joe suggested combining it with *kalua* pork. It was still bland. Laker slid his bowl unobtrusively aside to concentrate on the neatly folded *ti*-leaf bundles, which were delicious.

"In fact, Tillie's obit was written years ago, by my predecessor. I just had to update it. Fill in a few gaps. When it runs, it will be in a prominent place."

"Even though she left Honolulu more than half a century ago?"

"Local girl made good," said Joe wryly. "We feel way out on the edge here, and most of the time we like it, but there's still that fascination with somebody who's born here and becomes prominent in the nation's capital."

"Especially remarkable for someone from a pretty humble background. Missionaries' kid, I mean."

The reporter's eyes widened with pleasure at the prospect of straightening Laker out. "Not so humble."

"Oh?"

"The missionaries who settled here in the nineteenth century were the first *haoles* who came to stay. A lot of them bought land low and sold it high decades later."

"They did good and they made good."

"Yep. Tillie's family, the Brighams, especially. Her parents didn't carry on the missionary tradition. The father owned a shipping line. The mother was prominent in society, as they used to say."

"And Tillie was earning her living as a secretary at Dole. Wasn't that unusual?"

Joe nodded and excitedly pointed his chopsticks at Laker. The *ti*-leaf dumpling between them slipped out and plopped onto his plate. "*Very* unusual. A family like the Brighams was expected to send a bright girl like Tillie to the mainland for college. To Vassar to meet and marry a Yale man. Or Radcliffe to nab a Harvard guy."

"So what happened?"

Joe retrieved his dumpling and popped it in his mouth. Chewed leisurely. Reporters could never resist building up the suspense.

"I think Tillie rebelled. I think there was some scandal that got hushed up."

"You think?"

He gave a shrug and a nod. "I spent a long time in

the *Advertiser* morgue, read acres of fading newsprint. Found only one fact to support my theory, and that wasn't enough. My editor made me cut all that out of the piece."

"What was your theory?"

"Tillie wanted to stay here. Her parents insisted on the college and husband-hunting thing. There was a family blowup. She had to move out of the house and support herself."

Laker nodded. As she had shown in later life, Tillie had a mind of her own and a strong will. He could believe she had been a rebellious teenager. "But you couldn't find anything about her in the newspapers of the time?"

"I didn't say that. She was all over the society pages." Joe had one of those shoulder bags in which reporters carried their tape recorder and notebooks. He opened it and took out a manila folder, which he handed to Laker.

Laker had finished his meal. He set the plate aside and opened the folder. The first page was a photocopy of a newspaper page from 1939. A picture showed a girl holding a wooden tennis racquet and wearing a white dress that reached to just above her knees. She had nice legs. He looked at the face and at first saw no resemblance to the worn, wrinkled woman he had met in Maryland. Slowly a resemblance emerged: the high cheekbones and firm chin. And the eyes. Even in a black-and-white photo you could tell they were blue.

He paged through more photocopies: Tillie in a one-piece suit, surfing at Waikiki. In jodhpurs and boots, riding in the mountains.

"In the summer of 1940, she abruptly vanishes from the society pages," Joe said. "That was when she went to work for Dole. Must have been quite a jolt. From socialite to secretary."

"The family blowup. What caused it, do you think?"

"You may have noticed, she followed the fleet."

Laker had. There were pictures of dinners at various clubs, dances at The Royal Hawaiian hotel, showing Tillie, lovely in her long gown and above-the-elbow gloves, a corsage pinned to her bosom, and an ensign or lieutenant beside her, in white from his high, tight collar to his shoes, with a sword at his side.

"It couldn't have been unusual for a socialite to date Navy officers. There were plenty of them in Honolulu."

"True. But Tillie got serious about one of them. Too serious."

Laker sat back and folded his arms.

"You look skeptical," Joe said.

"You said earlier, you did find one fact to support your theory. I think now's the time for it."

"Tillie didn't stay at Dole. In the spring of 1941, she took a new job. At Pearl Harbor."

"To be closer to some naval officer, you think."

"In spring 1941, they would have known they were on borrowed time. Nobody was expecting an attack on Pearl Harbor, but it was inevitable there would be war between America and Japan."

Laker caught their waiter's eye and motioned for the check. "You're building a load of supposition on your one fact."

"Okay. Maybe I've seen too many of those old black-and-white movies, with Vivien Leigh and Robert Taylor. Betty Grable and Tyrone Power." Joe gazed out at the traffic on Ala Moana Boulevard without seeing it. His face was somber. "If there was an officer she loved, I think Tillie was right to stay here with him."

"Borrowed time, you said."

"In May of 1942, Tillie moved to Washington, never to return. In December of '44, she married Mr. Moneybags Ephraim North. To me, that means her naval officer was killed, in the attack on Pearl, or in one of our lost battles of early '42."

"It could also mean there was no naval officer."

"You think I'm nuts."

"I think you should write a screenplay."

"Nah. Tyrone Power's dead."

9

The only Honolulu hotel Ava knew the name of was The Royal Hawaiian, so that was where she was going to stay. The moment the van pulled up in front of it, she was pleased with her choice. It was a six-story pink palace topped with a cupola, right on Waikiki Beach. Long rows of windows with awnings looked out to sea. It was old-fashioned and charming. All the other beachfront hotels were new skyscrapers.

She fully intended to be a good girl and do as Laker said. At first, anyway.

After checking in, she returned to the front desk with Tillie's journal. The helpful clerks offered to copy it for her, but she insisted on being taken to the copying machine in the office to do it herself. Then she had the journal placed in the hotel safe.

Twenty minutes later, she stepped out on the pool deck, wearing a bikini, terrycloth wrap, and sun hat purchased from a boutique in the lobby. Stretching out in a lounge chair under a pink-and-white striped umbrella, she promptly fell asleep. It had been a long trip from Washington.

An hour later, she awoke refreshed. Restless, in fact. Looking at the people on the deck and in the pool, she thought they were all the carefree vacationers they appeared to be. Laker's notion that she would be watched or approached seemed far-fetched.

Anyway, she was a typically pale-skinned redhead, with a tendency to burn. Even with the protection of a beach umbrella and sun hat, she didn't feel like lying out here any longer. Especially as she was bored out of her mind.

She returned to her room and examined the photocopies she'd made of the journal. On a careful rereading, the Japanese lines stubbornly refused to make any more sense. What had the young Tillie been trying to do? Write poetry? Some of the entries were short enough to be *haiku*, but didn't meet the metrical requirements. Maybe she was trying a literary experiment of a different sort. Most entries were so filled with repeated words they suggested Tillie was trying to emulate Gertrude Stein.

Giving up on the Japanese lines, she turned to the headings. A date and an address. Laker had recognized some of the street names. Would it be possible to pick up her grandmother's trail? She spread out the map provided by the hotel, and quickly found two of the streets from the journal, Lemon Road and Punchbowl Street.

The names were enticing. Ava thought she just might find out something.

She called down to the lobby and ordered a rental

car, then changed into chinos and polo shirt. With cell phone in hand, she hesitated. Laker was bound to call to check up on her. She could lie to him, say she was at the hotel as instructed, but why should she lie? He had no right to tell her what to do. But she didn't want to get into tiresome explanations or arguments, either. She decided to leave the phone in the room.

The first address she checked, 318 Nahua St., was only a few blocks away from The Royal Hawaiian. The even-numbered side of the 300 block consisted of a hotel, a McDonald's, and a Walgreens. In fact nothing she saw on Nahua Street had been there in Tillie's day, except the Ala Wai Canal at the end of it.

That was how her search went, for a discouragingly long time. Again and again, she got out of the car at an address and looked at a new building. Some addresses proved unfindable; the numbering system must have changed. A few street names had changed, too.

At least she was seeing a lot of Honolulu. She liked Chinatown, with its busy street markets and small, peak-roofed temples. She stopped at a restaurant for a late lunch of *lomi lomi* salmon.

Going back downtown she found a pleasant area of palm tree–lined streets, parks, and old buildings. On the street Tillie had named, no building bore the number she had written. But on the other side of the street stood an old survivor, a Protestant church built of rough gray volcanic rock. Its large wooden doors were framed by white pillars, and a rectangular, battlemented clock tower rose from the slate roof. Ava guessed that it had been here since the nineteenth century.

She went in. The plain interior was pleasantly dim and cool. Carved into the wall inside the door were the lines

Thou shalt love the Lord thy God with all thy heart, and with all thy soul, and with all thy mind. This is the first and great commandment. And the second is like unto it, Thou shalt love thy neighbour as thyself.
On these two commandments hang all the law and the prophets.—Matt. 22: 37–39

in English and Hawaiian. It was possible that Tillie had looked upon this inscription, so Ava copied it in her notebook.

This was beginning to seem like a waste of time, but she was too stubborn to give up. She got back in the car and headed for the next address. In the rearview mirror she saw another car turn left at an intersection and get behind her. It was a white Subaru, as nondescript as her rented Honda, except that it was missing its front left hubcap.

She had seen that rusty, lug-nutted wheel before. Could the white Subaru be following her? But no sooner had the thought formed than the car turned off. Ava had to smile at the way her heartbeat had speeded up. Honolulu's street pattern was a grid, and the way she kept crisscrossing and doubling back, it was no surprise that she should see the same car twice.

Laker was making her paranoid, that was all.

10

After dropping off Joe Kalapalea at the *Advertiser,* Laker tried Ava. She didn't answer her cell phone. He left a message. Then he pointed the Mustang's long hood toward Pearl Harbor. It was a beautiful half-hour drive along the coast. Leaving the highway, he pulled over and tried her again. No answer on the cell or her room phone, so he called the desk. The staff of The Royal Hawaiian lived up to their reputation for courtesy and helpfulness, but were unable to find Ms. North at poolside.

For a moment he seriously considered going to the hotel, turning it upside down in search of Ava, calling the police if he couldn't do so. It was possible she was in serious trouble. Then he decided that he was overreacting.

Ava clearly believed that her grandmother's sacrifice had not been in vain. The murderers were fooled; they thought the journal had been destroyed in the explosion. And no one else knew of its existence. Maybe she was right. Laker hoped so.

He also hoped Ava would call him back soon.

He drove on until he came to the turnoff for the Admiral Clarey Bridge, where he pulled onto the shoulder and got out of the car to admire the view. A strong salty wind peeled back his jacket. Brilliant sunshine sparkling on the waves made him narrow his eyes.

Across the water, near Ford Island, a curving white memorial stood above the wreck of the *Arizona,* sunk by the Japanese with the loss of more than a thousand men. But, as Laker had noticed on previous visits, if you wanted to put the catastrophic defeat of Pearl Harbor in the right perspective, Pearl Harbor was the place. On his own side of the water was the naval base, much bigger than it had been seventy years ago, with the tank farm, the administrative buildings, the cranes and docks where the sleek gray warships were moored two by two. An enormous aircraft carrier, with planes lined up on its flight deck, was being poked and prodded into the channel by three tugboats. It was far away, but he could hear the tugs' engines laboring as their screws churned up wakes behind them. The sight made him think of the carriers *Yorktown*, *Hornet,* and *Enterprise,* which with the rest of the Pacific fleet had sailed from here only six months after the Pearl Harbor defeat, to inflict on the Japanese navy a blow from which it would never recover.

His gaze drifted back to Ford Island and the long gray shape, bristling with guns, of the battleship *Missouri,* on whose deck the Japanese had surrendered, only four and a half years after Pearl Harbor. Only days after Hiroshima and Nagasaki had been devastated by nuclear bombs.

Laker was no flag-waver or misty-eyed patriot. He

had risked his life for his country too many times and come too close to losing the gamble. And had done things for his country that it troubled him to remember. But at moments like this, he thought, if you have to fight a war—any war, open or secret, declared or undeclared—you better win it.

And America would, if he, Tom Laker, had anything to say about it.

He drove across Halawa Creek and stopped at the gate of the naval base to present his credentials. He parked the Mustang where the guards pointed and walked toward the cluster of administration buildings, preparing to be condescended to. Laker had worked with military people closely in the Middle East, and had managed to win their respect, but it hadn't been easy. Military people seemed to start with the assumption that a civilian was a little soft, a little sloppy, always looking for corners to cut and expecting to be pampered.

The first man behind a desk he spoke to explained it all to him. Records of BuPers—the Bureau of Personnel, the 1940s name for the Navy's Human Resources Department—were not kept at Pearl Harbor but in the Records Depository in St. Louis. It was no problem, because they could be accessed online.

The clerk did so, and told him that Matilda [none] Brigham had worked as a clerk-typist in the Office of Commissary Supply from 5 May 1941 to 15 January 1942. That was all. No, there would be no more information on record here at Pearl. So why are you still standing here, wasting my time?

He didn't actually say that, but Laker got the message. He moved on, office to office, building to building. He learned nothing more, and encountered attitudes ranging from stiff courtesy to undisguised boredom. Nobody made the connection between Matilda Brigham and Tillie North.

Emerging into the sunshine, Laker walked down to the docks. He looked out to sea, where the aircraft carrier was now hull down on the horizon, then toward land, where the clutter of buildings and roads climbed part way up the green flanks of the hills.

This was looking like a wasted afternoon. What traces was he expecting to find here, of Tillie's presence a lifetime ago? How could he even begin to answer the question of why this bright and beautiful girl had defied her parents, refusing to go to America and attend a Seven Sisters college and meet an Ivy League man, the way those of her favored class were expected to do?

Then there was the fact that Ava hadn't called him back. He couldn't help worrying about her, thinking he ought to go to The Royal Hawaiian.

He didn't return to his car, though.

It was a funny thing about Laker. Official reports ascribed his successes in the field to courage and persistence. He didn't buy that. What he had was a willingness to trust his luck. When it seemed that he was getting nowhere, when it seemed that he was getting in trouble, he would push a little harder. Things were going to break his way.

The key encounter or revelation was just around the corner.

He turned and walked into the entrance of the nearest office building and read the directory. It said that in the basement he could find the Office of the Base Historian, Capt. (ret.) Ernestina Penderghast.

He descended the steps. The door was open, so he walked in. It was an old-fashioned sort of government office with fluorescent strip lighting, linoleum floor, and walls painted light-green. The only window was high up on the wall and provided a view of khaki-clad legs walking past. Tall shelves were solidly lined with document boxes.

A white-haired woman was sitting at a desk under a big map of the harbor, examining a *katana*, a Japanese sword.

"Captain Penderghast?"

She looked up. She was about seventy years old, and the lines in her face indicated that she had spent more of them frowning than smiling. Steel-gray eyes appraised him. "Can I help you?"

"I have an idea that you can. In fact I wish I'd found this office earlier. You know, you're kind of inconspicuously placed."

"Tell me about it. I used to have larger quarters. Even a staff. But when Pearl Harbor became part of Valor in the Pacific National Park, they turned historical responsibilities over to the National Park Service."

"That's a shame. The Navy should have its own history office."

It was the right thing to say. Captain Penderghast was one of those people who warmed to you when you shared their complaints. She put down the *katana* and rose to approach him. She was wearing civvies—dark blue slacks and light blue shirt—but with razor-sharp creases.

"The NPS serves tourists, and they're only interested in December 7. The rest of our history is being lost. But the higher-ups won't listen to my complaints. I've made myself unpopular around here." She smiled with sour satisfaction, proud of making herself unpopular. "Every time a department puts its records on the Cloud, or wherever they put them, I pester them to give me their files instead of throwing them away."

"It would be a shame to lose those files. When people enter information on a computer, they're just filling in blanks on a form. Back when there were files, all sorts of interesting papers got tossed into them."

"Are you a historian, Mister . . . ?"

"Oh, just kind of a researcher. My name's Laker."

"And what are you researching today?"

"A civilian employee who worked here in 1941."

Captain Penderghast gazed at the ceiling while consulting her memory. "It's possible I'll be able to help you. What was his name?"

"It was a young woman. Matilda Brigham, no middle initial."

The gray eyes dropped to meet his. "Tillie North? She worked here?"

He nodded.

"Would your—uh—research be connected with her recent death?"

He shrugged.

"Not too forthcoming, are you, Mr. Laker?"

He reached into his coat pocket. "If you'd likc to see my ID—"

"Would it tell me whom you really work for?" She went on without waiting for an answer. "I've been stationed at the Pentagon several times. I know the ropes.

And I'm willing to bet that you're from Washington. Or Langley. Or Fort Meade."

She was smiling. Laker smiled back.

"If this is a matter of national security," the captain continued, "let's get to work."

She led him down an aisle of shelves, peering at labels on document boxes. "Do you know her job title and department?"

"Clerk typist, Commissary supply. Which is kind of odd in itself."

"How so?"

"She spoke Japanese. You'd think that in 1941 the Navy could have found something more useful for her to do than order cutlery and napkins."

"The Navy didn't have much respect for the accomplishments of women in those days." She knelt and pulled a document box from a bottom shelf. Lifting off its top, she riffled through the manila folders inside. "This is where she ought to be. But no Brigham."

"Oh."

"Don't despair, Mr. Laker. They made a terrible mess of the files when they shipped them over. We'll just have to dig."

For the next hour, they sat on the floor back-to-back, pulling boxes off the bottom shelf and going through them. Many boxes emitted a smell of mildew when the lids were lifted. Tiny red bugs crawled over the papers. But Laker didn't doubt the search was worthwhile, because the files were thick. The manila folders were stuffed with faded carbon copies of reprimands and commendations, approvals and refusals. Given the military's devotion to paperwork, he was confident that if they could find Tillie's file it would tell him a lot.

Captain Penderghast was just as determined as he was. Dragging another box onto the floor and lifting the lid, she said, "Any idea why she came to Pearl to work, Mr. Laker?"

"I spoke to someone this morning who had a theory," he said, and related Joe Kalapalea's tale of a doomed romance with an officer.

The captain snorted. "And was your informant by any chance a man?"

"Yes. Do you have an alternative theory?"

"By summer 1941, everybody knew war with Japan was inevitable. Hawaii would be on the front line. Maybe instead of retreating to the mainland, Tillie chose to stand and fight."

"As a clerk typist in Commissary Supply?"

"That was about all the Navy would allow a woman to do." Her fingers, which had been flicking steadily through the labels of files, stopped. "Ah. Brigham, Matilda [none]."

She pulled a folder and handed it to Laker, It was disappointingly thin. He opened it, and found only one piece of paper. The captain peered at it and frowned.

"That's just her initial placement form from BuPers. I'm sorry, Mr. Laker. I've never seen a personnel file that had only the one form in it. I suppose it doesn't tell you anything?"

Laker closed the file and handed it back. "Thank you, Captain."

He rose, dusted off his pants, offered her a hand. She didn't take it. The gray eyes were boring into his. "You're *not* disappointed. The file did tell you something, didn't it? Like that Tillie needed a job title to get on the payroll. But she never sat at a desk in Commissary supply."

Laker smiled but didn't answer.

"You're thinking the Navy had a different use for her. Maybe she was in the same line of work as yourself. What did you call it? 'Research'?"

"Research will do."

11

Ava drove out of town on a wide road that looped up a mountainside. The views were exhilarating. When the road curved left, she looked down on the skyscrapers of Honolulu and beyond them to limitless blue sea and sunny sky. When it curved right, she looked up a lush green slope to the mountaintops. Dark clouds seemed to have snagged on them. It was raining up there.

She was looking for 3217 West Manoa Road. According to the map spread on the passenger seat, she was on Manoa, but it was hard to read addresses. Buildings were far back from the road, obscured by palm trees, Norfolk Island pines, brilliantly blooming hibiscus bushes. Most of them were large, and no doubt expensive, houses of coral stone and redwood. They didn't look very old. She had the feeling she was in for another disappointment. She wouldn't be able to find the address her grandmother had written down seven decades ago, or if she did it would be a different building.

But this time it turned out to be easy. She came around a curve and saw a driveway entrance ahead, with a sign beside it: Kapa'a Kauii Inn, 3217 W. Manoa Rd.

She took the turn. The drive was lined with tall mango trees. When the building came into view, Ava was excited to see that it looked old. Beautiful, too: a large wooden house with porches—*lanai*, she corrected herself—running all the way around the first and second floors and a steep tiled roof. Guests were sitting in wicker chairs on the ground-floor *lanai*. An elderly couple was descending the steps to a waiting taxi. Several cars were parked along the drive. She stopped behind the last one and walked to the building.

The lobby wasn't air-conditioned, but slowly revolving fans far up on its high ceiling kept it cool. There were reed mats on the polished, broad-planked wood floor. Hawaiian calabashes filled with ginger flowers stood on Chinese lacquered tables. On the walls were large, framed black-and-white photos. They seemed to be of the building itself.

She was approaching one for a closer look when a young man in white shirt and black tie came around the registration desk toward her. His features looked Japanese; his voice sounded American. "Welcome to the Kapa'a Kauii Inn. Do you have a reservation, ma'am?"

"No—um—I'm not checking in. The hotel looks like it's been here a long time?"

He nodded. "My family has been operating it since the 1970s."

"The building looks much older."

"Oh, yes. It was built in 1928 as a private house. By

the time my folks bought it, it was in pretty bad shape. They had to put a lot of work into it."

"Really? Do you happen to know if it was a private house in the 1940s?"

"No. The army requisitioned it. Used it as a rest home for wounded officers. Here, you can see."

He led her over to one of the photos on the wall, which showed the house with Jeeps parked in front and a flagpole flying the stars and stripes. Pajama-clad men in wheelchairs were being pushed past an enormous tree. It was a banyan, the tree that sent out long branches that grew their own trunks until it constituted a grove in itself. "They were here from '42 to '46. Left the place in quite a mess, apparently."

"Any idea who owned the house before them?" She was hoping there was another photograph.

"It belonged to Tadashi Kurita. In fact we've restored it to look the way it did when the Kurita family was here." The man's expression had changed as he spoke. The mouth was set, the eyes narrowed to slits.

"I'm sorry—have I offended you in some way?"

"No, ma'am. Nothing like that. But it's a sad story. The government took over the house when they sent the whole Kurita family to an internment camp."

"There were internment camps here, like there were in California? I didn't know that."

"It was forgotten, or hushed up, until recently. But there were. People of Japanese ancestry made up a third of the population of the islands. Many had been here for generations. But after Pearl Harbor everybody was scared of invasion. Martial law was imposed. Thousands of Japanese-Hawaiians were rounded up and interrogated. An unlucky few got locked up in a camp."

"Including the Kuritas. Why?"

"Probably because they entertained members of the Japanese diplomatic community here. Which was hardly a crime prewar. In fact it was hard to avoid if you were Mr. Kurita. He owned a sugarcane company that did a lot of business with Japan. But the *haoles* suspected he was a spy. He was eventually exonerated and released, but he never recovered. Excuse me, ma'am."

An Asian couple was approaching the registration desk, laden with luggage and small children. The young man went to assist them. From the set of his shoulders he was relieved. Ava's questions had depressed him.

She walked to the front door and looked out. The vast, labyrinthine banyan tree was gone without trace. She opened her purse and pulled out the sheaf of photocopies, found the relevant entry:

6/27/41
3217 W. Manoa

Don't have it anymore
must have lost it under the banyan
It's time we
the banyan
lizard so still so quick lizard

It didn't make any more sense than the first time she'd read it. But it was confirmation Tillie had been here. And now she knew the name of someone who had known her. Tadashi Kurita. The races had not mixed much in old Honolulu. Why had Tillie made the acquaintance of a Japanese-Hawaiian sugarcane magnate? She had no idea, but she was looking forward to the expression on Laker's face when she told him what she'd found out.

She walked back to her Honda, pressing the unlock button on the key fob. The lights didn't flash. She must have forgotten to lock it. She got in behind the wheel, consulting the list of addresses she'd made. There was another, farther up Manoa, if she remembered right. In fact it wasn't an address but a crossroads, Manoa and Route 51. Seventy years ago, Honolulu had been much smaller, and buildings that far out didn't have street numbers. She wondered what she'd find there. Now that she was on a roll.

She laughed as she fastened the seat belt. Noticing the glove compartment lid had fallen open, she shut it before starting the engine.

Above the Kapa'a Kauii Inn, the grade was steeper and the road took a series of tight switchbacks. Her ears popped. The road straightened out, and she realized she was atop a ridge. The sky was darker and tropical-size raindrops were plopping on the windshield. She turned on the lights and wipers. The road was lined with an unbroken wall of foliage. She had left buildings behind, too.

She passed a sign that said JCT 51 and coasted to a stop at the crossroads. No buildings here, but there was a cleared space on the other side of the road. A Realtor's sign was facing away from her. The lot was for sale. Maybe the Realtors would be able to tell her what had been there.

She pulled the car onto the shoulder and got out. The wind was strong. She crossed the road blinking as warm raindrops smacked her in the face. The sign wasn't for a Realtor. It was an advertisement for a gas station two miles ahead. Disappointed, she turned to head back to her car.

Another car was approaching. It pulled onto the shoulder behind the Honda. It was a white Subaru, missing its left front hubcap.

Ava froze. Realized she'd been preoccupied and careless. She had only noticed this car twice, but it must have been following her all day. The glove compartment door had been open because the Subaru's driver had searched her car while she was in the Kapa'a Kauii Inn.

The driver's door was opening. She spun and ran into the rain forest. After only a few seconds of blundering through the dense, wet foliage she was soaked. A root yanked her foot out from under her, and she pitched onto her face in fallen leaves and mud. Now that she'd stopped making noise, she could hear her pursuer crashing through the forest. He wasn't far away.

She scrambled up onto her knees, then rose to her feet and kept going, pushing limbs away from her face. There was no way of moving quietly. He had only to stop and listen to track her. Maybe she would be better off to stay still, but she was too scared to stop running.

The going was becoming a little easier. Not because the foliage was thinning. She realized she was descending a slope. She picked up her pace, batting frantically at the limbs in her way.

Abruptly the screen of leaves parted. She found herself poised on the edge of a steep bank above a stream. She tried to stop, but her feet slid in the mud and she fell. Grasped at roots but couldn't hold on. She skidded into the water. It was warm but deep, with a strong current. It caught her and bore her along. Thrashing with both arms she was able to fight her way closer to the bank. Seeing a fallen limb she caught hold of it and pulled herself up and out onto the mud.

She made herself stop gasping and listen. The rushing of the stream, the patter of rain on leaves, the calls of birds that were strange to her . . . that was all she heard. No sound of anybody crashing through the undergrowth. Her pursuer had given up.

She hoped so, anyway.

She crawled up the bank, reached level ground, and stood listening. Heard the engine of a truck laboring uphill. That told her where the road was and she headed for it. She could see nothing around her but green leaves. Her shoulders were hunched. Any second she expected a blow from behind.

She came out by the side of the road. Looked both ways: no vehicles, no one on foot. She walked uphill, and soon the crossroads came in sight. Only her car was there. She ran to it, jumped in, and started the engine. Her nerves were still raw. She made a screeching U-turn and headed back toward the city. Soon she reached the stretch of switchbacks.

"Get a grip, Ava!" she shouted. She was going too fast. For no reason, there was no one behind her. She forced herself to slow down. When the sign for the Kapa'a Kauii Inn came into view, she turned into the driveway and stopped.

Opening the Honda's door, she stood on trembling legs. Took slow, deep breaths until she calmed down. She was soaked to the skin and covered with mud. A glance in the car's side mirror showed some scratches on her face. Otherwise she was fine. She hadn't even lost her shoulder bag. She opened it. The photocopies of Tillie's journal were a sodden mess.

It was possible that she had panicked for no reason. Maybe that was what Laker was going to say when she told him about it. Her pursuer had just been some guy from Washington. Maybe even a fellow employee of the NSA. He'd known nothing about the journal and meant her no harm. Just wanted to ask her a few questions about why she had chosen to visit her grandmother's hometown at this particular time.

It was possible. But Ava did not believe it.

Her pursuer was Tillie's murderer. He knew she had the journal. If he'd caught her, he would have killed her.

She got back in the car and started the engine. But she wasn't quite ready to get back on the road. For a long moment she sat gazing through the rain-spattered windshield, down the drive lined with tall mango trees.

Then she dropped the transmission into Drive.

12

June 27, 1941

The mango trees are only half as high. The drive is a dirt road.

Night has fallen and white cones of headlamps precede the big cars, one an Oldsmobile, the other a Packard, as they lumber through the dust. When they reach the house, servants in white jackets are waiting to open the doors.

Tadashi Kurita waits on the *lanai* to welcome his guests. Light from the front door makes his pomaded black hair glisten. He is short but stately in his double-breasted gray suit. He exchanges bows with the owner of the Olds, shakes hands with the couple from the Packard. They go into the living room, where the other guests are sipping drinks. Kurita signals to his butler to announce dinner.

Soon the guests are seated at the long table. The Kurita house is one of the few where Japanese and Americans continue to socialize. These men are owners of sugarcane and pineapple plantations, executives of shipping firms, managers of hotels and restaurants. They come to the Kurita house to talk about how the impending war is hurting their business, to discuss ways of keeping civil order in Honolulu. Though the Japanese-Hawaiians assert their loyalty, ugly incidents in the streets indicate growing American suspicion.

Halfway down the left side of the table sits a pretty girl with golden hair in a French roll and blue eyes. Her crimson lipstick sets off her white teeth as she smiles in response to a remark by the man on her left. Her posture is erect, her expression attentive. She seldom speaks.

Tillie Brigham understands that her role is to be decorative, like the centerpiece of breadfruit and green leaves, the sideboard bouquets of yellow hibiscus and calla lilies.

She is the youngest woman here by years. By decades. And the only unmarried one. The wrinkled wives of the businessmen look at her with suspicion. Word has gotten around about the Brigham girl who has turned down a place at Vassar to live alone in a Honolulu apartment and earn her own living. There can be only one explanation: she is a gold digger. Her escort tonight is Herbert Lansdowne, vice president of Dole. Herb is an eligible widower, fifteen years her senior. He has explained to several people that she used to be his secretary before she went to work at Pearl Harbor, and they continue to be friends. No one believes that's all there is to it.

From time to time, not too often, Tillie glances at Hirochi Ryo. He is the guest of honor, seated on the hostess's right. He works at the consulate, and for a representative of the Imperial Japanese government, he is surprisingly well-liked by Americans. He is almost as tall as a white man, lean and broad-shouldered. He does not squint through thick spectacles, the way most Japanese do. Or most Americans believe that they do. The black eyes under heavy lids gaze steadily at the man across from him. Tillie thinks he is aware of her look, but he will not return it. He and the man are talking about Joe DiMaggio's hitting streak, speculating how long it will last. His English is fluent and unaccented. He studied at the University of Chicago and was stationed at Washington for several years. He's also been at the Moscow embassy. In fact he has not lived in his homeland since the military government took power. His public comments about General Tojo's policies are diplomatic in the extreme.

He looks around, smiling, as the servants enter bearing many small trays of dark wood. Tillie knows he likes Hawaiian food, strongly inflected as it is with Japanese influence. On the trays are pink oval slices of fish on a bed of shredded greens. The guest on Tillie's right informs her that he is a meat-and-potatoes man and says that this fish looks *raw.* She confirms that it is. He finds the next course, cucumber salad served with a bowl of soy sauce with white radish slices floating in it, equally unappealing. She murmurs sympathetically as she watches Ryo's long fingers deftly manipulate his chopsticks. When the next course arrives, her neighbor asks hopefully if it is meat. She informs him it is *sukiyaki*, a platter of beef on a bed of Kikuna leaves, with *enoki* mushrooms and *nana negi* onions.

"They're like leeks," Tillie says. All the time her head has been turned away from Ryo, she has sensed his gaze on her. But when she glances at him, he is talking to their hostess.

Her boredom and tension increase as the meal goes on. Once the Japanese have had their tea and the Americans their coffee, she hopes that the party will end. But the guests linger over their cigarettes. Conversation shows no sign of flagging. Mr. Meat-and-Potatoes has discovered that the man on her left is a kindred spirit. They have been talking politics across her through dessert, both apologizing that the subject must be boring to a pretty young girl.

Two bald heads get between Tillie and her cup as the men lean close and whisper. "The Nips aren't going to be satisfied with their gains in China," says Mr. Meat-and-Potatoes.

He explains that with the European powers at each other's throats, their Pacific colonies rich in rubber and oil lie open to the Nips. Now that Russia has been invaded by Germany, the only white nation left in the Pacific to counter the Nips is America. The other man opines that FDR was smart to bribe Japan with oil and steel, but Mr. Meat-and-Potatoes vehemently disagrees, saying the steel has gone to build battleships and the oil to fuel them for the inevitable day when they sail to invade Hawaii.

As the argument goes on, Tillie watches the cigarette smoke thicken and stir in the blades of the ceiling fans. Then she looks at the servants in their white jackets, standing against the walls with their hands clasped behind them. They have nothing to do and look as bored as she feels, except for one who is staring intently at the opposite wall. She follows his look. In among Mr. Kurita's display of Malay weapons is a solitary gecko, as still as if nailed to the wall. Tillie smiles. You never can keep the geckoes out. The servant, unable to stand it anymore, makes a move toward the gecko, and it skitters across the wall out of reach with astonishing speed. You never can catch a gecko, either.

Finally the guests begin rising from the table. Tillie wipes her sweaty palms before dropping her napkin. The evening is ending for the others. Not for her.

On the *lanai* she and Herb stretch out their thanks and good nights to the Kuritas as the other guests move off through the noisy tropical night to their cars. The Kuritas go inside. Herb takes her arm and leads her along the broad *lanai* and around the corner of the house. He offers her a cigarette. She shakes her head. She has already sweetened her breath with a mint.

"Are you okay?" he asks.

She nods.

"They'll call me when I get home. They always do. Any message?"

"No."

He starts to go, hesitates. "Sometimes I'm sorry I ever told the Navy about you."

"I'm not."

He squeezes her shoulder and walks off toward his Buick. Tillie turns back to the house. Long pale rectangles are cast on the *lanai* by the floor-to-ceiling windows. They disappear as the lamps inside are turned off. She walks until she comes to the side door. Mrs. Kurita's maid is waiting, eyes downcast. As Tillie enters, she whispers, "Upstairs, second door on right."

Arrangements have been made correctly, and there is no one to see Tillie as she climbs the steps and walks down the corridor. Without knocking, she opens the door. There is only a single lamp on the dressing table, but she can see Ryo in the dimness. He is in bed. As he raises himself on an elbow, the covers fall away from his muscular shoulder and arm. He does not speak. They like to pretend that she does not know he is in the room. It is a game.

One of their games.

She turns her back to him. He'd set the scene carefully, the lamp off to the side, the tall mirror above the dressing table facing her. He likes to see her front and back. She unzips her dress and lets it fall. Slides off her shoes.

Now she makes him wait, sitting at the mirror, pouring water from the ewer to the basin, washing off her mascara and lipstick, patting her face dry with a soft towel. Then pulling the myriad of pins from her tight French roll, allowing her blond hair to fall around her shoulders.

She stands, hooks her fingers under the straps of her slip, slides them off her shoulders, lets the slip fall. Bending to one side, then the other, a movement she knows he likes, she thumbs her stockings from their garters. Sitting in a chair by the lamp, she lifts her right leg and eases the silk hose down her thigh.

It is no easy task to remove stockings gracefully. A Chinese courtesan was brought over from Macao by Captain Jenkins and Commander Mannion to teach her how to do it. Along with other tricks.

Glancing over her shoulder she can see the moonlight reflected from Ryo's eyes as he watches from the shadows.

She stands to remove her girdle. Another task she'd

had to learn how to do for an audience. She'd always hated wearing a girdle and had many fights with her mother, who thought it was indecent to go without one. Her mother would be so pleased to know she is decent tonight.

Now she is down to her peach satin panties and brassiere. Ryo's breathing is becoming audible. She stands at attention, arches her back, brings her hands up to undo the two sets of hooks. Peels the cups away from her small, high-riding breasts. The aureoles of her nipples are unusually large. She used to worry that when she bent over in a bathing suit, a bit of pink might show. The anxieties of a virgin seem so far in the past.

She bends to lower her panties. As she steps out of them and begins to straighten up, Ryo breaks the silence. "Oh, not yet! Hold still. People say that the sweep of Waikiki beach to Diamond Head is the loveliest curve in the islands, but they haven't seen your behind."

She chuckles as she lets him look for another moment. Ryo's sense of humor was a surprise to her. His fluent English and his years in Chicago and Washington had been explained in the briefings, but not his jokes that seem so American to her.

She crosses the room. Ryo throws back the covers and sits on the edge of the bed, displaying the evidence of how much he has enjoyed the show. In his hand is the familiar short ivory stick. She opens her mouth, accepting it as obediently as her horse used to accept the bit. It's necessary; otherwise she can't keep from making noise. The Kuritas and their maid know what she and Ryo are doing, but the rest of the household does not. It must be kept that way if they hope to meet here again. And she does. Otherwise they have to meet in Honolulu, in a borrowed apartment or a hotel room, and the arrangements are difficult and tense. A mixed-race couple draws stares.

He pats the bed beside his thigh. She puts one foot there. Then he slides to the floor, kneeling between her legs. Soon she has to bite down hard on the ivory. The Chinese courtesan, while teaching her all the ways to please a man, told her that the man's efforts to please her would be perfunctory at best. But Ryo likes to bring her to her first climax before she is even in bed.

The courtesan was wrong about something else: how the lovemaking would end. She said that the man would lose interest in her the instant after he spent his seed. She should expect him to turn over and fall asleep. But Ryo props himself on an elbow over her and gently mops the sweat from her brow with the corner of the sheet and runs his fingers through her tangled hair, all the while murmuring endearments. He wishes her sound sleep and lightly kisses her closed eyes, as if she is a child.

When she reports to Captain Jenkins and Commander Mannion, she tells them everything Ryo does and says. Except for this.

Ryo's head lies on the pillow next to hers, his face turned toward her. She can tell by the rhythm of his breath against her cheek that he has fallen asleep. She is wide awake. Her vigil is beginning.

She knows the day has been tiring for him. His duties at the consulate are grueling, and these dinner parties, when he has to weigh every word before he speaks, wear him down. She hopes that he will sleep deeply. That there will be nothing for her to do tonight.

But no. She will not be spared. It begins as it usually does. He stirs, rolls onto his other side, then onto his back. She opens her eyes to see that his brow is furrowed. Beneath his lids his eyes are moving. His mouth opens. First there are only mumbles. But gradually he begins to form words. Japanese ones.

Whoever had tipped off Captain Jenkins and Commander Mannion that the Japanese attaché talked in his sleep had also known that he spoke in his mother tongue. That was how she got this job.

There are plenty of beautiful girls in Honolulu, Jenkins said. There are a few who are also intelligent, brave, and patriotic. But there is only one who in addition to having these qualities speaks fluent Japanese.

Tonight, what Ryo says is as usual a jumble. Some small anxiety of his day at the office continues to haunt him. He mentions the banyan tree outside the Kuritas' house. And the gecko on the dining room wall. That amused him, too. Eventually he grows quiet and still. There will be no more tonight. She slips out of bed, retrieves the journal from her purse, carefully records his babblings before she forgets them. For all the good they will do the U.S. Navy.

Don't worry, Jenkins and Mannion will say when she reports. Some night he'll reveal something big. He's well thought of at the consulate, a rising man, a confidant of the consul himself. He knows secrets and he'll let them slip.

One time Jenkins sent Mannion out of the office.

Put his hand on her shoulder and looked her in the eye. "We know what you're undergoing. The—the degradation. You feel the dirt can never be washed away. But it will be worth it in the end."

But I don't feel degraded, Tillie thinks now. Ryo's hands have touched every inch of my body, and I don't feel dirty. I won't feel dirty until the day he lets the secret slip and I bring it to you.

Until I complete my betrayal of him.

13

"Laker."

"Boss."

"Are you on a secure line?"

"Yes."

He was in a small office in the Customs and Immigration wing of Baltimore–Washington International Airport. He and Ava had come here straight from their plane, and Laker had used his Department of Homeland Security creds to obtain the use of a secure landline.

"You've been in Honolulu with Ava North. Where her grandmother grew up."

"How did you know?"

Mason grunted. Or possibly laughed. "Not from you. As usual, you did not inform me of your plans. Well done."

"Sir?"

"Your reputation in this town for handling matters your own way is the only thing keeping my battered old bureaucratic ass out of a sling."

"People have been asking you what I'm up to."

"The sort of people it's hard to say no to. So it was a good thing I could plead ignorance. Now they've started asking the Secretary for Homeland Security."

"Oh."

"Our boss. That's undesirable, Laker."

"What do you want me to do?"

"Are you making progress?"

"I think so. I've found out—"

"No. Don't tell me. We're not having this conversation."

"Okay."

"I will continue to cover for you for as long as I can. But Laker? When I call, prepare to do what you're told. For a change."

The line went dead. Mason preferred landlines to cell phones. Partly because they could be made more secure. Mostly because he liked to hang up on people, and it was much more satisfying when you could slam a receiver down on a cradle.

Laker replaced his own receiver and turned to Ava. She was sitting in an uncomfortable plastic chair by the door, her russet head bowed. She'd fallen asleep. It had been a tiring couple of days.

"Ava."

The head came up and she blinked at him.

"Apparently the word is out."

"About our trip to Hawaii? So you were right. Somebody—maybe my own esteemed employer—peeked into the airline reservation computers."

"Yes. They found your name. And they penetrated my alias. Which bothers me."

"That guy who followed me was probably from the field office of the FBI or whoever and he only wanted to ask me some questions. Now I feel twice as dumb for panicking and running away and falling in a river."

"You said your instincts told you he was your grandmother's murderer."

She sighed and looked down. "Yes. But what are my instincts worth? I'm an amateur. As I demonstrated by not following your advice. I should have stayed at poolside."

"The main thing is, you're okay."

"And we've still got the journal."

He considered for a moment. "Somebody is probably waiting at your apartment. To haul you back to Fort Meade for debriefing."

"It's inevitable, isn't it? What do we have to fear from being questioned by our own people? Apart from the tedium."

"It'll put us in a dilemma. Either we run off a string of lies, or we tell them about the journal."

"We tell them, and they'll demand we turn it over."

"Once it's out of our hands, it could just disappear. Don't rock the boat is rule number one in this town."

"And cover your ass is number two. Laker, I don't want to give up the journal till we find out what it means."

"Better not go home, then. I recommend a hotel. Unless you have a friend you could stay with."

Ava smiled. "I have you."

He turned his good ear toward her.

"You and I are in this together, Laker. And I don't want to get any of my innocent BFFs in trouble. I guess I'll have to buy some clothes and things."

"There's a coffee shop on the corner, a block west of

my building. Meet me there in four hours. We should go to my place together."

She glanced at her watch. "They'll be watching your place, too."

"Possibly. But there's a sort of gentleman's agreement among the D.C. spy shops. They don't try to pull each other's agents in off the street."

"Sensible arrangement. I have the feeling that trying to pull you in off the street might be hazardous to one's health. What will you be doing with the next four hours?"

"Old Washington saying. If you know nothing, people will tell you nothing—"

"But if you know a little, they'll tell you a lot," Ava finished for him. Her face became grave. "So you'll be trying to leverage what we found out in Hawaii. That Tillie was a honey trap."

"Ava, all we know for sure is that your grandmother worked for Naval Intelligence."

"We also know how intelligence agencies use beautiful, innocent young women. I expect it was the same in 1941."

14

Laker was sitting in a small, windowless conference room off the newsroom of the *Washington Post*. It was unimpressively furnished—just a battered wooden table surrounded by old office chairs—but this was where politicians who were about to announce their candidacy for office, or wanted coverage for some other reason, came to meet with editors and reporters. Something about the atmosphere reminded him of the old movie *Cat on a Hot Tin Roof,* and Burl Ives as Big Daddy wrinkling his nose and saying, "There's an odor of mendacity in here."

The door swung open. Joshua Milton stood glaring at him a moment before entering.

One of Washington's most famous and choleric investigative reporters, his face was familiar to Laker from the Sunday morning news shows: long graying dark hair flopping over his forehead and curling up from the tops of both ears so that he appeared to have horns, dark eyes with heavy bags under them, a mustache drooping over a downturned mouth.

"I was told a guy wants to see me, and he claims to be Thomas Lakcr. Which I find implausible."

The odor of mendacity must be getting to him, too. Working here, you'd think he'd be used to it. "Want to see my ID?"

"I know what the IDs of people like you are worth. I also happen to know Laker used to play ball for Notre Dame. So our sports editor will be sending up a photo in a minute. You want to tell me who you rcally are?"

"Let's wait for the photo."

Milton shut the door and slumped in a chair, looking balefully across the table at Laker. "You turn out to be Laker, I'm gonna be disappointed. Taking on a bullshit errand like this one—"

"What do you think I'm here for?"

"C'mon. It's that screwup in Pakistan two years ago. I've been working on the story ever since. Now it's ready to go. You guys don't want us to publish. You're here to ask nicely. Then there'll be the appeal to patriotism. Then the veiled threats. Let's skip it. Have your lawyers call our lawyers, and I'll see you—or somebody—in court."

The door opened and a copy boy came in. Were there still copy boys, Laker wondered. If so, they probably didn't call them that anymore. In any case he was a harassed-looking kid, and he handed Milton a folder and left.

Milton opened the folder, and Laker saw a photo of himself upside down in pads and number jersey. Looking as young as the copy boy.

"So you are Laker," Milton said.

"I'm not here about Pakistan."

"What, then?"

"In this case it's a who. Tillie North. I'd like to ask you a few questions."

Milton closed the file and tossed it on the table. "I don't like answering questions. Especially about Mrs. North."

"Ten years ago, you were working with her on an authorized biography."

"Yeah. She was charming. Told me lots of anecdotes about the rich and famous. I kept saying, c'mon, Tillie, you got to rip the lid off. We want to sell some books here. But she wouldn't give me the real stuff. The project was canceled. I had to give the advance back. Which was inconvenient, considering I'd spent it."

"You were pissed. So you set to work on an *un*authorized biography."

"I deny that. I have nothing to tell you about Tillie North. Unless you want to hear her funny story about the time Hubert Humphrey got drunk."

"I want to know about an earlier period in her life."

"Oh?"

"When she was an asset of the Office of Naval Intelligence at Pearl Harbor. Assuming they used that term in 1941."

Milton smiled for the first time. "You live up to your rep, Laker. That was buried deep. You find out about Mannion and Jenkins, too?"

Laker raised his eyebrows. He figured that was all it was going to take. Milton had been waiting for someone he could tell this story to for a long time.

"Commander J. T. Mannion, just beginning a long and distinguished career in ONI. At Pearl in '41, he was trying to turn a diplomat named Hirochi Ryo. Smart man, esteemed at the consulate, sure to have actionable intelligence on Japanese war plans. He'd spent years in America. Liked Americans."

"So did Admiral Yamamoto. That didn't stop him from masterminding the Pearl Harbor attack."

"No. Ryo was cut from the same cloth. Loyal to the emperor, even if he had doubts about General Tojo. Mannion was getting nowhere. Finally he tried a kind of honey trap."

"Entangle Ryo in a romance, then blackmail him?"

"Not exactly. Try to blackmail Ryo, and he'd just commit hara-kiri. There was a twist to this one. Captain L. B. Jenkins, Mannion's boss, was a digger. He tracked down Ryo's roommate at the University of Chicago, who told him Ryo talked in his sleep."

Laker thought of the seemingly meaningless lines in the journal. So they were the unconscious murmurings of a Japanese diplomat. He said, "Mannion and Jenkins went looking for a beautiful girl. With no known connections to Naval Intelligence. Who spoke Japanese."

"Tillie gave her body for her country. Repeatedly. Faithfully turned in all Ryo's mutterings. But he was a professional diplomat, on guard even when asleep. He let no secrets slip. That's what Mannion told me."

"You interviewed him?"

"In a hospice in Arizona. He was ninety and riddled with cancer. He was dead by the time I found out he'd lied to me."

"You mean, the operation was *not* a failure?"

Milton's dark eyes burned into Laker's. "My source for this part is still alive. So don't even try to get the name out of me."

"Okay."

"On November 27, 1941, Jenkins sent a top-secret

cable to his superior in Washington. According to Tillie's report, Ryo's blathering of the night before included the words "*kido butai* has sailed" and something she couldn't understand about the Aleutians. Not much but it was enough. *Kido butai* means striking force. The Japanese attack fleet, which did in fact set sail from Hitokappu the previous day. The U.S. had an airbase in the Aleutian Islands. The Japanese were worried a patrol might spot the fleet. Jenkins said that meant the Japs were approaching Hawaii from the north. He urgently recommended air patrols of the northern approaches. If his recommendation had been acted on, the Japanese would have been sighted and Pearl would have been ready."

"Have you seen Jenkins's message?"

"No, and nobody ever will. Same with the response from Washington, which was stand down, nothing to worry about, negotiations with the Japs are going just fine."

"Washington was complacent."

"Laker, how dumb can you get? FDR himself had decided to let the attack happen, to bring America into World War II, something he'd been trying to accomplish for years."

"This is old news, Milton. The 'FDR knew' rumors started before the war was even over. There have been—what?—ten official investigations."

"They've investigated coded cable traffic, radio transmissions, stuff like that. Jenkins's operation has never surfaced."

"It would have. If you could prove what you say."

Milton conceded with a shrug. "I'm not ready to publish yet. But I've found out what happened in the later lives of Ryo and Tillie, and it all fits."

Laker leaned forward, turning his good ear. "What happened to Ryo?"

"On December 7, Ryo and the other Japanese diplomats were arrested and put in an internment camp. On April 5, 1942, he was returned to Japan. He went to work at the Foreign Ministry in Tokyo, where he was apparently doing something important and hush-hush. The records are incomplete, but apparently he'd resumed his rise in the diplomatic service. A year later, he suddenly disappeared."

"Disappeared?"

"It wasn't until years after the war that his family found out what happened to him. March 10, 1943, he was committed to Hoisin Prison near Tokyo. On January 4, 1944, he was executed there."

"You think his superiors somehow found out about his affair with Tillie? How he'd almost given the game away?"

"*Somehow?* What kind of spook are you, Laker?"

"You mean Mannion and Jenkins sent word through a back channel."

"Yeah, they burned him."

"Why?"

"Why not eliminate a rising enemy foreign service officer? Especially if you can get the enemy to do it for you."

"Mannion tell you that?"

"He didn't have to. Then there's what happened to Tillie."

"She moved to Washington."

"In the summer of '42. As a reward for services rendered, Jenkins arranged an office job in the War Department. There she met an army lieutenant named Ephraim

North. They got married in early '44, and by the end of that year North was a major stationed at the Pentagon. By '46, he was a lieutenant colonel attached to the White House. The Norths' long career as a D.C. power couple had begun."

"You're saying they blackmailed FDR."

Milton rolled his eyes. "Laker, don't be crude. We're talking about two of the most subtle political operators this town has ever seen. They dropped hints in the proper ears that a secret—even the biggest secret—was safe with them. And they were rewarded."

Laker nodded. He could see a few soft spots in Milton's version of events, but didn't see any point in arguing with the reporter about them. He did have one more question, though.

"Do you think Tillie ever knew what happened to Ryo?"

Milton laughed harshly. "She'd forgotten all about him by then. She'd managed to make the marriage of the season, even though she was shopworn goods by the standards of the time. Now she was starting her climb to the top of Washington society. She never looked back at that sordid episode in Hawaii."

15

Ava missed their rendezvous at the coffee shop. He called, but her cell phone was off and her in-box was full. He went home. An hour later, his intercom buzzed.

"Laker," Ava's voice said. "Let me in before somebody sees me."

His building had no lobbies or corridors; the elevator—actually the freight elevator of the old pin factory—opened directly into his apartment. A minute later, the doors slid back to reveal Ava with a suitcase and duffel bag. She looked frazzled.

"God, what a day I've had. Pour me a big glass of that wood stripper of yours, would you?"

She staggered past him and flopped on the couch in the living area, leaving him to cope with the luggage. She was a North, after all. The suitcase was heavy. The duffel was light, but it clanked.

"What's in here?" he asked.

"Pup tent. Fresh from the outdoor store in the mall."

"You're going to pitch a tent?"

She indicated the spaciousness of the loft with a sweep of her arm. "This place gives me agoraphobia. I can't sleep out. And I'm certainly not going to share your teepee." She raised her eyebrows at him. "I hope you haven't been getting any ideas?"

"About you being my squaw? No."

He put the luggage down and went to the safe he used as a liquor cabinet, where he poured two glasses of Speyside Cardhu. He handed one to Ava and sat down opposite her.

"Sorry I missed you at the coffee shop." She kicked off her shoes, crossed her legs, and began to massage her left foot. "My feet are killing me. I was trying to hail a cab on N Street when Becky Johnson of CNN spotted me. She and her camera crew chased me as far as Constitution Avenue before they gave up."

"I notice you've turned off your phone."

"Had to. My section chief at NSA kept calling me about coming in to answer questions. It started with requests and escalated to demands. Then threats to pull my security clearance."

"Has anybody mentioned the journal?"

"Still our little secret, as far as I know. It's in the suitcase."

"Good."

"This town is having a panic attack, Laker. Everybody's remembering something they once said to Tillie North and shouldn't have. They can't concentrate on their work. And these are the people who guide the destiny of the world, or think they do. We're ants to them."

"Sam Mason has our backs."

"That's not much comfort to me."

"It would be if you knew Mason."

She tossed off her scotch and held out the glass. He got up to refill it.

"Who did you go to see today? Thanks," she said as he handed her the glass.

"Milton, at the *Post*."

"Josh Milton. The original poison pen." She took a long swallow of scotch.

"He had some information." Laker sat down across from Ava. "You're not going to like it."

"I haven't liked anything that's happened to me in a while. Except you."

She smiled at him over her glass. Laker forced himself to concentrate and told her the story. She listened gravely, and did not speak till he was finished.

"Okay. Milton is full of it. First, his only proof that Ephraim North blackmailed his way to the top is that he reached the top. Which he actually did by being brilliant, loyal, and hardworking. And having Tillie at his side."

"Factors a conspiracy-monger like Milton overlooks."

"Second, I know that journal practically by heart. And there is nothing in there that even hints at a coming Pearl Harbor attack."

"True. In fact the journal breaks off more than a month before December 7. Any thoughts on that?"

"They realized they were wasting their time. Ryo wasn't going to say anything useful. I don't have to tell you, Laker. Most intel ops fail."

"But if the journal is just a by-product of a failed operation, why did your grandmother keep it? Why did she want you to have it?"

Ava leaned forward to put the glass on the table. Wearily rubbed her eyes. "I don't want to know the answers to those questions, Laker. I'm afraid I'm going to find out something horrible about Tillie."

Laker said nothing. After a minute, Ava lowered her hands. "Okay. Sorry. I know I have no choice. And I know what we're going to do first thing tomorrow."

"Which is?"

"We're going to see the person Tillie trusted most in this world."

16

Erlynne Bendix was napping when they arrived. The garden of the Dillsworth Long Term Care facility in Reston, Virginia, was a peaceful spot on a warm July morning. Marigolds, petunias, and tiger lilies were blooming in the greenery surrounding the small patio. Bumblebees and honeybees browsed among them.

Mrs. Bendix, as Ava called hcr, was an African American woman in her late eighties. Her forehead was deeply scored and her cheeks sagged, but her pure white hair was still dense. The eyes behind her bifocals were shut, the head bowed. She was breathing deeply but silently.

"She'll be irritable if we wake her," Ava whispered. "We'll just have to wait."

"Okay."

"I don't know how this will go. Some days she's forgetful. Other days she pretends to be forgetful because she can't be bothered with you."

"You seem a little intimidated by her."

"When I was a child, she ruled the Chevy Chase house with an iron hand. She'd come to work for my grandmother right after the war, as a teenager. She was her maid for almost fifty years. It was funny, Tillie knew hundreds of people. Brilliant, talented, powerful men and women. But in a way, Erlynne Bendix was her closest friend. Grandmother knew anything she told her would go no further."

"Hard to find a friend like that in Washington."

The old lady stirred. Raised her head. Blinked at Ava. "Miz Maureen?"

"I'm Ava, Mrs. Bendix. Maureen's daughter."

She thought it over. "That's right. Maureen died ten years ago." At Mrs. Bendix's age, you were not squeamish talking about the dead. The head turned slowly, the aureole of white hair catching the light. The eyes behind the thick glasses came to bear on Laker. "I don't remember you. You're not Ava's husband?"

"No."

"No reason I should remember you, then."

"None at all. My name is Thomas Laker, ma'am."

She turned back to Ava. "Your grandmother's dead, too. I saw it on the TV."

"Yes, Mrs. Bendix. We've come to talk about my grandmother. We have questions about her early life, when she lived in Hawaii."

"That was long before I came to work for Miz Tillie. I don't know nothing about Hawaii."

"Yes, but she may have spoken to you about it. She was working for officers at Pearl Harbor, Commander Mannion? Captain Jenkins?"

"Before my time," Mrs. Bendix said stubbornly.

"They asked Tillie to do something for them," Ava

said. "For her country. It was important work and only she could do it."

Mrs. Bendix was watching a bumblebee land on a petunia and crawl over its petals. Ava leaned closer and began to tell her about what Tillie had done for her country. She didn't get far.

"Ava, who have you been listening to? Your grandmother would never have gotten mixed up in a thing like that."

Laker said, "It was wartime, ma'am—"

"A lady is a lady, peace or war. I don't want to hear no more about it."

Ava sat back, lifted her purse onto her lap, and took out the journal. She held it out to Mrs. Bendix, who looked at it for a long moment but did not take it.

"She kept that with her all the time," Mrs. Bendix said. "If you have it now, she must've wanted you to know everything."

"Yes. It's very, very important."

Mrs. Bendix took an interest in the bees again. A full minute passed before she said, "I don't like to talk about it. It was a terrible thing they made her do."

"It's all right, Mrs. Bendix. We know most of the story. Mannion and Jenkins. And Hirochi Ryo."

The last name brought the old woman's eyes back to Ava's. "Hirochi Ryo," she repeated. "Yes, that was his name. I'd forgotten. I'm not good with foreign names."

Ava held the journal out to her again. "Did you ever look in this book?"

"Once, maybe. Didn't mean nothing to me."

"Did my grandmother ever tell you why she stopped writing in it?"

"Why she stopped?"

"We're thinking it must've been because they realized Hirochi Ryo wasn't going to reveal any secrets. Mannion and Jenkins, I mean. They told Tillie she didn't have to do it anymore."

Mrs. Bendix's gaze drifted back to the bees again. The silence stretched on. Laker thought she was not going to answer. But then she said, "You don't know what kind of men Mannion and Jenkins were. They spared Miz Tillie nothing."

"She had to keep . . . meeting with Ryo? Reporting to them what he said? But why did she stop writing in the book?"

"Because she wasn't going to betray the man she loved, Ava."

Ava flinched. *"What?"*

"She'd go to Mannion and Jenkins, and they'd ask her what Ryo said, and she'd make up some nonsense. She was in love with that man, and she shared his bed until December 7, when they locked him up in an internment camp. Far as I know, she never saw him again. Years later, she found out he'd been sent back to Japan, and he died in the war. I was with her when she heard the news. By then she was a married lady with two children, but she was heartbroken. That's when she told me about him. Now I've told you."

The long gust of speech seemed to leave her exhausted. Her shoulders sagged, but she kept her head up, her fierce gaze fixed on Ava. "That's all I know. Now let me rest."

Ava rose unsteadily and murmured something, maybe thanks, maybe apology. She turned away.

Laker said, "Mrs. Bendix, we need to know why the

book is so important. Did Mrs. North ever say why she kept it by her all these years?"

The old woman seemed to think this was a stupid question. She said, "Because it was all she had left of Hirochi Ryo."

17

Back in the loft, Ava took the journal out of her purse, dropped it on the coffee table, and stood staring at it.

"Now we know. Tillie couldn't betray her lover," she said. "What we don't know is, could she betray her country?"

"We haven't found any evidence that she knew about December 7. Nor that Ryo himself knew about it. The Japanese navy had a spy in Honolulu tracking fleet movements. Even he didn't know when the attack was coming."

"Well, Laker, that's what I would like to believe. That Mannion and Jenkins's brilliant scheme produced no intelligence. Had no effect, apart from breaking a young girl's heart."

She dropped on the couch, hunched over with elbows on knees. "But where does that leave us? What's in this book that Tillie had to die for it? And who was that guy who chased me through the forest in Hawaii?"

Laker had no answers to these questions, so it was

just as well that the phone rang. It was the landline phone on his desk. The secure line. He walked quickly over and picked it up.

Sam Mason didn't give him a chance to say hello. "You'll remember, I told you you would get a call, and you'd have to do as you were told for a change?"

"Yes."

"This is that call. I need your report. I can't cover for you any longer."

"I'll be there in half an hour."

"Not here. The Mall, third bench down from the reflecting pool."

Mason hung up.

"Your boss?" Ava asked.

Laker nodded. "Our time is running out."

The high white dome of the Capitol building loomed over its reflection in the broad rectangular pool. As usual tired tourists were resting on the wall that surrounded the pool. Some looked as if they were contemplating a dive into the water. It was late morning and unbearably hot already.

Laker crossed the street to the wide lawn lined with trees that was the National Mall. Farther down toward the Washington Monument, he could see banners and crowds and hear amplified music. An event was going on. There was a festival or a demonstration or both on the Mall every day of the summer. But this end was fairly quiet, as the crowds of office workers from Capitol Hill hadn't arrived yet to take their lunch breaks.

Mason had the third bench to himself. He'd put on a

Washington Nationals cap to protect his bald head from the sun. It jarred with his dark blue business suit. Laker jogged over to him and arrived sweating.

"Why aren't we meeting in your office?" he asked as he sat down.

"There are two guys from the Bureau permanently stationed in my waiting room, with orders to take you in for questioning."

"I'm surprised you put up with that." Mason had even more disdain for the FBI than for the CIA and the NSA.

"The guy who put them there has the power to cut our budget. To the bone."

"Oh."

"You'd be flattered if you knew the names of the people who've told me to turn you over to them or they'd have my head on a plate."

"Have any of them mentioned a book? A journal?"

"No. Is that good?"

"It means we're still a step ahead. The book is what this is all about."

Laker told the story from the beginning. Mason did not interrupt. He was still and expressionless. The man had remarkable powers of concentration. You never had to tell him anything twice.

When Laker was finished, he thought it all over, polishing his spectacles with his tie. "First off, Josh Milton of the *Post* is a conspiracy nut."

"We can forget about the 'FDR knew Pearl Harbor was coming' business?"

"FDR is dead. World War II is over. This is about something that matters *now*. I'm an expert on D.C. shitstorms, and the one we're in is a Force 5."

"Ava says there's nothing in the journal but the nighttime mutterings of a Japanese diplomat who's long dead and forgotten."

"She must be missing something. I'll have our specialists go over the journal. Maybe there's a coded message that Ava missed. Or something sewn into the binding. A microchip, maybe."

"Possible. But Ava isn't going to want to let go of that book."

"She'll have to. You two have hit a dead end."

"Once word gets out that the journal exists, there'll be a mad scramble for it."

"Word won't get out. The Outfit is the most leak-proof shop in town. You know how many people I've fired to keep it that way."

Laker did. He said, "All right. I'll bring the book in. I want a moment alone with you in your office to put it in your hands. Then I'll be happy to let the Feebs drag me off to their headquarters for a few hours of chat."

Mason gave one of his rare, brief smiles. "When it comes to bullshitting the Bureau, Laker, you're a past master. Just don't let on how much you're enjoying it."

18

"I'll let you have it," Ava said. "On one condition."

This was better than Laker had expected. He'd worried she wouldn't surrender the journal without a fight. He'd found her in his kitchen, making coffee in a press and heating milk to go with it. She gave him a mug and they sat at his dining table, a long, plain wooden refectory table that looked as if it had come from a monastery. He could host a dinner party for a dozen guests, but since he rarely did, the table provided space for books, magazines, and projects. There was a sailing ship model that had reached the rigging stage and a disassembled carburetor from the 1964 Mustang he was gradually restoring. Next to the chessboard lay Tillie's journal. Ava gazed at it as she sipped coffee.

He said, "I'm glad you understand. It really is the only thing we can do now."

"Your boss is quite right." There was an edge to Ava's voice. "Of course my grandmother was able to come up with a code so subtle and ingenious that I, a mere NSA cryptographer with a Ph.D. from MIT, failed to break it. Or even recognize that it *was* a code."

"Mason didn't mean to be insulting, just—"

"No, no, I'm amused by his notion that my grandma was up on all the latest spycraft. Microchips sewn into the binding. Give me a break. But you can take him the journal. *After* I go through it one more time."

Unsure he'd heard right, Laker turned his good ear. "You've gone over it many times. What else is there to look for?"

"Something so simple that I've overlooked it up to now."

Reaching for a magnifying glass that lay next to the ship model, she shifted to a seat where the sun came over her shoulder. She opened the book.

Laker left her to it. He went to his walking desk, flicked the switch on the treadmill, and moseyed along at one mile an hour while he dealt with his email. Any faster and he made typing mistakes. A lot of people who'd been unable to reach him by phone had sent him messages. They weren't happy with him.

"Laker."

She was sitting with her elbows on the table and hands folded, propping up her chin. The journal lay open before her. "Please bring me a pencil."

"You found something?"

"Yes."

"In the Japanese or the English?"

"In the blank pages."

He went over to the table. Handing her the pencil, he looked over her shoulder at the journal. He saw only white paper. Ava picked up the book, angled it to take the light. Now he saw a few faint scratches.

"Tillie must have made them with a pin," Ava said. "It would have been difficult for her, with her arthritis."

"The marks were made recently?"

"Yes. It's a message to me."

She was rubbing the page with the side of the pencil point, to make the angular block letters stand out:

AVA LAST BDAY

"I don't understand," Laker said.

"North family shorthand for birthday."

"Ava's last birthday."

"Grandmother warning me I'll never see my next birthday? That's a cheerful thought."

"Let's assume she's using 'last' in the sense of 'previous.'"

"Let's do. My previous birthday was just a few weeks ago. May 11."

"Did Tillie give you anything?"

"A present? I'm trying to remember." She sat back and closed her eyes. "I had a lot of work that day. And I was thirty, so I didn't feel much like celebrating anyway. Friends from the office bought me a drink, and I went home and to bed. I didn't visit Tillie. Didn't even talk to her on the phone."

"A card?"

"She'd stopped sending birthday cards. Afraid she'd forget a date and offend somebody."

"Anything else you remember about the day?"

She sat still, eyes closed and brow furrowed, for a couple of minutes. Then she gave an impatient toss of her head. "What did your esteemed boss say? That I'm at a dead end? He was right."

She snapped the journal closed and handed it to him. He slipped it into the side pocket of his suit coat and went back to the office area, where he knelt in front of a low shelf.

"So you have a real safe," Ava said. "In addition to the one you use as a liquor cabinet. It's kind of small. What's in it?"

He spun the dial to the last number and opened the safe. Withdrew his service weapon. Like the Army, the Outfit issued the Beretta M9.

"Oh," Ava said.

He slid a magazine into the butt, jacked a round into the chamber, made sure the safety was on. Then he took off his jacket and shrugged into his holster. Laker favored a shoulder rig, with the gun slung butt down at his left side. Belt holsters seemed too cowboy to him.

Ava was hovering, looking worried. "Are you expecting trouble?"

"No. But I told Mason I'd put the journal in his hands. No one else's. I'm making you the same promise."

19

After Laker left, Ava had a spell of restlessness. It was a good thing his loft had plenty of room for pacing. She was able to do laps around the exterior walls, by the windows, getting up a good head of steam.

She told herself to stop thinking about the journal. She should be sending texts and making calls, trying to mollify her superiors at the NSA. But she kept being distracted by the feeling that she was failing her grandmother. She imagined Tillie taking a pin or paperclip in fingers made shaky and clumsy by the years, painfully scratching a message that was meant for Ava alone. Only Ava just didn't get it.

On her tenth or eleventh circuit of the loft, a new possibility occurred to her. Maybe Tillie hadn't been referring to Ava's birthday, but to her own.

It was easy to remember, because it was even more recent than Ava's. June 2 was Tillie's birthday. It had fallen on a Tuesday. Ava had stopped by the Cheltenham Long Term Care Community after work. The visit had been brief, because Tillie was always tired in the evening.

But otherwise she was feeling good. Ava had brought her earrings—Tillie still loved earrings, even though she needed help to put them on—and an audio book. It was the latest rip-the-lid-off-Washington bestseller. Tillie thanked her for that, too, saying she enjoyed such books now that she could be fairly sure she wouldn't be mentioned in them.

But had Tillie given *her* anything?

Not a present, of course. But she and her grandmother exchanged paperwork on every visit. Doctors, lawyers, and investment advisers were prodigious generators of correspondence. Ava always arrived with a big envelope filled with letters to explain to Tillie, documents for her to sign. What papers had they huddled over on June 2?

Weary of walking and straining to remember, Ava lay down on the couch, closed her eyes, and emptied her mind. Sometimes things came to her when she stopped trying to remember.

The trick worked. On Tillie's birthday, Ava always prepared for her signature a new living will. Tillie feared that she would lapse into a coma and be kept on life support for weeks or months. She wanted to make sure her wishes were made clear in a document that was up to date with the law.

But the living will was just a few pages of legal boilerplate. It couldn't have any larger significance.

Abruptly Ava swung her feet to the floor and sat upright. The scene in her grandmother's room on June 2 had just flashed into her mind, bright and clear. Tillie was in bed, the papers resting on a tray on her lap. After going over the living will, she had left it with Tillie to read over and sign. They were expecting Ava at the nurses' station, to talk to her about Tillie's medication. It had taken some time. When she returned, Tillie was asleep. She had glanced at the last page to make sure it was signed, then put the will in the envelope. When she got home, she'd filed it away. She hadn't looked at it since.

Ava was sure that if she paged through the will, she would find a piece of paper that Tillie had slipped into it. She was going to have to return to her apartment. Laker had warned her that the building would be under surveillance by the NSA. She'd have to slip by the watchers somehow. Or talk her way past them. What was the worst thing that could happen? That she'd end up in a conference room at Fort Meade, answering questions. Just as Laker would be doing.

She grabbed her purse and took out her iPhone to text for an Uber car. Once she was in it and on her way across town, she would text Laker. She wanted him to know where she'd gone.

Once it was too late to stop her.

20

The Gray Outfit's headquarters was located on Capitol Hill, in a row of ornate Victorian-era townhouses with mansard roofs and bay windows and minuscule front gardens behind low wrought-iron fences. The plaque by the heavy wooden front door said, National Alliance of Auto Parts Distributors. It was calculated to inspire disinterest in passersby. Generally it worked as intended, but every couple of days a member of the public would press the intercom, wanting to know if the Alliance could help him locate some hard-to-find auto part.

After stating his business, he would be buzzed into the paneled front hall of the mansion, where Joanie, the receptionist, sat at an antique desk. She was supposed to give visitors a phony brochure about the good work being done by NAAPD and send them away. But she'd fielded so many inquiries over the years that by now she actually knew a lot about rare auto parts and could be helpful.

As he opened the door, Laker was thinking he ought

to ask her where he could find a replacement headlight for his vintage Mustang.

He found himself facing not Joanie, but a security man in a Kevlar vest, holding a Heckler & Koch MR556A1 at port arms. The door swung shut behind him. He glanced over his shoulder at another armed man.

"It's Laker all right, everything's cool," the man in front of him was saying into the mic clipped to his vest. "Hi, sir."

Laker recognized the shaved head and long, crooked nose of Brad Bartel. "What's up, Bartel?"

"One of the roof sensors flashed us a warning light. I went up there and didn't find anything. Probably a pigeon, but we have to stay in perimeter mode defense for another twenty minutes. Better hang your creds, sir."

As Laker took out his ID and slipped the tab into the breast pocket of his suit coat, Bartel stepped closer and whispered, "You know the Feebs are waiting for you?"

He nodded and patted Bartel's shoulder as he went past. Joanie, who was stout and gray-haired, was trying to maintain her dignity as she scrambled out from under her desk. They exchanged waves as he mounted the staircase, which made up for its narrowness with a red carpet held in place by gleaming copper rods and a banister held up by curved wooden balusters.

A stocky African American man in a blue suit appeared at the top of the stairs, in front of the large bay window. "Hi, Tom."

At least it was Ray Hilton, one of his friends at the Bureau, who'd be escorting him across town. "Hello, Ray. Sorry to keep you waiting."

"No problem. I've been catching up on current

events." He held up a copy of *The Economist.* "The kid here has been wasting his time playing games on his iPhone. Boothroyd, this is the celebrated Thomas Laker. Try not to genuflect."

Boothroyd, a young man with a blond buzz cut, smiled and shook hands.

"Who's going to be grilling me, Ray?" Laker asked.

"Deputy Director Frances Wilson."

"Wilson herself?"

"She gets mad whenever the Outfit operates on American soil and doesn't coordinate with us. Personally, she likes you. You could do worse."

"I'd like to report to my own boss first."

"DD Wilson is champing at the bit, so don't take long."

As the Feebs sat down on the bench in the bay window, Laker turned and walked down the short paneled corridor to Mason's office. The door was open, Mason at his desk. The office had been a back bedroom and its one window looked out on a blank wall, so in his rare moments of idleness, Mason gazed up at a stained-glass panel in the ceiling. No daylight reached it, and he had ordered an electric light put in the attic, so the clusters of grapes, and birds against an azure sky showed up clearly. Laker closed the door and advanced to the desk, taking the journal from his pocket. "One development since we last talked—"

There was a crash and pieces of multicolored glass showered down on them. The roof panel had shattered. Laker looked up to see something drop though the hole, bounce on Mason's desk, and explode. It was as if a bolt of lightning shot across the small room, simultaneous with a crack of thunder. Laker was blinded and deafened. Losing his balance, he collapsed to the floor. *Stun grenade,* he thought.

After a few seconds his vision came back, dim and blurry. A man in combat boots and dark clothing was standing atop the desk. He wore a flak vest and balaclava mask and held a machine pistol in his hands. A ribbon of spent shells unfurled from it. Laker couldn't hear the reports.

He swiveled his head. Hilton and Boothroyd were in the doorway. He saw the muzzle flashes of their automatics but heard nothing. In the next instant blood was gushing from Hilton's chest, and Boothroyd's young face turned into red mush as the hail of bullets from the machine pistol found their marks.

Laker managed to get to his knees and reach for the killer's boots in an attempt to pull his legs out from under him. But he was too slow. The killer jumped to the floor and scooped up something that was lying there.

The journal, Laker thought.

Mason saw too. Blinking and grimacing from the effects of the grenade, he surged up from his chair and threw himself bodily at the killer, who pivoted and swung the metal stock of the machine pistol at Mason's head. Blood sprayed across his white shirt and he collapsed.

Now the killer turned on Laker. The mask hid his face except for his blue eyes. Grasping the edge of the desk, Laker was pulling himself to his feet. He saw the killer drop into a crouch and knew the kick was coming but couldn't get his muscles to respond in time. The kick landed hard on his chest, knocked him flat on his back. He started to roll away, knowing it wouldn't do any good.

The bullets he expected did not strike him. He looked up at Bartel in the doorway, standing over the bodies of Hilton and Boothroyd, firing his HK. The bullets ripped into Mason's desk, sending splinters flying. The killer was behind it. The hand holding the machine pistol came up. He fired blind, swiveling his wrist, unleashing a scythe of bullets. A line of holes was punched in the wall and blood jetted from Bartel's thighs, below the Kevlar vest. He dropped.

Instantly the killer was on the move, rounding the desk, jumping over the bodies in the doorway. Laker struggled upright and lurched after him. He was running down the corridor toward the bay window, firing. The heavy glass shattered. The man leapt through it and dropped out of sight.

One hand on the wall, the other on the banister, Laker was able to stay upright as he followed. He reached the window in time to see the killer, who had landed in the soft earth of the flower beds in the small front yard, rolling over and regaining his feet. He bounded over the low fence to the sidewalk.

It was a fifteen-foot drop, and Laker was in no shape for it. He ran down the stairs, passing more guards coming up. He could hear them shouting at him but not make out the words. He shouted back that Mason and Bartel needed help right away, especially Bartel, whose femoral artery was probably severed. He ran on, passing Joanie, who was talking on the telephone and looking at him with wide, shocked eyes.

Outside frightened passersby were taking shelter behind parked cars. Traffic was tangling. Looking down the sidewalk, Laker could see the running man. He had a big lead already. Laker's hand touched the butt of his

Beretta, but his vision was still blurred and jumpy, not good enough to take a shot. He started running.

His thoughts were in tumult. God, what a shambles. Ray Hilton and that poor kid Boothroyd were dead. He could have no hope for them. Brad Bartel was going to bleed out if help didn't reach him in the next few minutes. And Sam Mason? Laker had no idea what shape he was in.

At least the effects of the grenade were wearing off. With every stride he felt more sure of his footing. He was a block away from the Outfit now, and the usual street life of Capitol Hill was humming along obliviously. People stared at the two running men, more curious than afraid, and were slow getting out of the way. Laker called on years of football experience to dodge pedestrians on the sidewalks and vehicles and cyclists at the street crossings. He was hoping to gain on the killer, but the man was fast and sure-footed. His lead was holding up.

His arms were pumping freely. He'd put away or discarded the machine pistol. Sunlight glistened on his black hair. He'd taken off the balaclava, too.

They were now running through a parking lot, weaving among people burdened with bags or pushing carts. A car backed out right in front of the man but it didn't faze him. He threw out his arms, planted both hands on the trunk lid, and vaulted over the car, effortlessly regaining his footing as he landed.

The Beretta in its holster slapped Laker's ribs with every stride. His vision was good enough to aim now, but there were too many people around to risk a shot. He realized they were approaching Eastern Market.

In front of the old brick market hall, the row of

white pavilions where farmers put out their produce was thronged with lunchtime shoppers. The man slowed to a jog, picking his way among them. One hand and then the other slid up inside the back of his flak vest, came out holding things. Laker couldn't make out what they were. The man put the thing in his right hand on his head. It was a baseball cap. Then he went in the entrance to the market hall.

Laker followed. The man had disappeared. The aisles between display cases of cheese and meats and beds of ice on which lay staring fish were packed with people, and half of them were wearing baseball caps. Laker had three aisles to choose from. He guessed straight ahead, moving among the people with the overhand motions of a swimmer, muttering apologies, scanning the crowd ahead.

After a few moments he stopped, realizing it was futile. The thing in the killer's other hand must have been a jacket he could put over the flak vest. Laker didn't know what color it was. Even if he saw the man, he wouldn't recognize him.

He turned and made his way slowly to the entrance, getting his breath back.

His vision was normal except for an occasional flicker, and he was no deafer than usual.

He took out his phone and put it to his good right ear.

Joanie came on the line. "Laker?"

"I lost him. Eastern Market, just a minute ago." He gave her a description, pitifully inadequate, to pass on to the police.

She said, "Better come back, Tom. DC cops are here. And the Bureau. They have two dead."

"Bartel and the boss?"

"Just left in the ambo. Both still breathing. That's all the medics would say."

Thank God for that, anyway, Laker thought. "On my way," he said.

Stepping into the sunlight, he spotted a cab parked in the market's forecourt and beckoned. As it maneuvered toward him he glanced at his phone again. He had a text. It was from Ava. She said she'd figured out what her grandmother had given her, and was on her way to her apartment to retrieve it.

The cab pulled up beside him and Laker got in. He gave the driver, a turbaned and bearded Sikh, the address of the Outfit's headquarters. As he sank back in the seat and the cab pulled away, he tried to assess the damage.

The journal was in enemy hands. Whoever the enemy was. Dates in 1941, addresses in Honolulu, the mutterings of a sleeping Japanese diplomat. Would it mean any more to the enemy than it had to them?

Laker sat bolt upright as the realization hit him. The killer was probably going through the journal now. The blank page Ava had rubbed graphite on would leap out at him. Tillie's message might not mean anything to him, but it would tell him that Ava was the key.

She was now at home. The first place he would look for her.

Laker slid forward on the seat. "Take me to 1108 New Hampshire Avenue."

The Sikh half-turned with a doubtful expression.

"It's just off Dupont Circle. As fast as you can get there," Laker said, touching Ava's number on his phone's keypad.

21

Ava heard the incoming-call tune from the phone in her pants pocket, but let it go to voice mail. This was a delicate moment.

She was approaching her home on foot. It was an old ten-story apartment building of tan brick with a maroon canopy at the entrance. The curb was solidly lined with parked cars, and right in front of her building was a white Chevrolet Impala, straight from the NSA pool. There were two motionless figures in the front seats. Waiting to take her back to Fort Meade for debriefing.

As usual she was wearing a hat with a wide floppy brim to protect her delicate skin. It also hid her red hair. With luck they hadn't noticed her yet.

Putting her head down, she walked quickly, but not too quickly, up the side path and along her building to the back. There was a parking lot surrounded by a high fence. Taking out her keys, she unlocked the gate and went through, then climbed the fire escape stairs to her floor, the sixth, arriving breathless. She went through the back door into the kitchen, turned left into the second bedroom she used as an office. There was a tall gray government surplus filing cabinet. She slid open the top drawer where she kept Tillie's papers and fingered through the tabbed folders.

She'd followed routine when she got back from Tillie's on June 2. Right where it should be was the latest living will, still in its manila envelope. She really ought to get out of here, but she couldn't resist opening the flap and pulling out the papers.

And there was her grandmother's personal message. Between the first and second pages, one sheet of paper, densely covered with print. The letters were a bit blurry and some were heavier than others. It had been typed on the old manual typewriter Tillie'd kept in her study at the Chevy Chase house. Before the arthritis worsened, she'd been an excellent typist. Priding herself on her speed and accuracy, she said she didn't need an electric typewriter, let alone a word processor. The letters formed meaningless groups rather than words. Ava had no difficulty recognizing a basic substitution code, the sort that could be used even by a bright middle-school kid. Once she found the key text, she would be able to decode it in a couple of hours.

A sound was nibbling away at a corner of her mind. Now she identified it. Someone was jiggling the doorknob of her back door. She jumped up and ran into the kitchen. The doorknob was turning back and forth. Clicks and rattles indicated somebody was trying to pick the lock.

Ava backed away. The watchers in the car must have been more alert than she'd hoped. They'd seen her go by and followed her up. She wondered how they'd gotten through the parking-lot gate. Well, she didn't want to talk to them. Folding the sheet of code, she trotted through the living room and out her front door. She locked it behind her and pressed the elevator call button.

The elevator must have been original equipment with the 1920s building and seemed to take forever when you were in a hurry. The click of a lock made her look over her shoulder. The knob of her door was turning.

The NSA guys had picked the lock of her back door, failed to find her inside, and now were coming after her. If they were the NSA guys.

She wasn't going to wait around to find out. Throwing open the heavy fire door she started down the stairs. Her rapid footfalls echoed in the dim concrete stairwell. She could hear other footfalls, too.

She came out in the small lobby, wishing her building had a doorman. But there was nobody, just an empty room with a tile floor and the tenants' mailboxes inset in the wall. She opened the door and started down the front walk. The NSA guys were still sitting in their Chevrolet parked at the curb, just as before, heads back against the headrests as if they were napping. But they'd be armed. They'd protect her from her pursuer.

She ran toward the car, waving. They didn't look her way. She shouted for help. Still no response.

She pulled open the door. The man in the passenger seat flopped over. From the motion of his head she could tell that his neck was broken. She looked at the man in the driver's seat: eyes shut, mouth hanging open. He was dead, too.

She cried out and backed away, scanning the sidewalks for somebody—a dog walker, a jogger—but no one was nearby. The door of her building opened. Relieved, she saw that it was one of her neighbors. She didn't actually recognize the face, but it was a paunchy man in a dark suit, with gray hair and sunglasses. He was talking on his phone and paying no attention to his surroundings. Just another civil servant, come home from the office to let a repairman in or something.

She actually took a step toward him before she realized that this might be her pursuer. The killer of the men in the car.

She started running toward Dupont Circle. The man dropped his phone and started after her. She dug into her pants pocket, pulled out her own iPhone, shouted at it, "Call Laker!"

"Sorry, I didn't get that," it replied.

She turned it so the microphone was next to her mouth, enunciated, "Call Laker."

A few steps later the line opened. "Someone's after you," Laker said.

No time to ask how he knew. "He's chasing me down New Hampshire."

"You're headed for the Circle?"

Someone was shouting in the background on his end and it was hard to hear him. "Almost there."

"I see you. Ava, you can't stop, he's too close. Run into the street."

"Into traffic?"

"Don't look at the cars. Run a straight line, no stops or turns, and they'll avoid you. Ava, do it!"

Cars were whirling around the multilane roundabout. Oh God. She leapt off the curb and kept going. Looked straight ahead at the trees in the center of the circle. Heard horns sounding and brakes screeching. A car skidded sideways past her. A pickup truck rammed it in the side. She could see the driver pitch forward into a blooming airbag. Behind her people were shouting and cursing.

Laker had a good view from a hundred feet away. His cab was pulled to the curb and stopped and he was standing on the hood. The Sikh was out of the car, yelling and gesticulating at him. Laker wasn't paying attention. Ava was halfway across the street. Cars were screeching and plunging to a stop all around her. Everybody was staring at her, which was what Laker'd had in mind.

But her pursuer wasn't giving up. A gray-headed man in a black suit, he was dodging and weaving among the cars. He looked middle-aged but moved like a young man. He was closing the distance to Ava. Laker reached for the Beretta, but he didn't have a clear shot.

He jumped down from the hood and started running. Ava had reached the green island in the middle of Dupont Circle. She didn't slow down or look back, just kept running through the trees. Good girl! Laker thought. Pedestrians were standing at the curb, some turning to stare after her, others gaping at the onrushing pursuer. Even that didn't make him shy away. He ran through the cluster of people, closing in on Ava.

Laker reached the curb just as she neared the large fountain in the middle of the island. She turned to skirt it but the pursuer was too close. He swung at her head and knocked her to the ground. People sitting on the wall of the fountain were standing up, crying out, pulling their phones from their pockets, but they kept their distance. Nobody wanted to be a hero.

Which was fine with Laker. He had a clear shot.

He drew the Beretta, thumbed off the safe, dropped into a shooting crouch with both arms out. The bead of the sight was wavering. He was breathing too hard. He fired once.

And missed. The bullet kicked up a jet of water in the fountain to the pursuer's left. He spun around so fast that his sunglasses flew off. He hadn't been aware of Laker until now. He bent and scooped Ava up. Her head lolled—she was unconscious. The man handled her as if she were weightless, making a shield of her. Laker charged him. At the last moment he thrust her toward Laker, who had to drop the gun as he caught her. He laid her down and turned. The pursuer was running around the fountain. Not fast enough.

Laker took two bounds and tackled him.

They went down in a heap. The pursuer scrambled to his feet, a split second faster than Laker. He pivoted and high-kicked at Laker's head. Laker ducked just in time.

As the pursuer recovered, Laker closed in and threw his right fist. The man managed to get an arm up to block it. He was fast. Now his own hand was coming up in a blur of motion, palm up, aimed at the underside of Laker's chin. Laker pulled back so he missed by a fraction of an inch. If he'd made contact the blow would have broken Laker's neck.

They were face-to-face. The pursuer had blue eyes. He was the same man Laker'd lost at Eastern Markct. His left fist leapt at Laker's face. Dropping into a crouch so the blow went over his head, Laker punched low. His fist landed solidly in the man's sternum and should have knocked out his breath and left him helpless, but the man only grunted, fell back a step, and recovered his balance. Laker closed in.

This time Laker didn't see the blow coming. Only felt it, a bomb exploding inside his head. He sat down hard on the concrete. It would be a kick next. He tried to get his arms up to protect his head.

But the fight was over. The pursuer had turned his back and was running away. Laker realized he could hear sirens. He turned to see a D.C. patrol car with lightbars flashing pull over to the curb. He got up, tasting blood. Wiping his chin he staggered toward Ava. She was conscious, sitting upright, bracing herself with both arms.

A crowd of tourists surrounded them at a safe distance. Everybody seemed to have a phone out. Some were making superfluous 911 calls. Others were taking pictures of Laker. Two cops were running toward him, guns drawn. He slowly raised both arms.

It would be damned annoying to get shot now.

22

The nurses told Laker that Sam Mason was a difficult patient. Which didn't surprise him. Once Mason came to after surgery, he'd refused further painkillers. They told him he wouldn't be able to stand it, but he wanted his mind clear to deal with phone calls. So far, he'd stood it.

Laker's turn to report came an hour before dawn. He'd been in meetings all night. He entered Mason's room to find him sitting up in bed, talking on the phone. The left side of his face was covered in bandages. The surgeon had told Laker that the blow had caved in his cheekbone and eye socket. More surgeries would be needed. He might never recover the sight in that eye.

Laker felt his hands curl into fists. He didn't like it, that the enemy had been able to break into the Outfit's headquarters. To kill his friends and wound his chief. Didn't like it at all.

Mason glanced at him as he put the receiver down. Read his face. "Don't get mad, Laker. How many times have I told you, anger's worse than useless in this business. Breeds mistakes."

Laker sat in the chair by the bedside. Unclenched his fists and rested his open hands on his thighs.

"How's Brad Bartel?" Mason asked.

"Stable. But it'll be a long time till he's able to walk again."

"Any idea who we're up against yet?"

"Lot of theories. Few facts."

"These were highly trained, deeply committed operatives. They had to be from the intelligence service of a hostile nation. Or a stable, well-funded terrorist organization."

"I don't think it's 'they.'"

"What?"

"I think that it's the same man."

"But the descriptions don't match up. The guy you chased to Eastern Market was five-nine, one-sixty, black hair. The guy at Ava North's place was six-one, two hundred, gray hair."

"Yes. Only the blue eyes are the same. And even they can change."

"You've lost me."

"The Maryland cops brought in all the workmen at the North estate, the day Tillie was killed. Questioned them, ran background checks. Found nothing and released them. But they kept working on the backgrounds, and one ID has fallen through. The guy who was closest to the garage before it blew up. Name of Earl Richardson, except that there turns out to be no such person."

Laker handed over the photo the Maryland police had taken of the man. Mason studied it.

"Bad teeth. Brown hair. Brown eyes."

"Contact lenses."

"You think this same guy killed Tillie North?"

"And followed us to Hawaii. Although Ava never saw the guy who was after her, so I'm going on instinct."

Mason returned the photo. "You saw his face yesterday."

"I saw one of his faces."

"But you think it's the same guy?"

"Yes. At the meeting this evening, somebody came up with a name for him. The Shapeshifter."

"So what are the implications? That he's a lone wolf, working for no one?"

"It's a possibility. But I don't think so. I think you're right. A terrorist group or an enemy service. Too early to say. But one thing seems clear to me. He has a better idea what this is all about than we do. How the journal fits in."

"And now he's got it. *Shit.* Anybody have any ideas why he went after Ava? He had the journal. Why was he still interested in her?"

"First thing the journal told him was how important she was." Laker explained about the living will and Tillie's coded message. "She says that as soon as she finds the key text, she can decode it."

Mason's one visible eye was watching Laker coldly, steadily. "I get the feeling you haven't mentioned this last part to anybody else."

"No."

"Why not?"

"Because the Outfit has been penetrated."

Mason looked down. Took a deep breath and slowly let it out. "You're right. Kills me to say so, but you're right. This guy—the Shapeshifter—he knew when you were bringing the journal in. How to beat our security. He has a source in the Outfit. Whom we will have to find. And when we do I'll rip the guts out of the son of a bitch."

"Anger's useless, remember?"

"Worse than useless." Mason sank back into the pillows that supported him. "What are your plans?"

"I'm taking Ava and leaving town. Cutting all ties. Until we find and plug the leak, I'm going to stay out of touch."

"So you'll be on your own." Mason smiled bleakly. "Just the way you like it."

23

It was hot on the platform of the East 23rd Street subway station. Laker could feel the sweat beading on his forehead, trickling down his ribs. He was wearing a straw hat, oversize sunglasses that disguised the shape of his face, and a loose white *guayabera* that made him look fat around the middle.

Headlights glared in the tunnel. The northbound local was pulling into the station. The crash and bang of the subway took some getting used to when you were accustomed to the smooth, quiet Washington Metro. As did the heat of the unair-conditioned stations. But the train was so chilly that his sunglasses misted over. He grabbed the overhead bar as the train lurched forward.

It was necessary for Ava and him to drop out of sight, and one of the world's best places for doing that was just 200 miles north of Washington: New York City. They had ditched their cell phones and boarded a city bus to Union Station. They weren't encumbered with suitcases, which was just as well, because they switched from train to bus to taxi to ferry across the

Hudson. They checked into a large, anonymous hotel near Penn Station, using a fake driver's license that Laker had secured on his own, not one issued by the Gray Outfit.

But he wasn't going to underestimate the Shapeshifter and the organization he served. He devoted the morning to anti-surveillance precautions, riding the subway far uptown, backtracking by bus, traveling crosstown by cab. By the time he went to meet Ava at the New York Public Library, he was sure he wasn't being followed.

Almost sure, anyway.

He walked along the block-long Fifth Avenue frontage of double columns framing round-arched windows, mounted the broad steps between the lions crouching on their pedestals. It was noon, and the steps were occupied by office workers and tourists, sitting and eating lunch. He picked his way among them. Even though Ava was right where she'd said she'd be, leaning on the pedestal of the south lion, he did not recognize her until he was just a few steps away.

When they parted this morning, he'd suggested that she dress like an Orthodox Jew. He was pleased to see how well that had worked out. Flat shoes lowered her height, thick, dark knee-socks, long navy skirt and loose, long-sleeved white blouse disguised her willowy figure, and a plain headscarf covered her red hair.

"You blend right in," he said as he came up to her.

"But I don't think my rabbi would want me hanging out with you. You look like a Miami street hustler."

"Thanks."

"Really, Laker, I'm impressed. Your walk is completely different. And you're not turning your good ear toward me the way you usually do."

"That was a hard habit to break."

"Well, sit down. I got you a hot dog from the cart. Guessed you were a sauerkraut and spicy mustard kind of guy."

They sat side by side and she handed him the hot dog. She had only a small bottle of water. Noticing his look, she said, "My insides are all tied up in knots. You're used to this, I'm not. Not being Ava anymore, I mean. Shut out of my own life."

"It's necessary for your safety."

"I know."

"And we can hope it won't be for too long."

She sighed and put the cold bottle to her forehead. "I wish I had some progress to report. But I've wasted the whole morning. The frustration's driving me mad."

"I realize it's a big handicap, not being able to go on the Internet—"

"It's okay, Laker. I understand. Everything a person does on a networked computer can be tracked. I'm using only books and periodicals. And I'm finding everything I'm looking for. Obviously I'm not looking for the right thing."

"The key text."

"I thought this was going to be easy. I can tell by the look of Tillie's message, it's in a simple substitution code. A mono-alphabetic cipher. Each letter is standing in for another letter. All you need is the key text to tell you c is really f and so on."

"You thought you could guess what text she used."

"I knew my grandmother well. I tried her favorite hymn, 'A Mighty Fortress is Our God.' Her favorite poem, Arnold's 'Dover Beach.' The speech JFK gave at his inauguration, which she attended. The preamble to the 1965 Voting Rights Act, which she and Ephraim had a behind-the-scenes role in passing . . ."

Her voice trailed off. Laker waited while she opened the bottle and took a long swallow. Then said, "Other possibilities will come to you."

"I can sit in this library playing with texts for months. But I admit I'm losing hope. Tillie meant this message for me. How can it be so hard to decode? Maybe I'm not as smart as she thought."

He touched her shoulder. "You're plenty smart. Give it the rest of the day. Call me if anything happens that worries you. I've programmed my number in this phone." He handed her one of the two cheap burners he'd bought at a Duane Reade.

"Where are you going?"

"Shea Stadium. There's an afternoon game."

"You can't be serious."

"As you said, we're locked out of our lives. Might as well make the best of it."

He rose and walked away. But only to the bottom of the steps. He watched Ava go back into the building, then followed her as far as the cool, echoing marble lobby, where he sat on a bench by the wall as she mounted the staircase. He didn't want her to think he was worried about her. But he also wanted to be nearby if she called.

24

At the end of the day he climbed the stairs and entered the main reading room. It was a vast space. Chandeliers hung by long chains from a high, coffered ceiling with a central painting of blue sky and cottony clouds. Shelf upon shelf of books stretched around the room under the tall, round-arched windows. A couple of hundred people sat at the long wooden tables, reading books or working on computers.

Ava was sitting at the end of a table in a far corner of the room. Books and papers were stacked in front of her, higher than her head. She'd taken off the dowdy headscarf, and her hair shone coppery-red in a sunbeam that slanted through the window. Laker's heart lifted. Then he sobered up and made a mental note to remind her to tie the scarf back on before they went outside.

She raised her head, saw him, and smiled. Her mood had improved since lunch.

He pulled a chair close, sat down and whispered, "You've found something?"

"Oh, yes."

"The key text?"

"No. I put that aside and went back to the journal."

Laker was puzzled.

"The only part of it we still have, I mean. My translations from the Japanese." She tapped the lined papers in front of her, covered with her large, clear, looping handwriting. There were many marginal notes in different color inks. She'd been working hard.

"How come you went back to Ryo's midnight mumblings?"

"You think I'm wasting my time."

"Maybe not. The Shapeshifter must have thought there was something to them."

"Exactly. We gave up on the journal too soon. Josh Milton's Pearl Harbor red herring distracted us. Ryo's sleep-talk doesn't tell us anything about that. But it tells us about Hirochi Ryo. A person dreams about the things he manages to suppress when he's awake."

Laker glanced at the stack of stout books by her elbow. "Have you been consulting Jung and Freud?"

"No, Laker. I don't practice psychoanalysis without a license. Especially on dead people. But Ryo's memories are interesting. Want to hear?"

Chairs were scraping the floor as people pushed them back and rose. Books clunked on carts as librarians rounded them up for reshelving. Patrons were powering off their laptops, loading their briefcases and backpacks. It was almost closing time. Nobody seemed bothered by their conversation.

"There's a lot of stuff about his childhood," Ava went on. "He grew up poor, on a farm. His mother died young and his mean father beat him. But I won't bore you with that. It's this bit I'm interested in."

She pointed at the lined pad in front of her. Laker craned his neck and read:

"'Girl . . . maiden with a rifle between her legs . . . man with a dog. Shiny nose.'"

"Pretty cryptic," he said. "Who has the shiny nose, the man or the dog?"

"He makes clear elsewhere that it's the dog. He talked about it four times, at intervals of weeks or months. The only other memory he goes back to that often is the time the *daikon* harvest was bad and his father beat him and cracked a rib."

"Maiden with a rifle. Dog with a shiny nose. There's no way of telling what he's talking about."

She picked up a large book and laid it open in front of him. He looked down at a color photograph: an arched portal, two larger-than-life size bronze statues in niches on either side of a marble corridor. One was of a slender girl in a thin shift, hair falling to her shoulders, holding a hunting rifle, resting the butt end of the stock on the ground between her bare feet. Across the corridor, a man crouched and looked at her. His own rifle was slung. He had his arm around a sitting German shepherd. Its muzzle was shinier than the rest of the bronze. The corridor seemed to run on endlessly. It had a high ceiling and chandeliers. "What is this?" he asked "Some palace in Europe?"

"It's a station of the Moscow subway."

Laker nodded. He'd read that Stalin had ordered that the stations be made palaces of the people, and spared no expense. "What's with the nose?"

"Thousands of people pass every day. There's a long tradition of rubbing the dog's nose for luck."

"Obviously it made a big impression on Hirochi Ryo."

"Moscow was his first post abroad. He was a junior clerk in the trade section of the Japanese embassy. You wouldn't believe how many microfilmed issues of *Pravda* I had to go through before I came across a mention of his name."

"You speak Russian, too?"

"Read it, anyway."

"Impressive. Where does this get us?"

She leaned close and dropped her voice. He noticed that while she'd changed everything else, she was still wearing her favorite perfume.

"Ryo was a double agent. Working for Moscow."

Laker sat back in surprise. He stared at her.

"You're skeptical. But the Soviets did have deep-cover agents in Tokyo, you know. Like Richard Sorge."

"Sure. They were old enemies. The Japanese beat the Russians badly in a 1904 war. Tensions flared regularly after that. But just because Ryo was stationed in Moscow—"

"I'm not finished yet."

"Go ahead."

Ava tapped the color photo in front of her. "This station is Ploshchad Revolyutsii. It's the nearest one to the office of the NKVD, a forerunner of the KGB."

"Okay. Ryo must have traveled under NKVD headquarters. Along with several million other people."

She pulled a photocopy of a microfiche out of a manila folder and laid it before him. It was the front page of *Pravda*. She pointed to a small headline near the bottom of the page.

"What does it say?" he asked.

"'Japanese Businessman Killed in Accident.'"

"Accident?"

"He fell in front of a train. At Ploshchad Revolyutsii station. Only he wasn't a businessman. He worked at the Japanese embassy. That only came out later, when the Moscow police wanted to investigate and the Japanese refused to cooperate, saying they were satisfied it was an accident. It was quite a little diplomatic storm."

"What did he do in the Embassy?"

"The Japanese preferred not to say."

"You think he was a spy."

"A security man. He was tailing Ryo, who was on the way to or from a meeting at the NKVD. Ryo spotted the tail. Dealt with it. And obviously managed to evade suspicion. But he'd killed a man and it festered in his memory. Those statues are just down a flight of steps from the platform from which the man was pushed."

"It's ingenious, Ava. But it's guesswork."

She met his eye. Held it. "You've killed people, haven't you, Laker?"

He looked down. "I wouldn't be here if I hadn't."

"And you still have nightmares about them. As Ryo did."

Laker kept his head down for another moment. He said, "Okay."

"There's more. In 1939, Ryo, now stationed in Washington, takes leave to attend the funeral of Professor Charles Jordan at the University of Chicago.

Jordan was a brilliant economist, and Ryo had been his student in the 1920s. Jordan was killed in Spain, fighting the fascists. He made no secret about being a member of the Communist party. But it wasn't until the 1950s that a biographer found out he was an NKVD agent."

"He recruited Ryo in the '20s."

"Yes."

"Your theory's firming up."

"Then there's the fact that Ryo met the end of a double agent. Suddenly vanished from his Tokyo ministry in 1943. Imprisoned, tortured, executed in secret, his family not even informed."

"Yes," said Laker. "That's the way double agents end up, all right."

25

Ava was sleeping, her head on Laker's shoulder, as he gazed out the window. For two hours the train had been traveling north along the Hudson. The river had slowly narrowed as the train had emptied. The sun had dropped below the mountains on the far side of the river.

She stirred and sat upright. Blinked and smiled at him. "That was such a nice nap. You make a good pillow."

"Thanks."

The smile disappeared. "You haven't slept at all, have you? You've been keeping watch. Every time the train stops at a station and people come in the car, you have your hand on your gun."

"Don't worry. I haven't seen anybody suspicious."

"You know what? I think I'd actually feel better if I knew what you were worried about. Specifically."

"Cameras."

"You mean spy satellites?"

"Not just those. CCTVs are everywhere. We probably passed through the field of view of a dozen of them, when we walked from the library to Grand Central Station. If the enemy can get access to the feed of those cameras and is analyzing it with facial recognition computers—"

"I was wrong. I don't feel better."

"Sorry. But I have to assume the worst, since I don't know what kind of resources this organization has, or how deeply they've penetrated our agencies."

"The organization the Shapeshifter works for?"

"Yes."

"What if there is no organization? Suppose he's on his own?"

"Sam Mason said he's an agent of either an enemy nation or a terrorist organization. He serves a cause."

"Maybe it's his own cause."

He turned his good ear. "I'm not sure I follow you."

"I'm not sure where I'm leading."

"It's futile to speculate until we have a better idea what he's after."

"He's achieved his first goal. He has the journal."

"Yes. Although I don't know if he'll be able to get out of it all that you did."

His tone was so calm and offhand—so Laker—that she didn't register the compliment at first. Then she actually blushed. "Thanks. I've been wondering, did my grandmother ever know that Ryo was a double?"

"To tell her would have been to put his life in her hands."

"Erlynne Bendix said they were in love."

"Mrs. Bendix was—is—loyal to your grandmother."

"You mean, you think she wasn't telling us the truth?"

"She was, but maybe not the *whole* truth. I think

there are some of Tillie's secrets that she's still guarding."

They were silent as the train rumbled a few miles farther north. Then Ava said, "One thing we can be sure of. Those two master spies at Pearl Harbor, Captain Jenkins and Commander Mannion, they had no idea who Ryo was really working for."

"No idea."

"It's ironic, isn't it? If Ryo had known anything about the Pearl Harbor attack, he would willingly have passed it on."

"Moscow would have given the okay."

"What a hopeless op they dragged poor Tillie into."

"A lot of field agents have died for their case officers' blunders. But this op, misconceived as it was, started something. I'm hoping to find out more about that."

"We're going to see someone, then?"

"Tomorrow. A defector I helped debrief when I was a very green CIA agent."

"Where are we going tonight?"

"A place where I'm hoping to get some sleep."

26

Everything was closed at the little station where they got off, and they had to wait a long time for the taxi that took them across the river and up into the hills. It was late when they reached their destination.

She stood up from the cab. There were no lights, but by the time Laker paid the driver and the cab was rumbling away down the dirt road, her eyes had adjusted. There was no moon but the stars were bright. They were in a clearing in the woods, with a circle of cabins with cars parked beside them. The only sounds were crickets and tree frogs.

"Laker, what is this?" she whispered.

"A fishing camp. I was here with some army guys, years ago. Doesn't look like things have changed any. Just decayed a little more."

He took her arm and helped her down a rutted path. The wooden handrail had so many gaps it was useless. The wooden walls of the cabins were all a few degrees off plumb, and their shingle roofs were sagging. The cabins looked as if they would collapse if they didn't have stout stone chimneys to lean upon. Over the chirping of crickets she could hear water rushing.

"A stream?" she asked.

"Full of bass and perch. To the dedicated angler, it makes up for the rustic accommodations."

"Congratulations, Laker, I think we're truly off the grid now."

The door of the nearest cabin opened and a man appeared, tugging on a cap. He approached them, whispering vehemently. "No headlights after 9 pm! Didn't I tell you that on the phone?"

He was short and bent over with age, and Laker towered over him. He poked Laker in the sternum with his forefinger as he continued his sotto-voiced tirade.

"You're waking the whole camp and these folks have to be up before dawn! I told you on the phone—"

"Sorry, Mr. Bentley. But we didn't talk on the phone."

"No reservation?" The bearded face turned to Ava. "You can't expect me to accommodate a female without a reservation."

"That's too bad. I was here, years ago. Enjoyed my stay."

Bentley's hairy chin was upturned, bristling against the starry sky, as he thrust his face closer to Laker's. "I remember now. You caught that twelve-inch perch. Fine fish. Major Anders brought you. You're Captain . . . somebody."

Laker only nodded. Bentley did not inquire further. "Got one cabin left. It'll be kinda rough and ready. We don't get many *ladies* up here."

Ava wanted to tell him she'd hiked the Appalachian Trail from Maine to New Jersey, but he was already asking Laker where their rods and creels were. His annoyance deepened at the news they weren't here to fish. But he led them across the clearing and threw open the flimsy door of a cabin. It smelled as musty as if it was being opened up for the first time after a long winter. Bentley turned up the gas on a camping lantern, handed it to Laker, and left them with a gruff, "No more noise."

"I guess the wild and crazy sex is out, then," Ava blurted, then turned away, embarrassed by her own joke. In fact she was blushing like a schoolgirl. In the silence and seclusion, the close confines of the room, she was keenly aware of Laker's tall, powerful body. She went into the bedroom. There was only one bed, piled high with blankets and comforters.

He hadn't followed her. He called softly, "Good night."

She returned to the other room. He was sitting on the lumpy sofa, untying his shoes. Aside from a rickety wooden table and chairs, that was it.

"Laker, you can't sleep on that sofa. Unless you double your legs up under your chin."

"It's okay. 'Night."

They were both too weary for more discussion. She retreated to the bedroom. Not bothering to undress or pull down the bedclothes, she lay down and fell instantly to sleep.

When she awakened, it was much colder in the room. She ought to get under the covers, but first she'd have to get up, and she was too sleepy. She lay motionless on her back. The crickets and tree frogs had gone quiet. She listened for the whisper of the river but couldn't hear it. There was complete silence.

But not quite. A soft noise, but close. A whirring.

Something was in the room with her. It circled the room. Then approached the bed. She felt the stirring of air as it passed over her face.

"Laker!"

The door flew open. He advanced into the room, both arms out-thrust. In his left hand was the lantern, in his right the gun. He turned in a circle, then looked at her.

"What is it?"

The light had shown her the room was empty.

"I'm sorry. I must have been dreaming. I thought there was—I don't know—some kind of killer drone in here, circling, looking for me."

He tucked the automatic into his pants and turned up the lamp. Then he smiled and said, "You weren't dreaming."

He pointed and she saw, clinging to the window curtain by its talons, a small gray bat. Its black eyes shone in the light.

"Oh, the poor thing. It's frightened. Don't shoot it, Laker."

"I wasn't going to."

"But we have to get it out of here."

He nodded. He went around the cabin, pushing back curtains and opening windows, as well as the front door. Returning, he handed her a towel. He had one, too. They flapped them at the bat. It took off and circled the room. They kept flapping and it kept circling, scrupulously avoiding all doors and windows. Finally they gave up and stood panting. The bat returned to its perch on the curtain. It was panting, too.

"What the hell are you people doing?" It was the fierce whisper of Bentley. He was standing outside the front door. "If you've got to have lights on, at least keep the goddam curtains closed!"

Laker surreptitiously shifted the automatic to the small of his back and went out to talk to him. "There's a bat in here."

"Well, you better not hurt it."

"What?"

"They're a federally protected species."

"I don't think federal law requires us to turn our cabin over to it. Can you get it out of here?"

"And how do you expect me to do that?"

Ava came up beside Laker. "Mr. Bentley, I can't sleep with a bat flying around the room."

"You should've thought of that before you talked your husband into bringing you along. This is no place for ladies. Now I've got a campful of *real* fishermen who'll expect their breakfast in an hour, so no more fuss from you two." He stalked away, muttering.

Laker turned to her. "I suppose you won't let me shoot him, either?"

She had to put a hand to her mouth to stifle a guffaw. Turning, she went back into the bedroom. Startled bats rose from all corners of the room and began to circle the ceiling. There were at least half a dozen.

"Hm," said Laker behind her. "The light must have attracted them."

"They're holding the bats' Indy 500 in my bedroom! What are we going to do?"

"You're expecting *another* idea from me, as good as open the windows and turn up the lamp?"

This time there was no holding her laughter in. She stepped close to him, linked her fingers at the nape of his neck, and brought him down from his great height.

Their lips met. He put his arms around her. I could stay like this forever, she thought.

A moment later she thought: No, I couldn't. I want more of him. And to give him all of me.

She led him by the hand into the outer room and pulled the door closed, leaving the bedroom to the bats. Then she pushed him down on the sofa and stepped back, looking into his eyes.

"Have a seat, Laker. Relax and enjoy."

There was another camping lantern resting on the table. She turned the flame down, but not too far. She was still wearing her Orthodox Jew disguise from the city. Her rabbi *really* wouldn't like this next part, she thought. Unfastening the long skirt, she let it fall. She balanced on one foot, then the other to slip off the coarse knee-socks. Began to undo the buttons of the blouse, then lost patience and pulled it over her head. She could feel the soft golden light eddying around her breasts and hips as she cast off the last scraps of clothing. Laker's gaze felt just as warm.

He gave a long, appreciative sigh. Stood up. "My turn," he said.

The first thing he took off was the gun.

27

By the following afternoon, they were back in the Hudson Valley. They checked into a motel on the outskirts of the little town of Schuylerville. Laker showed his fake ID and paid in cash. Then he looked out the window while Ava explained to the clerk that they wanted a room with one large bed, not two small ones.

In the room, he put on a fresh shirt. They had acquired a change of clothes and a small suitcase.

"You're going to see this defector?" she asked.

"Yes. He probably won't be happy to see me. Best if you don't come along."

"Fine. I want to take another crack at Tillie's coded message to me."

"I thought you said you'd tried every possible key text. You were stymied."

"True."

"So what's different today?"

"Laker. *Everything's* different today."

She sat on the bed and smiled at him. Laker figured that if he was going to see Ilya Berilov today, he'd better get going.

Route 9 in Schuylerville could have been any road, anywhere. He walked past fast-food franchises, a muffler shop, a supermarket. The road curved away from a high stone wall with an arched portal. He stepped through it into another world. Tree-lined paths crossed broad lawns, leading to noble old buildings of red brick and gray stone. Summer term was in session at Burtondale College. Under a spreading sycamore tree, a group of young men and women with suntanned limbs sat on the grass in a ring around their professor, a gray-haired woman who was holding forth on the metrical patterns of John Donne. Laker walked past the group and into a doorway. On its lintel was engraved: DEPARTMENT OF HISTORY.

He walked down a dim corridor, reading the names on doors. The door of Professor Ilya Berilov was open. He stepped in and said, "Hello, Ilya."

The man sitting behind the desk looked up. Berilov hadn't changed much, except that his abundant hair had gone from silver to white. He took the glasses from his bulbous nose and tossed them on the desk. His heavily bagged dark eyes looked at Laker.

Sort of looked at him. Berilov was almost comically shifty-eyed. Conversing with you, he seemed to be watching a tennis match that was going on behind you. He said nothing.

"You don't remember me."

"Of course I do, Thomas Laker." Berilov spoke fluent English, but it seemed to cost him a lot of effort to produce the foreign sounds. His lips and jaws moved as if he were chewing stale black bread. "I was locked up in that safe house in Virginia for my first six weeks in the West. You were the seventeenth person to interrogate me."

"You didn't make it easy for me."

Berilov's white tufts of eyebrow bobbed once, indifferently. "The CIA had emptied me of everything I knew. By that point, I figured they were only using me to give young agents some experience. So I provided you with a challenge."

Laker indicated the straight chair in front of the desk. "May I sit down?"

Berilov folded his hands upon his paunch, which strained the buttons of his woolen cardigan. There was a steaming cup of tea on the desk. The old building was unair-conditioned and stuffy, but the chill of Moscow winters was apparently still in his bones.

"You want a rematch? Laker, I know no more than I did last time. I've been out of the game for more than twenty years."

Laker stepped forward and sat in the chair. "Not a rematch. Just some information. Let's not make this difficult."

Berilov kept silent while his eyes tracked side to side several times. "I have provided more than enough information to pay for my safe harbor in the West."

"You think so? We pulled you out of Moscow when the Soviet Union was breaking up. Mobs were storming the Lubyanka. Tearing down Dzerzhinsky's statue. As a longtime KGB apparatchik, your future was not bright."

"So they told me. But I wonder. One of my former colleagues is now absolute ruler of the new Russia—

which day by day looks more like the old one. If I had stayed, perhaps I would be at his right hand now."

Laker swept a hand across the large office: the carpet with the college seal, the paneled walls and mullioned windows looking out on the green campus. "Things have turned out pretty comfortably for you, I'd say."

"I don't owe my professorship to you. There are few people alive who know as much about twentieth-century European history as I do."

"That's true. All we did was sanitize your CV. Burtondale College wouldn't have hired you if they'd known you acquired your knowledge in the file room of the KGB."

Berilov sighed. "What do you want to know about?"

"Hirochi Ryo."

Berilov's eyes measured the span of Laker's shoulders a dozen times before he spoke. "So you finally found out about Ryo. How?"

"If you give me answers not questions, we can get this over with more quickly."

"Very well. It was quite a coup, recruiting a source in the Foreign Ministry in Tokyo in 1942. Stalin was very worried about Hitler's attempts to persuade the Japanese to invade Russia from the east, and—"

"Let's try again, Ilya. Ryo was recruited in Chicago in the '20s. By Charles Jordan."

"Was he? I didn't know." Berilov actually managed to look surprised. He was a little rusty, but still a professional. "It makes sense, though. Jordan was a true believer, in the days when the Revolution was new. Communism would bring the world a bright future. Equality and brotherhood. No more war. Ryo was the same. Do you know, Laker? I envy them. I served my country, but I didn't believe I was fighting for a bright future. If I had, maybe I'd have fought harder."

"Ilya, you're blowing smoke. Tell me what Ryo was doing for Moscow."

"I told you. He—"

"Not in Tokyo. In Honolulu, before the war."

Berilov sighed. "Do you know, Laker—"

"No more ruminations."

"But this is hard. Other sins, they get easier as you go along. Lying. Adultery. Murder. But giving up the secrets of your service, betraying your country—"

"We're talking about 1941. A long time ago."

"True." Berilov pulled himself out of his slouch. "You can probably work it out for yourself anyway. Ryo arranged to get the Japanese Foreign Service to post him to Honolulu because it was the perfect place to carry out his assignment from Moscow."

"Which was? Come on, Ilya."

"To build a network of agents in the American armed forces."

"I see. Did he have any success?"

"You sound doubtful. I assure you he did. Ryo was a brilliant recruiter. He didn't go in for the usual lures—bribery, blackmail, seduction. He was a true believer, as I said. He appealed to the idealism of these young officers, these graduates of Annapolis and West Point. He convinced them that only Communism could defeat Fascism."

"Did he really?"

For a moment Berilov's eyes ceased their shifting. They burned into Laker's. "It was the Red Army that beat the Nazis, Laker. Drove them back from Moscow, all the way to Berlin. While you and the British staged little diversions on the sidelines."

"You're telling me that Ryo built his network. Double agents in the U.S. Army and Navy. What did Moscow do with them?"

Berilov sank back into his chair. Again his eyes were looking beyond Laker, searching for more trouble coming over the horizon. "Nothing."

"Nothing?"

"You're a professional like me. You know how it goes. The winds of history blow, and the structures we have worked to build collapse. Pearl Harbor was attacked. Ryo was interned. By the time he got back to Tokyo, his agents were scattered all over the world. He was unable to communicate with them."

"Moscow didn't find someone else to run the net?"

"Soviet Russia and America were allies against the Axis. The network became unnecessary."

"Stalin never trusted anybody, especially not his allies. What did he do with the net?"

Berilov was sinking deeper in his chair. He put one foot up on the edge of the desk. He was wearing plaid Bermuda shorts that revealed a knobby knee and hairless calf.

"What do you want from me, Laker? Stalin and I were not intimates. I was just a child growing up in the Urals in the 1940s. All I know is what's in the file, and the file ends with Ryo's arrest. In October 1943, he made a small mistake, and they caught him. They tortured him for a long time before they shot him, but as far as Moscow could work out, he didn't tell them anything useful."

"His network outlived him. Didn't it?"

Berilov appeared not to have heard. “That must be the happiest death, don’t you think? The one at the end of torture, I mean. Not only are you released from pain, but you know you’ve won. They’re killing you because they couldn’t break you. I’m old. I’ll die within a few years, and it won’t be as happy.”

Laker’s patience was at an end. He stood, laid his hands flat on the desk, and leaned toward Berilov. “A network of officers in the American military. An incredibly valuable asset. What orders did Moscow give them?”

“The network was never activated.”

“Ilya—”

“If I knew any more, I would tell you. You are a very scary person, Laker, and I’ve forgotten how to be brave. You can go on threatening me, if you want to make an old man wet his Bermuda shorts. But you won’t get any more information.”

Laker straightened up. Let out his breath in a long sigh, and turned away.

28

Ava perched on one corner of the bed in the motel room, eyes wide, watching Laker pace. She said, "A spy ring of American officers, working for Moscow. This is it, Laker. The big secret. This is what it's all about. Now we know."

He paused, stood looking out the big window at the cars parked in the lot. When he didn't say anything, she continued.

"They were pledged to the Soviets, even if they were never activated. These men betrayed their country. If the secret comes out, even now, it will be enough to destroy reputations, send people to prison."

"No. The Shapeshifter hasn't killed five people just to keep a few old men from being dragged into court. Ryo's network survived him. It went off the books, into the black. But somebody in Moscow gave orders to those agents. And they reported back. Maybe it's still going on."

"Still going on? But the Soviet Union no longer exists."

“The current regime in the Kremlin isn’t what I’d call transparent. Or friendly.”

“Are you saying the Shapeshifter is a Russian agent? Trying to keep the lid on this ongoing operation, whatever it is?”

“That’s one possibility. I can think of others, equally bad. But we’re wasting time.” He turned to her. “We have to report what we’ve found out. To Sam Mason.”

“You mean crawl out from under our rock and go back to Washington.”

“Yes. I’m sorry. I know it will mean putting you in danger again.”

“I was put in danger when I was born with the name North. Let’s go.”

Laker rented a car with his own credit card—there didn’t seem to be any point in staying off the grid any longer—and pointed it south. Ava kept silent for the first hour of the drive, head back against the headrest, eyes shut. He assumed she was thinking about what awaited them in Washington. He was wrong.

She sat upright. “Laker, pull over.”

“I can’t.”

They were crossing the Hudson on the Tappan Zee Bridge. There was no shoulder, and traffic was heavy but moving fairly fast. He glanced at Ava. She was leaning forward, hands clasped and squeezed between her thighs, her whole being transformed into a dart of eagerness.

“What is it?”

“I have to get something in the trunk. In my suitcase.”

"What?"

"The key text. I just realized. I've had it all along."

They were still on the first section of the bridge, the trestled roadway low over the river, climbing slowly and sweeping in a broad curve to the cantilevered section, a framework of girders high above the middle of the Hudson. The sun had sunk below the hills on the far side. The water was black beneath them. For the moment there was nothing to do but follow tail lights. Ava was muttering to herself with impatience.

"You sure about this?" he asked.

"Yes. I've realized my mistake. I thought, this is a message from my grandmother to me. The encoding is only to keep others out. But it was meant to keep me out, too. For a while."

"I don't follow."

"Tillie was a Washington operator for fifty years. She knew that when a secret has to come out, you've got to prepare the ground, time the release of information, control the story."

"But this message was for you, not the DC press corps."

"She wanted to keep me on her side. Even if she had something . . . something awful to tell me. She didn't want me to know the whole truth, until I'd been to Honolulu, learned about Jenkins and Mannion and what they put her through. About Hirochi Ryo and her love for him."

"You mean the key text is something you stumbled on in Honolulu?"

"Right. One of the addresses where she and Ryo met—the building wasn't there anymore, but across the street was an old church from the missionary era. It was the first building I'd seen that would have been there in 1941, so I went to look at it. On the wall were some lines, some kind of exhortation to the faithful. I figured Tillie could have read them, so I wrote them down."

In the middle of the bridge, traffic slowed to a crawl and he feared she was going to jump out of the car and run around to the trunk, but she waited stoically, digging the heels of her palms into her jeans-clad thighs. Eventually the jam opened up and they coasted down the long slope of the bridge to the other bank. As soon as the road shoulder appeared, he pulled over and clicked the trunk release. Ava was already out of her seat, leaving the door open.

In a moment she was back, with her notebook and the typed sheets of the coded message. "Here's the cite. Matthew 22: 37–39."

He handed her the smart phone he'd bought on the way back from the car rental office. "I expect you want to download Chapter 22 of St. Matthew's gospel."

"Yes. Thanks. The decoding is going to take a while. You might as well drive on."

He checked his mirrors and pulled into the traffic lane. A mile went by. She hadn't pushed any buttons on the phone yet. He glanced sideways at her.

She took a deep shuddering breath. "Grandma figured I would be ready to learn everything now. I hope she was right."

29

April 2, 1942

In the lush hills of Oahu, Tillie has never seen a place so bleak as Honouliuli Camp. The rain forest has been scraped away, leaving hillsides bare except for scrub and tree stumps. The floor of the valley is covered with straight rows of wooden huts and canvas tents. The area is surrounded by twelve-foot-tall fences topped with barbed wire.

The bus she is riding in stops. Half a dozen MPs are waiting. The rims of their steel helmets shadow their eyes. Their M-1 rifles are slung. The door folds open and the visitors rise and descend. The MPs set them in line, roughly handling them, saying nothing. They seem to think these people, mostly Hawaiians of Japanese descent, can't speak English. Tillie wonders what they make of the one white woman in the group. Perhaps nothing.

In single file between the soldiers, they walk along the fence to a long Quonset hut. Tillie feels dizzy. She hopes she will not faint. She gave birth only four days ago. She feels not lightened but empty. Her strength is not returning; her confused body is directing its resources to the production of unneeded milk. Reflexively she looks down the front of her dress for stains.

After the glare of the noonday sun, it seems dim inside the hut, and stuffy. She labors to breathe in the press of sweaty bodies. There are long rows of wooden tables with benches. Picnic tables, probably moved from some seaside park that is now an observation post or machine-gun nest. Hawaii still lives in fear of Japanese invasion. They are ordered to sit. Tillie lifts one leg over the bench, an awkward movement in her long, tight skirt. It feels good to sit. The visitors become still, and now the buzzing of flies can be heard.

There is an addition to the rough wooden planks of the tables, a foot-tall metal barrier, on which is stenciled DO NOT REACH BEYOND.

Good advice, Tillie thinks. Reaching beyond was her mistake. Not contenting herself with what was expected of a girl of her class. Refusing her family's insistence that she go husband-hunting on the mainland. Accepting the Navy's call to serve her country. The vital job that only she could do, as Jennings and Mannion had put it.

Look where it has gotten her.

She squares her shoulders. Blinks and swallows. Hirochi is not going to find her in tears.

The prisoners—internees, she corrects herself—are filing in under heavy guard. There are happy exclamations as relatives see each other. Soon a roar of English, Hawaiian, and Japanese fills the Quonset hut to its curved metal roof. From both sides of the barrier hands reach toward one another, hesitate, are withdrawn.

Hirochi is standing opposite her. How tall he is. She'd almost forgotten. He has lost a lot of weight and his cheekbones seem sharper, his dark eyes more prominent. He has a rough prison haircut, semi-circles of bare skin showing above his ears, a spiky forelock projecting from his brow. He wears the same blue denim uniform as the other prisoners. Internees.

Sitting down, he places both hands flat on the table, fingers stretched toward her. She aligns her own fingers with his. They smile.

"You are as sweet a sight as ever. Your wonderful blue eyes."

The face so Japanese. The voice as American as her own. She's as startled as the first time she heard him speak. It has been a long time since she last saw him.

He stops smiling. "I hope you didn't suffer much."

"Not enough, according to the nursing sisters. They were disappointed I didn't pay the full wages of my sin."

"And the child?"

"A healthy girl. They let me see her. She takes after you."

"Unfortunate, considering the times."

"They told me there are many children of mixed race at the orphanage. But she will be raised an American and an Episcopalian. She will never know our names or anything about us."

Hirochi asks no more questions. Which is good, because she's told him all she knows. Their daughter has been born into even more unpromising circumstances than other illegitimate children. Lawyers for the Navy and the North family have agreed that the wall of secrecy that will separate her from her mother all their lives will have no chinks.

"How are you?" she asks. "So many months, locked up in this dreadful place."

"I have no complaints against the American authorities. If they hadn't arrested me on the morning of December 7, I would've been lynched by nightfall. And I deserve to be here. I'm the enemy. The rest of these poor people have done nothing wrong. They've been locked up only because they had a Japanese parent or grandparent. Tadashi Kurita is here, you know. In the bunkhouse next to mine."

She nods. She's heard that the friend who'd provided them with his beautiful house in the mountains for their trysting place was interned. She says, "Any idea how much longer you'll be here?"

"My status changed December 7. From diplomat to bargaining chip. Washington and Tokyo are negotiating an exchange of internees. I can only wait."

"I hope you wait a long time." She probably shouldn't say this, but can't help herself. "Even if they never let us see each other again, I like to think of you here. Safe."

"I'm eager to resume my work. My real work."

They gaze into each other's eyes. They can say no more. It's unlikely, but not impossible, that the wizened grandmother sitting next to her, weeping as she talks to her son, is an agent who will report their conversation.

She knows what his real work is. For the Communist cause. When she told him she was pregnant, all barriers dropped between them. They shared every secret. They never had any hope of a future together.

That only made it more important that they love and trust each other for whatever time they had.

He says, "My guess is that I'll be sent back fairly soon."

She bows her head to hide her expression. Only now does she realize how afraid she is for him. The risk of exposure and death he will run every day in Tokyo.

"You will be leaving soon yourself," Hirochi says. "Going back to the mainland."

"I suppose. Now that the baby's born. I don't much care, really. But there's a job waiting for me. They arranged it as a reward for services rendered. Jenkins and Mannion, I mean."

Hirochi's eyes narrow in warning. If the wizened grandmother is a spy, it was Jenkins and Mannion who sent her. As a professional, Hirochi disapproves of her indiscretion. She doesn't care. "It's Rear Admiral Jenkins and Captain Mannion now. I'm sure they're happy there's a war on. Good for their careers. Mine, too. They've arranged for me to be a secretary at the Navy Department in Washington."

Hirochi takes this in. "Your family—"

"Safe and sound in Boston. Ready to welcome me back into the fold. They're happy there's a war on, too. It'll drown out any whispers of my scandalous affair, they hope."

Hirochi is looking thoughtful. After a moment he smiles and says, "Washington. I enjoyed my time there. It will make me happy to think of you in Washington. The city will offer limitless opportunities to a person of your talents."

"Please. No. I can't bear to think about the future."

"Not now. But you have a long and glorious life

ahead of you. I'm sure of it." He hesitated again. "That is why I must burden you with something."

She pushes herself back on the bench. Away from him. She has an idea what he means. It terrifies her. "No," she says.

"Ah," he says, in a cheery tone meant to mislead an eavesdropper, if there is one. "You know what I mean."

He can only be talking about the names of the American officers he has recruited to serve the Soviet Union. She knows they exist, but that is all. She's made sure to learn as little as possible.

"I think, I hope that you'll never have to take any action in this matter." His tone is bland, as if he's talking about a minor chore that bores him. He's a professional. She's not. "But if for any reason I'm unable to—"

"Don't say that. I won't—I can't take this responsibility. You know what will happen to them if I ever—"

"No. I don't know."

His eyes implore her to say no more. So she keeps silent. Considers his words and realizes he's right. There's no telling what would happen to the men if she revealed their names. When they said yes to Hirochi, they committed treason. Agreed to serve a feared and hated enemy nation. But now Russia and America are allies against Germany. Soon Russia may join America against Japan. Does that mean the men are no longer traitors?

"The only thing I can predict about the future," Hirochi says, "is that you will see it."

No point in hesitating any longer. She can refuse him nothing. With the slightest nod, she accepts.

"Thanks," he says, in the casual tone meant to fool a

listener. “Just ask Bette for the briefcase I left with her.”

Now the MPs are moving down the aisles between tables, shouting. Visiting time is over. The roar of talk around Tillie stops for a moment, then resumes, even louder, as people rush to say the last things that need to be said.

Hirochi leans closer. Earnestly, softly, he says, “It’s good to have a secret. To know something more important than yourself. It gets you through the days, however you feel.”

The MPs are beginning to grasp internees by the arms, to pull them to their feet. Hirochi doesn’t wait for them to come to him. He rises and turns away, and doesn’t look back.

Tillie stands. Waits for the dizziness to pass, clambers ungracefully over the bench. Tomorrow she will go see Bette, Tadashi Kurita’s secretary, in her office at the Kurita shipping firm in Honolulu, and collect the briefcase. If there are other papers, she will burn them. She will keep only the list of names.

When she returns to the mainland, she will hide it where no one can find it. Hope she will never set eyes on it again.

Just as she will never see her daughter again.

30

Annette staggered into the lobby. Behind her the auditorium resounded with the applause of the rest of the audience. The splendors of the lobby of the John F. Kennedy Center for the Performing Arts—acres of red carpet, tall windows overlooking the Potomac, large bust of JFK on a pedestal—were wasted on her. She was blinded by tears.

Her nose would be running, too—it turned into a Niagara when she wept. She pawed in her bag for a handkerchief. She was going to drip down the front of her red frock and ruin it. She'd packed it so carefully back home in Wilkes-Barre, Pennsylvania, steamed out its wrinkles in the hotel bathroom—and for what? So she could feel overdressed and embarrassed. It turned out people didn't dress up for the opera in Washington, D.C. Everybody else was in slacks.

No handkerchief. Turning toward the wall, she wiped her nose with her bare forearm. And she'd only bought the opera ticket so she could wear the dress.

She'd never been to an opera and assumed it would be pretty boring.

If only it had been.

The beautiful music had swept out into the auditorium, picked her up and pulled her into the hopes and heartbreaks of Madame Butterfly. She'd had a pretty good idea how it would end, but that turned out to be no defense.

In the last moment before the curtain fell, Butterfly's poor little son, Sorrow, waved his American flag, as Lt. Pinkerton, his lying, conceited, irresponsible father—just like Annette's last boyfriend—arrived to claim him, and his abandoned mother plunged a knife into her breast. Annette burst into tears and fled up the aisle.

She was still crying. She'd have to pull herself together before she went outside and joined the line for taxis. Even when she was in good shape she could barely handle taxis. In Wilkes-Barre people drove themselves. Swallowing a sob, she turned away from the wall and straightened her back.

The auditorium doors opened and the audience poured out. There was that funny little man again, the Japanese tourist she'd noticed during intermission, walking around the lobby taking pictures with his expensive-looking Nikon. It made her feel better to see another lone tourist who was even more clueless than she. Annette was overdressed, but at least tastefully overdressed. This guy was wearing a necktie in a loud pattern that clashed with his plaid sport coat. He was almost a caricature of the Japanese tourists she'd seen all over the city, with his hunched posture, as if he was halfway into a bow, and his heavy-framed glasses and permanent bucktooth smile.

But now his smile faded. He'd noticed her sobbing and was heading her way.

Oh God, the last person she wanted to talk to was a Japanese! The opera had left her feeling embarrassed about being a countryman of Pinkerton.

"Miss? Don't cry."

She was about to turn away, but he was holding out to her a handkerchief, crisp white cotton, and it was just what she needed. She took it, brokenly mumbling her thanks.

"You should have stayed. You'd have seen, Butterfly was fine. She was smiling. Everybody was smiling as they bowed to the applause. Well, except for poor Pinkerton. A few people actually booed him." The Japanese tittered.

"Good," said Annette. "I hate him. Waltzing into Butterfly's house with his new wife, taking away her child—"

"His child, too."

"Poor little Sorrow. He'll grow up in a foreign land. With a woman who's not his mother and a father he ought to hate."

The Japanese took this in, nodding gravely. It seemed the opera had affected him, too. Then his mood changed. The smile returned and the narrow black eyes turned into slits. "But Pinkerton did him a great favor. Though he won't appreciate it for many years."

"What are you talking about?"

"Well, where does the opera take place?"

"I don't know. Japan."

The smile grew even broader. "Nagasaki."

She blinked at him, not understanding.

"It would have been Sorrow's fate to die at the age

of fifty, when the city was destroyed by an American nuclear bomb. Being in America, he probably lived another twenty years or more."

"Oh." How could anybody, especially a Japanese, make a joke like that? She wanted to get away from this guy. But his handkerchief was now a ball in her hand, damp and streaked with her makeup. She couldn't give it back to him like that. She didn't know what to do.

He gently took her arm. "Let me help you find a taxi."

Annette hesitated. She did need help. And though this guy had a twisted sense of humor, it was kind of him to try to cheer her up. She allowed him to draw her toward the doors.

31

Morning sun creeping under the window blinds of her hotel room awakened Annette. She opened her eyes. Tadeo's side of the bed was empty. Had he left?

No. She could hear water running. He was in the bathroom.

She wasn't sure how she felt about that. Usually it made her feel bad when a guy she'd hooked up with slipped away in the night. But in Tadeo's case it might have been for the best. The way he changed, once they got into the room last night—she'd been a little drunk at the time and just accepted it. But thinking it over now, it was strange. Scary even.

The first thing to change was his posture. He straightened up, and he wasn't "little" anymore, but rather tall for a Japanese. As they talked and drank, he dropped the toothy smile, took off the glasses. The hooded eyes, black and lustrous as jet, fixed on hers. She could hardly look away from them. In fact she hardly seemed to have a will of her own. Once they were naked, he told her what he was going to do to her and what he expected in return. She accepted and obeyed. Even though some were things she'd never done before. Others were things she'd never heard of.

She went over in her mind what had gone on last night in this bed. And on the desk. And when she was bent over the chair. At first the memories made her queasy. But as the sensations came back to her, her body gradually relaxed. Between her legs there was warmth and wetness. She sat up and threw the sheet off. She was naked. Tadeo's awful sports coat and other clothes lay on the floor. He'd be naked, too.

She got up, walked past the desk swept clean in their acrobatics of last night, the overturned chair. Well, they hadn't done it in the shower yet.

The bathroom door was ajar. She slowly pushed it open.

Tadeo was standing at the sink, his back to her. She ran her eye over the lean, muscular legs, the mounds of the buttocks, paler than the rest of him—one of many things she'd learned last night was that Japanese got suntanned—the smooth back tapering outward from waist to shoulders. In the mirror she saw his face come up as he realized she was there.

His eyes were piercing blue. Not black like last night. And something about them made her stomach squeeze up tight with fear.

A line from the opera came back to her, somebody questioning whether Sorrow was really Pinkerton's, and Butterfly's maid defending her, saying, "Whoever heard of a Japanese boy with blue eyes?"

It was Annette's last thought

* * *

The Shapeshifter whirled. His left hand caught the side of the girl's head, slammed it into the doorframe. She dropped without a sound. He knelt over her, fingers going around her throat, and carefully pressed both thumbs into the suprasternal notch, crushing the windpipe. In less than a minute she was dead.

He got to his feet and backed away, breathing hard. One of his tinted contact lenses was lying on the floor. He licked his forefinger and picked it up, returned it to its case. The other lens wasn't there. He dropped to hands and knees and crawled around the bathroom, searching for it. He hated unplanned killings. In the first minutes afterward there was so much to do, and any mistake or omission could be disastrous. Minor mishaps wasted time and, worse, clouded the mental clarity that was absolutely vital.

He'd been about to reinsert the contacts. Another minute or two, and he wouldn't have had to kill her.

He sat up on his haunches and shut his eyes. Regret. The most pointless and disruptive of emotions. He was going to have to take the time to work his way through it, or it would continue to sap his concentration and energy.

Last night had been self-indulgent from the start, doomed to end badly from the moment he decided to attend the opera. *Madama Butterfly* always amused him, the way the Italian composer portrayed the Japanese as delicate, weak, pathetic. It amused him even more to attend as a Japanese tourist, one of the horde who wandered around Washington, getting in people's way as they snapped endless pictures of each other in front of the monuments.

Then the final, unforgivable self-indulgence. Spotting the weeping but undeniably pretty girl and choosing to bed her. He deserved a night of relaxation and pleasure. This might be his last chance.

But the impulse was his own. Inconsistent with the character he was playing. And the girl had noticed the change in him, once they returned to the room. She wasn't as stupid as he'd thought. He sensed her wariness. Alcohol and desire overcame it. But even if she hadn't seen his eyes, it would have been unpardonably careless to allow her to go on living, remembering this night, becoming more suspicious. Conceivably, even going to the authorities.

The Shapeshifter methodically chased from his head both self-reproaches and self-justifications. Breathed deeply and evenly. When he opened his eyes, his mind was clear again. He'd refocused on his mission. And considering what it was, to brood about the death of a single American was absurd.

He found the missing contact lens behind the toilet, put it in the case. No need to reinsert them now. Going into the bedroom, he put on his clothes, retrieved his Nikon from the night table, his opera program from the trash can, his handkerchief from the girl's purse. He wiped clean any surfaces capable of yielding clear fingerprints.

Then he hesitated. What about DNA? He and the girl had used condoms for conventional sex, but the police would find his semen in her other orifices. And he'd probably left hairs in the bed, traces of saliva in the bathroom—trying to clean it all up would be a hopeless task. It didn't matter. His DNA was not on record anywhere.

It was not necessary to look at the naked body sprawled on the bathroom floor again. But he did pause at the door of the room, reflecting that most of the hours he'd spent here had been very pleasant. He thought of Lt. Pinkerton, leaving Madame Butterfly's house. *Addio, fiorito asil.*

He shut the door and hung the "do not disturb" sign on the knob.

It was early and there was no one to see him in the corridor or elevator. By the time he stepped into the lobby he had sunglasses and cap on. He crossed the lobby unhurriedly, nodding to the bellboy who was the only person who seemed to notice him, and stepped out into the warm sunshine of Constitution Avenue.

There were cars on the street but few pedestrians on the sidewalks. The Shapeshifter walked on. Once he got far enough away from the hotel, he'd toss the loud sport coat into a trash can.

His cell phone chirped. He looked at the screen and frowned. Raising the phone to his ear, he said, "Never call me from your own phone. Buy a cheap one at a grocery store. Use cash. Then call me."

He was about to press the off button, but she said, "Don't hang up. I won't call you back."

"You know the procedures. Follow them."

"I can't be bothered."

"Someone in your position cannot afford laziness."

"Oh, God. Spare me the words of wisdom. They're going to catch me. It's only a matter of time."

The Shapeshifter considered. Her insolence was intolerable. But what if he hung up and she really didn't call him back? Then he would have to take the additional risk of going to see her. Because he wanted to hear what she had to say. Her information had been excellent so far.

Spotting a bench in the shade of a building, he sat down. "What makes you think they suspect you?"

"They questioned me yesterday. A team from internal security."

"But they're questioning everybody, you said."

"Not for as long as they talked to me. I don't really care anymore."

He made his tone more gentle. "Don't talk like that. We know the sacrifices you're making. We appreciate your help."

"*We*. I'm not even going to ask who you really work for. It'd just be another lie. You've been lying to me from the start, pulled me in so deep there's no way out."

"Make your report," he snapped.

"There's talk of Laker being back."

"Talk? How credible, in your estimation?"

"Not very. It's coming from low-level personnel whose information is second- or third-hand. Morale is low in the Gray Outfit, what with the attack on headquarters and the internal security teams grilling everybody. Laker's the homerun hitter. Everybody wants him to step up to the plate."

"Why was this rumor worth reporting to me?"

"Because if it's true, and he's back in Washington, there's only one possible reason. He's found out something urgent and important."

"What would he do, in that case?"

"Report direct to Samuel Mason."

"Is Mason in any shape for such a meeting?"

"He hasn't been back to the office. But I don't think you hurt him as much as you think you did."

More insolence. "It was unnecessary to say that."

"Just keeping you informed," she said bitterly, and broke the connection.

The Shapeshifter lingered on the shady bench, reviewing the conversation. Her hostility to him was familiar. She'd been that way since his attack on the Outfit's headquarters. But the note of despair, of fatalism, was new. If she didn't care about being caught, then she should be. Should he eliminate her before it happened?

No, he decided. However she felt, she was still reporting to him. All that mattered now was to find out if Laker was back. And whether he'd made some important discovery.

32

Sam Mason, who used to be bald except for a gray fringe around the sides and back of his head, was now completely bald. His left eyebrow was shaved, too. A patch covered the eye. Pink, puckered surgical scars crisscrossed his forehead and right cheek. The staples looked painful. But he was listening with his usual concentration as Ava recounted to him what Tillie North had written in her encoded statement.

"Hold it, Ava," he said. "I can believe Tillie accepted the list of Ryo's agents from him at the internment camp. Emotions of the moment and so forth. But once she was back in Washington, she just sat on it? Didn't tell a soul?"

Ava, who was meeting Mason for the first time, gave Laker an exasperated look. He could've told her that when Mason slowed down a debrief, asking innumerable questions, it was a sign he was taking the matter seriously.

"Must we *plod*?" She burst out, leaning across the table toward Mason. "We've been talking for an hour, and we're still back in the 1940s. Things are happening *now*. Decisions have to be made *now*. Will you let me skip to the bottom line?"

Mason shook his head. "The decisions I make have to be the right ones. Go on."

"Do you want to read Tillie's statement yourself? Maybe you'll find it more convincing than my account."

"You're doing fine. Just answer my question."

They had arrived at Mason's house in McLean, Virginia, shortly after dawn. His nurse held them at the door, refusing access, until the man himself appeared, knotting his flannel bathrobe, saying that he couldn't sleep anyway. He led them down the basement steps. The best place for a secret discussion was an underground room with no windows.

The room had a battered couch before a big television screen, a small beer refrigerator, and a poker table. Obviously it had been Mason's man cave. But the Pirelli girlie calendar on the wall was five years old. He hadn't used the room much since his daughters got married and his wife died.

They sat down at the poker table after Mason turned on the overhead light that illuminated its green baize surface. Laker noticed that there were little silos of plastic chips inset in the table in front of him—red, white, and blue. He wondered if coffee was going to be brought down to them. At the Outfit, Mason banned coffee from meetings. He said it made people too comfortable, meetings too long. But the rules might be different at home.

They weren't. An hour had passed and no coffee had appeared.

Resignedly, Ava answered Mason's question.

"Yes, I believe she just sat on the list. She thought she was out of the world of big events and powerful men. She'd had enough of it. In 1942 she was a young single girl working as a secretary like thousands of others in Washington. Doing her bit for the war effort and keeping her broken heart to herself."

"That changed the next year," Mason said. "She met Ephraim North, brilliant army officer, moving up fast."

"In 1943, Ryo's network didn't seem to matter. The tide of war was turning in our favor. The Russians were helping us do it. American grandmothers were knitting socks for the Ivans at the front. People called Stalin Uncle Joe."

Mason turned to Laker. "You said Berilov told you Ryo's net was neglected, his agents scattered."

"I didn't believe him." Laker tapped Ava's decoding of Millie's statement with his forefinger. "And this confirms it. The net went off the books. It wasn't being run out of KGB headquarters anymore. It was being run from the Kremlin. Maybe even from Stalin's office. Ryo was replaced. The agents were kept ready. And in the closing days of the war, they went operational."

Rush hour hadn't ended yet on the Fourteenth Street Bridge across the Potomac. Cars choked the lanes bound for Washington. But the Shapeshifter, heading for Virginia at the wheel of an inconspicuous rental car, was moving at the speed limit.

It had taken him only a few phone calls, and a few elementary subterfuges, to establish that Samuel Mason was no longer in the hospital, and that he was not recovering at his retreat on the Chesapeake shore. He was at his house in McLean. The slackness of the enemy agency disgusted the Shapeshifter. Had they already forgotten he'd penetrated their headquarters?

Laker's the homerun hitter. People want to see him step up to the plate.

The words of his source at the Outfit kept coming back to him, nettling him. He'd stood face-to-face with Laker and traded blows with him. *Beaten* him. Laker'd dropped helpless at his feet and only the arrival of the police had saved his life.

Reaching the Virginia bank of the river, the Shapeshifter eased his grip on the steering wheel, shrugged the tension from his shoulders. Always respect the opponent, he reminded himself. To underestimate him is to give him an unearned advantage.

The Shapeshifter had read the journal many times. It hadn't told him what he needed to know. But Laker must have found something out, the Shapeshifter's source had said. He, or the woman, Ava North. They were a step ahead of the Shapeshifter.

A situation that would have to change.

33

"I don't think we need waste time reviewing the world situation in 1945—" Ava was saying.

"Give me the key points, as Tillie saw them," Mason said.

Ava's cheeks were burning with impatience. "Fine. We plod on. July 1945. The Potsdam Conference. Churchill, Truman, and Stalin met. Germany was beaten and the Grand Alliance was falling apart. Stalin was grabbing up countries in Eastern Europe. Didn't care to be reminded of past promises. Truman was frustrated. Then, July 16, he got the news from Los Alamos. The Trinity test was a success. The A-bomb worked. Some of the scientists were slapping each other on the back and guzzling champagne. Oppenheimer was muttering, 'I am become Death, the destroyer of worlds.'"

"Truman's reaction was on the backslapping, champagne-guzzling side," Laker said.

"He's just been given the biggest saber of all time, and he rattles it a bit." Ava said. "Hints to Uncle Joe that the U.S. has a new and terrible weapon."

Mason said, "To Truman's surprise, Stalin blew him off. But there was a reason he wasn't curious. He'd been following the progress at Los Alamos for months, thanks to Klaus Fuchs, his spy there."

"You *do* know all this," Ava said.

"Keep plodding."

"At Potsdam Stalin played dumb. Didn't acknowledge that Truman's hint was a veiled threat. Because his land-grabbing ambitions weren't limited to Eastern Europe. Now Japan was almost beaten, he wanted to be in at the kill, grab up the spoils. Soon as he got back to Moscow, he ordered a declaration of war against Japan and sent his troops into Manchuria. Truman was apoplectic."

Laker took over. "The day after Trinity, the casing and the works of Little Boy left Los Alamos in an army truck convoy. They went to Hunter's Point Navy Base near San Francisco. The uranium-235, the trigger that set off the nuclear chain reaction, arrived from Hanford, Washington. The casing and works were in two big wooden crates, the uranium in a small lead container. The crates went into the hold of the cruiser U.S.S. *Indianapolis*. The lead container was bolted to the floor of the flag lieutenant's cabin. On July 26, the ship arrived at Tinian Island, our forward airbase. Physicists had flown in from Los Alamos and were waiting to assemble it."

"Then Little Boy went on board the *Enola Gay,* which dropped it on Hiroshima August 6," said Mason. "Fat Man followed the same route to Los Alamos and Hunter's Point, arriving Tinian August 5, and was dropped on Nagasaki August 9. On August 15, Japan surrendered. Which was a good thing, because two bombs were all we had ready."

Ava said, "No."

There was no change in Mason's slumped posture. "I guess this is where we leave the history books behind," he said dryly.

"There was a third bomb. Bobby Soxer."

"That name sounds familiar," Mason said. He glanced at Laker. "It was in your report of Tillie's death."

"Yes," Laker said. "On the way to the Chevy Chase house, Tillie was quizzing us about World War II code names. We got Torch and Overlord. But she stumped us with Bobby Soxer."

Mason looked at Ava. "Your grandmother had a strange sense of humor."

"We'll never know what was going through her mind then," Ava said, meeting Mason's eye. "She knew her death was near. It was going to be a relief to her."

"Tell me about Bobby Soxer," Mason said.

"It followed the same route as the previous bombs," Laker continued. "At Hunter's Point, the crates and the lead box were loaded aboard the cruiser U.S.S. *Tulsa*. It reached Tinian August 10, to be used August 17 if the Japanese didn't surrender. But when the crates were opened by the physicists, there was nothing in them but scrap metal. No plutonium in the lead container, either."

Mason sat up straight. His one visible eye was blinking rapidly.

"Jesus H. Christ," he said. "So it was true."

"What was true?"

"About the empty crates at Tinian. I heard about them years ago, from a former director of Central Intelligence. Late at night, just the two of us, and he was drunk on his ass. I didn't take him seriously. I thought next he was going to tell me we had a jail at Area 51, full of alien UFO pilots."

"He was telling the truth," Laker said. "Bobby Soxer disappeared in transit."

Mason was silent for a long time. His fingers fumbled a chip out of the slot and began to tap it on the table. Laker'd never seen a nervous tic in Mason before. Didn't think he was capable of nervousness.

"And this was the work of Hirochi Ryo's agents?" he said at last.

Ava and Laker nodded.

"The biggest heist in history. How come it wasn't followed by the biggest manhunt in history?"

"Somebody at Tinian kept a cool head. Clamped a lid tight on the fiasco. Ignored the chain of command and reported straight to Truman himself," Laker replied.

"That must have been a swell phone call to get," said Mason. "Did Truman figure it was a Soviet op?"

"Yes," said Laker. "It fitted their MO. Their nuclear program was way behind. Spying and looting were their way of catching up. When the Red Army invaded Germany, they started grabbing Hitler's scientists, disassembling whole labs and factories and putting them on eastbound trains. Stealing Bobby Soxer was just one step beyond."

"With the side benefit that being in possession of the world's only ready-to-use A-bomb gave Stalin the window of opportunity he needed to complete his East Asian land grab," Ava said.

"It couldn't have been long till our next bomb was ready."

"Only a few weeks. But that was enough."

"Truman," Mason said. "That poor bastard. Everybody says the toughest choice he had to make was to drop the bombs on Hiroshima and Nagasaki. But this one—"

"He knew that if he ordered an investigation, the whole thing was going to leak out. And he knew where the trail was going to lead."

"Straight to the Kremlin," said Mason. "Who'd respond with angry denials and countercharges, of course."

"Things were already tense," said Laker. "There'd been incidents in occupied Germany, American and Russian troops shooting at each other. Patton wanted to turn his tanks east and head for Moscow. There were people who agreed with him."

"Only a few hotheads," Ava clarified. "The bloodiest war in history was coming to an end. Most people just wanted the troops to come home. And Truman was war weary too—he didn't say it publicly, but he was sickened by the slaughter at Hiroshima and Nagasaki."

Mason looked down. Seemed to notice for the first time that he was fidgeting with the chip. He put it back in its slot. "So what Truman decided to do was—nothing."

"The alternative was World War III," Ava said.

"But he had to let the traitors get away," Mason said. "American officers who'd done Stalin's bidding. The assholes."

"Give them their due," Laker said. "Ingenious and courageous assholes."

34

The Shapeshifter turned into Mason's street. What an odd country America was. The chief of one of its most secret agencies lived in a modest Virginia subdivision. Built in the 1950s, the brick and wood houses stood on rather small lots. Their lawns, of an unnatural greenness and density thanks to chemical treatments, ran into one another. No walls or fences between them, nor along the street.

He brought the car to a stop in front of Mason's split-level. There was a car parked in the driveway, a plain four-door sedan like the one he was driving, probably also a rental. The license plate was out of state. Orange. Was that New York? It didn't matter. The car had to be Laker's. He and the woman were in the house.

A cement path ran from the street right to the front door. An ordinary door, wood with glass panels on either side. The Shapeshifter's Heckler & Koch MP was in the glove compartment. He was afire to grab it, run up the path, kick the door in. The exhilaration of his assault on the Outfit came back to him, the hot weapon in his hands, the smell of cordite, the pouring blood and falling bodies,

Never underestimate the enemy, he told himself again.

He sat still and surveyed the street. As usual in the American suburbs on a weekday morning, there were not many people around. An AT&T van was parked two houses away, and the repairman was up a telephone pole, leaning back against his safety strap as he worked. Two kids were playing basketball in the driveway next to him. Across the street, a housewife was busy in her front garden, showing him a broad, jeans-clad rump as she knelt and bent over with her clippers.

No threats in sight. But the Shapeshifter reminded himself that days of planning and observation had paved the way for those minutes of pleasure at the Outfit. He watched and waited.

One by one, he noticed the false notes. A man was sitting in the passenger seat of the phone company van. Real repairmen did not travel in pairs. The two kids shooting hoops were not teenagers but young men, and they were wearing sweatshirts on a hot day, to conceal their guns. The gardener straightened up, placing both hands against the small of her back as if it ached. She gave the briefest of glances over her shoulder. At him. She took a cell phone out of her pocket.

A minute later, when a police car came around the corner, the Shapeshifter wasn't surprised. The car came toward him slowly, no siren, no lights. The cop was going to park behind him, come to his window, ask him in a friendly way what his business was.

But somebody would be aiming a gun at his head, just in case.

The Shapeshifter started his engine and drove unhurriedly away. The cop did not follow. Mason had been clever to make his security detail unobtrusive, the Shapeshifter thought. He was all but inviting another attack, and the attacker would blunder into a trap.

The Shapeshifter would have to find someplace else to park his car.

And wait for Laker to come out.

"Tillie knew nothing about Bobby Soxer then, of course. She was the bride of a junior army officer," Ava said. "In August 1945 they were as ignorant of what was going on as—well, the rest of the world."

"When did she find out?" Mason asked.

"Nineteen fifty-six. Ephraim was well established as an adviser and fund-raiser and golfing buddy of Ike. Tillie was Washington's most fashionable hostess. When the White House put a back-channel query about Bobby Soxer to the Kremlin, he heard about it. There was a momentary thaw on. Stalin was dead and Khrushchev had taken over. The Sputnik scare hadn't happened yet. Even so, the White House was surprised when it got an answer. The Russians admitted the theft of Bobby Soxer was their operation. But they said it never got to Moscow. The transport problem was too much for their agents. Bobby Soxer ended up at the bottom of the sea."

"What do you think of that, boss?" Laker asked. "Credible?"

Mason ignored the question. He said to Ava, "Ephraim North confided all this to Tillie. What did she do?"

"She leveled with him. Until then she'd kept what happened to her in Honolulu before they met a secret from him. But now she told him all about Hirochi Ryo. She offered to turn the list over to him. Her statement says she'll never forget that night. He was in his study, chain-smoking. She was lying in bed staring at the ceiling. In the morning he said he didn't want the list."

Mason grunted but said nothing.

"Tracking down and prosecuting those men would have exposed the whole scandal," Ava said. "Set off the drumbeat for war. The problem was the same as in 1945, except both sides had more and bigger bombs. They decided to let sleeping dogs lie."

"Let sleeping dogs lie," Mason echoed, with a grim smile at Laker. "The Third Commandment of Washington."

Laker nodded. "After 'Don't rock the boat' and 'Cover your ass.'"

"You're being too easy on your grandparents, Ava," Mason told her.

"But the traitors had had eleven years to create new identities or escape overseas," she protested. "It wasn't worth risking nuclear war."

"I think the risk to themselves was what the Norths were thinking about," Mason said. "It would've been damn hard to explain why she'd been given the list and sat on it all these years. Maybe she could have stayed out of jail, but her reign as Washington's most glamorous hostess would've been over. Along with Ephraim's days of golfing with Ike."

"Is he always this hateful?" said Ava to Laker.

"I'm sorry," said Laker. "But I have to agree. Power and fame and riches were just too nice to give up. So she kept the list hidden and wrote that message to you."

"Kick the can down the road," said Mason bitterly. "The fourth commandment of Washington."

"Why did she do it?" Ava asked Laker. "That's something I still don't understand."

"You mean set up this twisting, turning breadcrumb trail that would lead you to the truth after her death?" Mason said. "That's simple. She wasn't sure Bobby Soxer was on the bottom of the ocean."

"You mean the Soviets lied?" Ava said.

"They'd been known to do that," Laker said.

"Or it could have been a half-truth," Mason went on. "The bomb never made it to Moscow. And that was all they knew."

"A loose nuke," Laker said. "The nightmare of every intelligence chief. And there's been one for seventy years."

Ava shook her head. "It couldn't still be capable of exploding."

"That depends on where and how it's been stored," Laker said.

"But the trigger—the plutonium. Doesn't it have a time limit?"

"Some plutonium has a half-life of twenty-five thousand years," Mason replied. "Lots of people would say that's long enough."

"No," Ava said. "This is impossible. Like you said, it's seventy years. In all the time, somebody would've found out about it."

"The Shapeshifter did," Laker said.

* * *

The Shapeshifter had learned, from a map of Mason's subdivision that he brought up on the car's dashboard screen, that the street plan was typical of a '50s subdivision: a cluster of intersecting loops. The entrance he had come in by was the only way for vehicles to get in or out. So he'd returned to it and parked, to wait for Laker's car to appear. But after only a couple of minutes, he noticed something that didn't fit. Across the four-lane road was a public school. A guard in an orange vest was standing at the crosswalk. In America crossing guards were usually senior citizens, but this man was young and fit-looking. And he was still there, even though it was mid-morning and no more children were arriving.

Another member of Mason's security detail. Who would spot and report him if he stayed here.

The Shapeshifter started his engine and drove out the subdivision entrance. Which way to turn? He chose left and drove until the road curved, taking him out of the watcher's view. Turned again, into the small parking lot of a Walgreens, and parked.

If Laker turned right out of the subdivision, headed back to Washington, the Shapeshifter would miss him. If he turned left, headed deeper into Virginia, he would drive by the Walgreens.

Fifty/fifty.

The Shapeshifter thought it over but couldn't think of any way of improving the odds. He cleared his mind of indecision and watched the road.

* * *

"Who's the son of a bitch working for?" Mason asked. "We still have no idea about that."

"The Shapeshifter? My guess is a terrorist organization," Laker said.

"Or an arms dealer," Ava said.

The possibility interested Mason. "An international arms merchant with connections in the Russian Mafia. Whoever found out about Bobby Soxer would have to have high-level contacts in Moscow."

"Or in Washington."

Mason's one visible eye glared at Laker. Then his anger faded and he sank back in his chair. "You're right, goddammit. When I'm looking for a double agent in the Outfit, I can't say it's impossible we're dealing with rogue agents from one of our own spy shops. Anyway there's only one thing that matters about the Shapeshifter. That we get to Bobby Soxer before he does. Having Tillie's list of Ryo's agents gives us a headstart."

"Except that we don't have it," Ava said.

"What?"

"We can't find it," Laker admitted miserably.

Mason struggled to his feet, started pacing from the poker table to the big screen TV console with slow, painful-looking steps. "For fuck's sake," he said. "After telling you this whole story, Tillie didn't tell you how to find the list of agents?"

"She set it down in great detail," Ava replied. "She said the list was disguised as a seating chart for one of her dinner parties. What gave her the idea was the coincidence that there were fourteen agents in Ryo's network and fourteen places at her table."

"Okay. And where did she put the chart?

"In a blue folder labeled 'seating charts' that was kept in her social secretary's office on the ground floor of the Chevy Chase house."

"What happened to those files when she moved out of the house?"

"They came to me, along with the rest of Tillie's records."

Mason lurched to a stop. Raised his one remaining eyebrow at her. "You've had this chart all along?"

"No. Tillie seemed to think I had it, but I didn't."

"We went to Ava's apartment as soon as we got back to Washington," Laker explained. "There was no file labeled 'seating charts.' We spent the rest of the night going through all Tillie's papers. No luck."

Mason returned to the table and sank into his chair. "Tom?"

Laker gave a start. Mason'd never called him by his first name. "Boss?"

"There's only one course of action open to me. Shower, shave, and report personally to the Secretary for Homeland Security. Please tell me I don't have to report that we've got fuck-all."

"We have an idea," Laker replied. "Or maybe it's better to call it a hope."

"Erlynne Bendix," Ava said. "My grandmother's maid and confidante for fifty years. If anybody would know what happened to that file, she would."

Mason sighed. "It's better than nothing. Fractionally. Go."

35

At the Dillsworth Long Term Care Facility in Reston, Virginia, an attendant from the front desk led them to Erlynne Bendix's room. The staff was trying hard to brighten the lives of the aged residents, Ava thought. As they passed the lunch room, she looked in the doors to see that today's meal had a Mexican fiesta theme, with red and green streamers crisscrossing the ceiling, posters of Caribbean beaches and pueblos on the walls, and a mariachi band playing at the front of the room while a dancer stomped and swirled and clicked castanets. The blare of horns was deafening, the dancer energetic, but most of the wrinkled faces looked grim and indifferent as they chomped messily on their tacos and enchiladas.

A comfort dog was visiting, too. In the corridor, a beautiful yellow Labrador retriever was rolling on his back, paws in the air and tongue lolling in a doggy smile. A group of residents were trying to maneuver their wheelchairs close enough to reach down and stroke his furry chest.

Following the attendant, they cut through a spacious lounge where people on couches or in wheelchairs were facing a huge television showing a Washington Nationals game. More seemed to be dozing than watching. One corner of the lounge was occupied by a family gathering, a middle-aged couple showing pictures on their phones to their aged mother, while teenaged grandchildren were standing before cages on poles, trying to alleviate their boredom by getting the cockatiels inside to bite their fingers. But the cockatiels looked bored, too.

They went through a doorway and were now in Mrs. Bendix's corridor. Ava recognized it from previous visits. It was quiet except for two frail residents making their way along the wall slowly, hand over hand on the waist-high grab bar, and a nurse whose paunch bulged against his blue uniform. He had a patchy beard and glasses. He was wheeling a metal cart down the aisle, distributing meds to people in their rooms.

Erlynne Bendix was in bed, a book lying open on her chest, her glasses perched atop a wave of white hair. She wasn't asleep, but gazing out the window. The attendant waved Ava and Laker in and left. Mrs. Bendix turned to them and settled her glasses on her nose. Ava felt a twinge of her childhood shyness before her grandmother's formidable maid.

"Hello, Mrs. B," she said, smiling.

Mrs. Bendix did not smile back, but looked at her long and hard.

"Ava," she said at last, and her chin dipped with self-congratulation, as emphatic as a tennis champion's fist pump, at recalling the name. Her gaze shifted to Laker. "And you're the government man. You said I didn't have to remember your name. But here you are, back again. You going to bother me with more questions about Miz Tillie?"

Ava laughed nervously. She crossed the small room and pulled a chair close to the bedside. Laker remained in the doorway. "I'm afraid so, Mrs. B. There was something my grandmother meant me to have. A very important document. She wrote that it would be in her papers."

Mrs. Bendix shrugged her thin shoulders under her flowered nightgown. "You got all those."

"But we can't find this document. Do you remember a folder called 'seating charts'?"

"Social secretary kept all those. It was always some pretty girl who liked to make phone calls and had good handwriting and didn't do any real work."

"But you knew that grandmother kept the seating charts from her dinner parties."

The many lines in Mrs. Bendix's forehead deepened as she frowned in concentration. She was silent for so long that Ava turned to Laker with a despairing glance. Mrs. B would be no help to them. But he'd turned to watch the nurse rolling the meds cart down the corridor behind him.

Mrs. Bendix said, "Oh, yes."

"You do remember the seating charts?"

"I had to make sure, after the butler wrote out the place cards, to take the seating chart back to her. When the party was over, I'd bring her nightcap—always a small glass of straight bourbon—to her bedroom. And while I put away her clothes or brushed her hair, she'd make notes on the chart. Things like, 'Never seat Mr. R and Mrs. J next to each other again.' Or 'Captain X and

Miss Y are going to be engaged by next month, I bet.' or 'Never invite Dr. K to dinner again. Cocktails only.' We used to laugh a lot while she did that." She blinked and focused her eyes on Ava. "You here looking for gossip, child? It's mighty old gossip."

"I'm just trying to figure out, why didn't that file come to me with the rest?"

"I don't know. I was in here by the time Miz Tillie moved out of the Chevy Chase house. How would I know anything about that?"

"But when you were still working"—Ava struggled to put her question clearly—"is it possible somebody took the seating charts file? Did anybody ever have access to the social secretary's files?"

"'Course not. I'd have caught any of those college girls letting outsiders see Miz Tillie's private papers, I'd have handed her her walking papers."

"Ma'am?" said Laker from the doorway. "We understand you never let anybody near those files. But what about Miz Tillie? She ever grant anybody access?"

Mrs. Bendix wagged her head.

"Stop and think, ma'am, please. We're talking about a lot of years."

Mrs. Bendix shut her eyes. Again her brow furrowed with concentration. People usually did what Laker told them to do, Ava'd noticed. A full minute passed before Mrs. Bendix spoke.

"There was that one fellah. Talk about rude questions. He must've been from New York City. But Miz Tillie said he was helping her write her book. He was supposed to look at her papers only here." She broke off, annoyed with herself. "Not here. I mean, in the study of the house at Chevy Chase. But he was always asking to take papers home."

"We're talking about Joshua Milton," Laker said.

"That's the fellah. I was glad when Miz Tillie threw him out. He didn't go gracefully. He gave me the feeling—you know, when you fire a maid, and she slips some silverware in her pocket? Milton was like that. But I don't recall Miz Tillie and I ever went through the files to make sure he hadn't taken anything. We were both old and forgetful."

"But if we're looking for a missing file—" Ava said.

"Go to that Milton fellah."

Ava hurriedly thanked her. She rose to see that Laker was no longer in the doorway. He couldn't wait to go to the *Washington Post* and confront Milton, she thought. She hurried into the corridor, and was surprised to see that Laker was not striding toward the exit. Just standing there, looking the other way, and Ava followed the look. There was nothing to see but the nurse pushing his meds cart slowly down the corridor.

Laker's arm swung up. The Beretta was in his hand. He fired. Ava was stunned. He'd shot the nurse.

No, he hadn't. She turned to see that the nurse had ducked the bullet. In the same blur of motion he swung the cart around and shoved it at Laker. She realized that the patchy beard was false and the fat stomach was padding and this was the Shapeshifter.

Laker dodged the cart but lost his balance. He threw out his left hand to catch himself. That gave the Shapeshifter the split second he needed to run by them. Laker set his feet and dropped into a shooter's crouch, both arms straight out. But an elderly couple were making their way slowly down the corridor and he couldn't risk a shot. Tucking the automatic in his waistband, he set off running after the Shapeshifter. Ava followed.

The Shapeshifter was already a dozen paces away. He ducked into a doorway. She heard a crash and clatter of metal. Reaching the doorway a step behind Laker she saw that it was the lounge. The birdcages were rolling across the floor and the cockatiels were flying free. The teenagers were hiding behind furniture, their parents crouching beside their chairs. They were looking after the Shapeshifter with frightened eyes. But the grandmother was gazing at the brilliantly colored birds flying overhead, a smile on her face.

Now the Shapeshifter was running by the people sitting in front of the big screen. Nobody was watching the game anymore; all eyes were turned to him. He came to a sudden stop, grabbed the nearest wheelchair by both handles, and shoved it at Laker. The small, wizened woman in the chair cried out, her eyes wide with terror.

Laker sidestepped and pivoted to grasp the handles, then ran behind the chair a few paces, gradually slowing it to a standstill. He'd made the move as gracefully as a matador and some of the people in front of the television cheered.

But the Shapeshifter's maneuver had worked. He'd already reached the door on the other side of the room. He ran through it. Ava was five paces behind him. She heard Laker shout, "Ava, wait!" but didn't heed him.

The Shapeshifter was running down the corridor, skirting the cluster of wheelchairs around the comfort dog. The yellow Lab surged to its feet and bounded after him, barking. The Shapeshifter turned right and disappeared through another doorway. Laker barreled past her. The three of them chased the Shapeshifter into what turned out to be the lunch room. The dog got to him first.

With a final leap the Lab sank its teeth into his pants leg. The Shapeshifter cried out—the first sound she'd heard him make. He swiveled and clouted the dog hard on the side of the head. The dog whined and collapsed in a heap.

The trumpeters lowered their instruments and the guitarists froze in mid-strum. The dancer stood flat-footed, letting her castanets fall to the floor. The old folks recovered first. They pelted the Shapeshifter with tacos and burritos as he ran through the opposite door. Ava was glad to see that his left pants leg was bloody.

In the reception lobby all the personnel were on their feet with phones in their hands. They'd heard the gunshot. Nobody tried to stop the Shapeshifter as he crossed the room and pushed through the door. A moment later Laker followed, with Ava behind him.

Now he was outside, the Shapeshifter could put on speed. Leaning forward, arms pumping, he was sprinting across the parking lot. Laker drew his gun. He wouldn't miss at this range, she thought.

Focusing on the Shapeshifter, she didn't hear the approaching siren, didn't see the patrol car until it screeched to a stop in front of Laker. His shot spoiled, he ran around the car, but another pulled up, blocking him again. He stopped and turned. The cops from the first car were on their feet, pointing their pistols at him, shouting. Squeezing his eyes shut in frustration, he dropped the Beretta and slowly raised his arms.

Ava looked for the Shapeshifter but didn't see him. He must've already reached the other side of the parking lot and disappeared through the trees. She didn't know what to do.

She wanted to step forward, join Laker in trying to explain to the police. But they had him braced against a car with a gun to his head. Explanations were going to take a while. Too long. By now the Shapeshifter was probably in his car. Eavesdropping at Mrs. B's door, he couldn't have failed to overhear the name of Josh Milton.

Ava had to get to the *Post* reporter before he did.

Turning her back on Laker, she headed for their rental car, forcing herself not to hurry. Another police car approached, siren wailing and roof-lights rippling. The cops passed her without a glance.

36

"Mr. Milton is working remotely today," said the newsroom operator at the *Washington Post.*

"What does that mean? That he's at home?" Ava was driving south along the Potomac on Route 123, phone in hand.

"I can direct your call to someone else on the National Politics desk."

"I need to see Milton, right away. Give me his home address."

"I'm sorry but—"

"This is Ava North."

"Oh. Just a moment, Ms. North."

The receptionist was back in a minute with the phone number and address, which Ava only had to hear once to memorize; she'd always been good at that. She considered dialing his number, but the address was in Alexandria, only a few minutes away. She decided to just go there.

As she exited to U.S. 1, she wondered how Laker was doing. Nervousness was making her a little giddy, because she thought of *Notorious*, the scene where the motorcycle cop pulled Ingrid Bergman over for drunk driving. But Cary Grant showed his G-Man ID, and the cop saluted and groveled and followed Cary Grant's orders.

She hoped Laker had an ID like that.

Milton lived in the old part of town, in one of the narrow brick row houses built in the mid-nineteenth century. Nice, if you were into vertical living; people happily paid a couple of million bucks for one. Milton's latest rip-the-lid-off-Washington book must be selling well.

She looked both ways as she got out of the car, her stomach crawling. The street and the sidewalks were busy, and she lacked Laker's preternatural ability to spot the enemy. The Shapeshifter had only Milton's name. It would take a while for him to obtain the address.

She hoped.

Steep steps led to the house's front door. As she approached them, Milton appeared, stepping out of an archway under the steps. He was in a ratty old bathrobe over pajamas. His dark eyes were more heavily bagged than usual, and his graying mustache was droopier. Knowing the ways of writers, she figured he'd stayed up all night to beat a deadline.

"Ava. At last," he said, unsmiling but plainly glad to see her. "I've been expecting you."

"Your office called to alert you?"

"Even before that. I knew you'd realize it's time to tell your story, and I'm the one who will take best care of you."

He waved her into the door under the steps. It was a

service entrance leading to the kitchen. A long table was covered with papers, notebooks, back issues of the *Post,* a laptop, and a greasy carton containing half a pizza. Milton must have chosen to work here so that he could be close to his coffeemaker.

"Have a seat," he said.

"Sorry, Josh. I'm not here to give you an exclu."

"You're not?"

"I'm here to retrieve a file you took from my grandmother's house. Stole, really."

He squared his shoulders and narrowed his eyes. It didn't take much for Milton to get up on his high horse.

"Stole? I reject that term. We were collaborating on a memoir, until your grandmother got cold feet and reneged. A lot of papers passed back and forth."

"This was a folder labeled 'seating charts.'"

"I don't know what you're talking about," he said, looking genuinely baffled.

"You kept it because Millie had written gossipy notes about her guests on it."

Now he remembered, but pretended he hadn't. "I'm not with you yet. Tell me more."

"Give me the folder, Josh."

He plunged his hands into his bathrobe pockets. "Your grandmother fired me because she couldn't order me around. You can't, either."

"I'm in a hurry."

"You're flushed and breathing hard, I can see that. And it's not because you want me, unfortunately. By the way, are you sleeping with Thomas Laker?"

"The folder, now."

"Did he send you? I suppose this is a matter of national security and it's my duty to let you have it."

"I'm not going to appeal to your patriotism, Josh. Just your sense of self-preservation. A man is on his way here. He knows about the folder and will stop at nothing to get it."

"Oh, I'm about to receive a visit from an *enemy agent*?" He worked his heavy eyebrows sarcastically.

Ava wanted to fly at him and pound her fists on his chest. She shut her eyes and took a deep breath.

"Yes. An enemy agent. He's killed five people. He won't hesitate to kill you. If you have any sense, you'll get that file off your hands and take a long vacation in Valparaiso."

"What can be so important about seating charts for dinners that took place years ago?"

"Josh, listen. Your life is on the line."

He didn't reply, but after a moment's thought he led her up the stairs to the main floor. They crossed the hall and went into a formal dining room, which Milton's decorator had furnished in period style: crystal chandelier, paneled walls—with one panel open to reveal the chute of an old-fashioned dumbwaiter—French windows overlooking the street, and ornately carved antique furniture. Like the one downstairs, the table was covered with books and papers. As well as a few photos. She recognized her grandmother's face.

"So the rumors are true. You're continuing the book about Tillie on your own."

"Yep. When Laker came to see me, I figured there'd be a market for it. And I was right, wasn't I? She's going to be back in the news soon?"

Ava stepped closer to the table, scanning the clutter for the file she wanted. Milton planted his hand flat on a light-blue folder. She peered through his spread fingers. The label read *seating plans*.

"Which papers do you want?"

"Jesus *Christ,* Josh!"

"You can't expect me to turn over the whole file. There's great stuff in there. Tell me which papers you want, and why, and maybe I'll—"

She grabbed the folder and whipped it out from under his hand. As he overbalanced and toppled onto the table, she spun and ran.

He caught up with her at the top of the staircase. Grasped her arm with one hand while the other reached over her shoulder for the folder. She pressed it tight against her breasts. With him half on top of her, she struggled down a couple of steps, then stumbled to her knees. Losing his grip, Milton tumbled over her.

Her free hand caught the banister, saved her from falling. But Milton went head over heels down the steps and landed flat on his back on the tile floor of the kitchen. She hoped he was stunned and she'd be able to get past him. But as she descended he struggled to his knees, then his feet, and spread his arms to block her way.

There was a clink of breaking glass.

Milton's eyes met hers. She saw the dawning fear in them as he realized she'd been telling the truth. Then he swung around.

From where she was standing halfway down the stairs she couldn't see the door. But she heard the shot. A red plume of blood and brains arced from the back of Milton's head. He dropped in a heap at the foot of the steps.

Ava cried out and began to back up the stairs.

A blue-clad figure came into view below. The Shapeshifter, still in his nurse's scrubs. The glasses and beard disguised his face. His eyes fixed on the folder she was clutching to her chest. The gun was in his right hand. Another instant and he would raise it and aim.

She whirled and ran. Her back muscles tensed in anticipation of a bullet. But there was no shot. Just the sound of his footfalls on the steps as he pursued her.

She ran into the dining room. Slammed the heavy wooden door, yanked the chair from the head of the table and jammed it under the doorknob. A second later, the doorknob turned, rattled, then the whole door shook in its frame as the Shapeshifter threw himself against it. It wouldn't hold for long.

Setting the folder on the sideboard, she picked up another chair with both hands, swung it over her head, and threw it with all her strength at the French window. The glass shattered and the chair sailed through. She bounded over to it—but hesitated at the threshold. It was a twelve-foot drop to the sidewalk. By the time she got back on her feet—assuming the fall hadn't broken her ankles—the Shapeshifter would be through the door. As she tried to run away—hobble away—he'd shoot her in the back.

The door took another heavy blow. She darted frantic glances around the room. There was only one other way out. She ran to the dumbwaiter, peered down the empty chute. Lifting one leg then the other, she scrambled in to perch on the narrow ledge. Holding on with her left hand, she stretched out her right toward the folder on the sideboard.

Her left hand lost its grip and she went down the chute.

As she dropped straight down, both arms above her head, she could hear the door to the dining room splintering. He was in. And the folder was lying on the sideboard.

Fierce pains shot up her legs as she landed. The thin wooden platform of the dumbwaiter at the bottom of the shaft hadn't been built to withstand the weight of a falling woman. Her feet punched through it. She tried to bring her arms down, succeeded only in jamming herself tight in the chute. Her feet were caught in the ruin of the platform. She struggled, found she couldn't move at all.

Up in the dining room the Shapeshifter must be standing at the smashed window by now. Looking out, not seeing her. It wouldn't take him long to figure out where she'd gone.

A wave of hopeless panic rose in her mind. She fought it off. Made herself think.

It was her arms folded tight against her sides that were trapping her. No use trying to lower them. Instead she raised them. Better. She could breathe. Even bend her head so she could look down her legs to the broken planks of the platform. What was under them? Some sort of gears and cables. She tried to wriggle her feet free. Nothing happened except that the pain intensified until she almost fainted. It was dark in the chute. The kitchen hatch doors must be closed.

Too much time had passed.

Ava ceased to struggle. Slowly raised her eyes. She expected to see the head and shoulders of the Shapeshifter, leaning into the chute, pointing his gun at her. But there was only the empty chute. The folder was what he was after. He'd grabbed it and run. He was gone.

She took a long, shuddering breath. Only now did she identify a sound that she'd been hearing for a while: approaching sirens.

Laker must've had an ID like Cary Grant's after all.

37

Laker was in the lead squad car, riding in the front passenger seat beside Officer Rita Martinez. She had luxuriant chestnut hair pulled into a knot at the nape of her neck and wore a lot of blue eye shadow, but she was a kick-ass cop all the same. She'd enjoyed barreling down Route 123 at ninety mph. Noticing that he was hanging onto the grab handle above his door, she cracked that he could relax, she had every intention of making her daughter's Quinceañera tomorrow.

Siren whooping, lights flashing, they were now hurtling down the narrow streets of Old Town Alexandria between rows of parked cars.

Martinez hit the brakes, and the car plunged to a halt in front of Josh Milton's row house, brakes squealing. Laker pitched forward against his safety harness. He released the catch and threw open the door. As he jumped to his feet, the door at the top of the steps opened. He caught a glimpse of the Shapeshifter, still in his blue nurse's scrubs, but the Shapeshifter stepped back and pulled the door closed before Laker could aim his Beretta.

Martinez came around the front of the car, pistol in hand. Sirens were keening as more police cars arrived. As he ran up the steps, Laker noticed the smashed front window, the glass fragments and broken chair lying on the pavement. He'd assumed that Ava had gone straight from the retirement home to Milton's. Now he hoped she had gotten out of the house.

Martinez reached the door first. She fired two bullets into the lock. Laker shouldered the door aside and entered, both arms up, left hand bracing his gun hand. Nobody in the hall or on the staircase. Leading with her weapon, Martinez entered a doorway to her left. He took the one to the right. It was a dining room. He dropped to one knee and looked under the table. Nobody there. He glanced again at the broken French window that he hoped had been Ava's escape route and backed out of the room.

More cops were coming in the front door, weapons drawn. Laker crossed the hall, looked down the stairs. A body was sprawled in a red pool on the floor. "Man down!" he shouted, and descended the stairs. Halfway down he recognized Milton. No way he could have survived that head wound, but Laker checked for a pulse anyway.

Rising, he searched the kitchen, fearing he would find Ava's bloodstained body. But she wasn't here, thank God. Martinez was coming down the steps, followed by another cop. She carefully sidestepped the pool of blood, looked around. The ground floor was one large room. "No back door," she said. "Only windows are on the front side, and the street's full of cops."

"Only one way he could have gone, then," Laker replied. "Up."

The other cop was already climbing the stairs. Martinez followed. Laker was about to go after her when a muffled voice called his name. He swung back to the empty room, baffled.

"Ava?"

"See the dumbwaiter doors?" said the muffled voice. "Open them."

He did. He was looking at her jeans-clad legs. Her feet had broken through the thin wood planks of the dumbwaiter's platform.

She said, "I guess there's a humorous side to this fix, but I can't see it right now."

He was relieved that she sounded like herself. "Have you tried to free your feet?'

"Well, duh. They're stuck. Also they hurt like hell. I'm afraid the planks aren't all that got broken."

"Okay. We'll get you out. Brace your arms against the walls."

"Laker, just leave me. The Shapeshifter has the file."

"Shit."

"Sorry. All my fault. Go after him."

"There are a dozen cops chasing him. By now they'll have the whole block sealed off. He won't get away," Laker said, with more certainty than he felt. "Let's get you free."

It took several minutes. One foot was trapped under a metal strut, the other tangled in a cable. Her ankles were cut, bruised, and swollen. He knew he was hurting her, but she didn't make a sound. As she maneuvered into a sitting position on the ledge of the dumbwaiter's hatch, she said, "I'm happy as a clam, Laker. Go."

He hurried up the stairs, passing several cops on the way. He glimpsed others on the upper floors, looking under beds and in closets. The staircase ended at the low-ceilinged attic floor, where a door stood open on narrow, steep steps. Laker climbed them, scrambling out under the wide blue sky.

A gray-headed cop with sergeant's stripes on his sleeves and a shotgun in his hands nodded to Laker. Excited voices were babbling from the radio clipped to his epaulet. The cop said, "We figure he was trying to get away across the roofs. Now he's hiding somewhere."

There were parapets along the street frontage, but the flat roofs of the row houses joined smoothly side to side. Laker looked out across a plain of black asphalt, broken only by chimneys, ventilators, housings for skylights or stairways. Two lines of cops were moving steadily toward each other from either end of the block, pistols or shotguns at the ready, searching anywhere a man could hide. They were high up. Laker could see the Washington Monument and Capitol dome in the distance.

"He may try to break into a house," Laker said. "How else is he going to get back to the street?"

The sergeant nodded. That possibility had occurred to him. "We haven't found a broken skylight or kicked-in door yet. We'll get him, sir."

A deafening yell burst from his radio. Laker could also hear it through the air, because it was coming from a skinny young cop standing on a roof just two houses away. He was pointing down, into the alley behind the house.

"Say again, Kernan," the Sergeant called.

"It's him," Kernan replied, voice under control now. "Just lying there. Musta fallen."

The Sergeant set off at a run. Laker was right beside him. The cops in the nearer search line had also heard. They were straightening up, turning to look at Kernan, lowering their weapons.

Laker reached the skinny youngster and looked where he was pointing. It was the Shapeshifter all right, in his blue scrubs, lying facedown in the alley. He was motionless. Blood and other fluids stained the cobblestones around his head.

"All *right*!" the Sergeant exulted. "That's him. Right, sir?"

Laker opened his mouth to say yes. Hesitated. Where was the folder? It ought to be lying open on the cobblestones, the papers scattered all around. Maybe it was under the body. He narrowed his eyes, looked harder. Then he saw the knot of chestnut hair at the nape of the neck.

Officer Rita Martinez was not going to her daughter's Quinceañera tomorrow.

38

"The fucker simply put on Martinez's uniform and went back the way he came. The house was full of cops and nobody noticed. I may even have passed him on the stairs," Laker said.

They were back in Mason's man cave. All was the same as in the morning, except that now there was a bottle of bourbon on the poker table. Laker and Mason were drinking it straight, Ava with water. Her right foot was in a heavy black surgical boot, propped on a chair. She had broken a metatarsal bone. The left foot was only cut and bruised. They could hear the phones upstairs ringing constantly. Every few minutes one of Mason's security detail brought down a sheaf of messages. He dropped them on the table without looking at them.

"How'd the Secretary take your report?" Laker asked.

Mason laughed humorlessly. He was still in the suit and tie he'd put on to go see the Secretary of Homeland Security. "How do you think? When I told him there was a loose nuke, and we didn't know if it was functional or not, hadn't a clue where it was. That an able, ruthless enemy agent was after it, and we didn't know who he worked for or even what he looked like. Only that he was now a step ahead of us. Oh, and here's the best part, I can't offer much help because my agency is compromised."

He emptied his glass and refilled it. "I ever have to make a report like that again, I'll blow my fucking brains out first."

"Have we found out anything?" Laker asked.

"Not much. My security team logged a minor incident at 10:38 this morning. A car parked down the street, driver stayed at the wheel. He moved on soon as a cop car appeared."

"Did they get his license number?"

"Yes. Car was rented by Michael Nussbaum of Bozeman, Montana. Turned in at Reagan airport at 4:12 pm. We're checking out that ID. My guess is, it'll prove a phony."

"If it was the Shapeshifter, his source at the Outfit is still feeding him information," Laker said. "Accurate information."

Mason looked at Ava. "Is the Shapeshifter going to have any problem figuring out which of the seating charts in that file has the names of Ryo's agents?"

"My grandmother's statement said she wrote in name, rank, branch of service. And they're all men. The list's going to stick out from the rest of the charts."

Mason said, "It won't take the Shapeshifter long. Then he'll go looking for those men. The ones that are still alive."

"Or their descendants," Ava said.

Mason raised his single eyebrow at her.

"They may have passed on the secret, just as Tillie did to me." Ava sighed. "The poor bastards have my sympathy. Whoever they are."

"Holy shit." Mason picked up his glass, saw that it was empty already. He started to refill it, then put down bottle and glass and pushed them away. "It's impossible that these men or their children or grandchildren have been sitting on a secret like that for seven decades. The Shapeshifter won't get anything out of them. No, Bobby Soxer must've gone to the bottom of the Pacific in 1945. That's the only possible explanation."

"Is that what the Secretary thinks?" Laker asked.

"Yes."

"The Secretary's an optimist."

Footsteps on the stair made Mason turn his head. Laker looked, too. It was Joanie, the receptionist from the Outfit's headquarters on Capitol Hill. She looked more grandmotherly than ever in a green pantsuit that bulged around the middle. A scarf covered her gray hair.

Mason settled her in a chair and introduced her to Ava. He put the bottle of bourbon and a new glass in front of her, but she shook her head.

"I'm sending you into the field," Mason said.

Her mild hazel eyes became enormous. "Why me?"

"Because I'm 110 percent sure you're not a double agent. And there are not enough people I can say that of. Don't complain. The field means Hawaii."

Laker and Ava looked at each other. She figured it out first. "Tillie's illegitimate child?"

"Right." said Mason.

"What do you expect to find?" Laker asked.

"No idea. But it's a loose end. And when I have no real leads, I'll settle for a loose end." Turning to Joanie, he explained to her about the child.

"I don't know," she said. "Those are mighty old records. Assuming there ever was a record. Having a child out of wedlock was so shameful back then. The authorities figured kid and mother were better off if they never knew each other's names."

"If there is anything, you'll find it," Laker said with a smile.

He and Mason rose with Joanie. Even Ava struggled to an upright position. They all shook hands gravely to send her off.

"Let's wrap this up," said Mason, sinking wearily into his chair. "Laker, I can't offer you any intel or support—"

"Just an order," Laker said. "Go after the Shapeshifter."

"And a piece of advice. Watch your back. He may turn around and come after you. Now, Ms. North—"

"It's obvious what I should do. Go to the Pentagon. Or wherever they keep personnel records of Hunter's Point Naval Station, 1945. Maybe I'll be able to get a line on Ryo's agents."

"Pointless," said Mason. "We don't even know for sure Hunter's Point was where the bomb was waylaid."

"Boss," Laker said. "She's a smart cookie."

"No. Ms. North, you are an employee of the NSA. It's my duty to tell you to report to your superior there. They will provide protection while you convalesce."

She gave a firm headshake. "I'm not going to sit this out in some safe house in Maryland."

Mason sank deeper into his chair. He opened his hands. "Okay. I'm not in a position to reject any offer of help. Especially from a smart cookie."

39

Theo Orton noticed the naval officer walking parallel with him, three rows of headstones to his right: a slim, erect figure in dress whites from cap cover to shoes. He was wearing sunglasses, which Orton thought was maybe a bit disrespectful here.

This was Jefferson Barracks National Cemetery, on the Mississippi south of St. Louis. Plain white grave markers stood in long rows along the green hillside, which rose gently to the tall trees. Deer were browsing up there.

Sunglasses or not, the officer suited the dignity of the place a lot better than he did, Orton had to admit. He was an old man with bowed shoulders and potbelly, limping along the row of headstones, wreath in hand. His T-shirt had spots and tears he hadn't noticed when he'd put it on.

By now, after so many years of visits, he no longer had to count the headstones. Habit told him when to stop and turn to face his father's. MELVILLE ORTON, *Captain, USN Missouri* was all it said. Orton grunted as he bent to take the old, faded wreath and lay the fresh one in its place. Straightening, he stepped back. He didn't salute, not being a military man. But he wished he could do something. It was a long drive from his retirement community in North St. Louis County. It seemed to him he ought to say a prayer, or the Pledge of Allegiance, or just remember Dad. But Orton wasn't especially religious or patriotic, and his memories of his father, dead more than twenty years, were fading. So he did what he always did: stood for a moment with his bald head bowed, then headed for home.

A month had never gone by without his visiting the grave, even in the days when he'd had kids who wanted him to play ball, a wife who wanted him to do chores. It was important that somebody should pay tribute to Mel Orton, the truest hero resting in this cemetery, though no one else would ever know.

It was a long walk back along the row of headstones. The naval officer was nowhere in sight. His bad knee was throbbing by the time he reached the parking lot. Opening the door of his old beater, he stepped back, averting his face, as a wave of trapped heat rushed out. Only then did he notice that the left rear tire was flat. Cursing, he went around to open the trunk, swept away a layer of detritus to get to the spare. Just had to look at it to know it was flat, too. Orton had dropped his AAA membership to stretch his pension, dropped his cell phone because nobody was calling him. Leaning on the fender, he muttered a few more choice words.

"Trouble?"

He turned. It was the naval officer, at the wheel of a new gray sedan. He was smiling sympathetically.

Orton kicked his left rear wheel. "And the spare's flat. Could I borrow your phone for a minute, please?"

"Why don't I drive you to a gas station? We'll inflate the spare and I'll bring you back."

That was the cheapest way to handle it, and for Orton, cheap was good. He put the spare in the sedan's trunk, noticing the government plates. It was from some motor pool. The officer was on business.

Orton got in beside him. The interior was deliciously cool. He offered his hand.

"Appreciate this. Theo Orton."

"Bill Vincent."

His grip was strong. He still had his sunglasses on. Top-of-the-line Ray-Bans. He had high cheekbones and a long jaw. In his thirties, Orton guessed. Two gold bars on his collar tabs: lieutenant (s.g.). Above his chest pocket were a row of campaign ribbons and a badge of the earth impaled on a sword. Orton didn't know what specialty it represented.

He said, "You're far from the sea, sailor."

Vincent laughed as he put the car in gear. "Tell me about it. I'd kill for a cool breeze. I'm on an errand to the military records depository here. Thought I'd take the chance to pay my respects to an old friend. Marine. IED, outside Kabul. I guess you were doing the same?"

"Paying my respects, yeah." There was a clunk. Orton wasn't used to the noises new cars made, and it took a moment to realize that this was the doors, locking automatically.

"Your war would have been . . . Vietnam?" Vincent asked.

"Would have been. But I was 4-F. It's my father's

grave I was visiting. He was in the Pacific during World War II. Navy guy, like yourself."

"Coral Sea. Midway. Leyte Gulf. The battles we study at the Academy. Was he in any of them?"

"No. He was stateside. Logistics officer."

"Oh. Well sure, the fighting man can do nothing without rear-echelon support."

Orton didn't like the tone. He looked over, and sure enough, Vincent had a snide grin on his face. Stung, Orton blurted, "My dad was as much a hero as anybody who fought at Midway. More."

"You baby boomers kill me. Took your 4-Fs and your student deferments and let Vietnam be lost. Now you're old and feeling kinda guilty. So you idolize your dads. The Greatest Generation. Fighting the Good War."

"Fuck you, pal. Pull over. I'm getting out."

Vincent didn't pull over. Didn't say anything, either. When he slowed down to turn off the main road into a subdivision, Orton grabbed the handle and threw his weight against the door. But it was locked.

"Stop! Let me out!"

"Sorry, can't do that. I want to hear all about your dad. And the heroic deeds he did at Hunter's Point Naval Station."

The first ripple of unease chilled Orton's anger. "I didn't say he was stationed at Hunter's Point."

"You didn't have to."

"It's no coincidence, you picking me up."

"No."

They were driving through a run-down subdivision. The old ranch houses and split-levels had oil-stained driveways, cracked front walks, overgrown lawns.

Vincent pressed a remote clipped to his visor as he turned into a drive. The door of the garage attached to the house lifted. They drove in.

"What's going on?" demanded Orton. "Whose house is this?"

"Rented for the occasion. There's nobody here. We won't be disturbed." He pressed the remote again, and the door went down behind them, shutting out the light. Taking off his sunglasses, Vincent looked at Orton. His hooded eyes were blue. "I'm from the Office of Naval Intelligence. We've been looking into the career of Captain Mel Orton."

"Why? He's been dead for twenty years."

Vincent didn't answer. He got out of the car. So did Orton. The garage was dim, windowless, empty. No, not empty, he saw when Vincent flicked on the overhead fluorescents. In one corner stood a workbench, with vises of various sizes clamped to the edge, and neat rows of tools above it: saws, drills, screwdrivers, hammers. They were brand new and gleaming.

"You buy these?" Orton asked mockingly. "Planning to fix up the place?"

"No." Vincent leaned against a fender, crossed his immaculately white-clad legs at the ankle. "How much did your father tell you about his wartime service?"

"I don't have to answer your questions, Lieutenant. You're trying to intimidate me, and it's not gonna work."

Vincent ignored this. "Hope I don't shock you, Orton, but your estimate of your dad as a hero is maybe a little inflated. Just a little. He was really the worst traitor who ever wore uniform. Including Benedict Arnold."

The cold blue eyes studied Orton's face. He was

looking for a shocked reaction. Orton hoped he was disappointed. "Skip the theatrics. Just tell me what you know. Or think you know."

"At Pearl Harbor in 1940, your father was recruited as a double agent. For the rest of the war, he served the Soviet Union."

"He *never* served the Soviet Union."

"Interesting statement. Maybe you'd like to explain."

"You're kinda slow, lieutenant. I'm not gonna cooperate with you. I mean—what is this shit? The war's over, the Soviet Union's gone, my father's dead."

"True, we can't give him what he deserved. Meaning court-martial and execution. But we can remove whatever's left of him from Jefferson Barracks National Cemetery."

Orton swallowed hard. "No! You're not gonna desecrate my father's grave!"

"You think a traitor deserves to rest beside men who served their country?"

"He was not a traitor."

"You're going to deny he was recruited into a spy ring run by a deep-cover Soviet agent named Hirochi Ryo?"

Orton flinched at the name. So ONI *did* know. How the hell had they found out, after all this time? "He was recruited. But the ring was never activated. My father never did one fucking thing for Communist Russia."

Vincent uncrossed his ankles, put both hands on the fender and pushed himself to a standing position. He looked disappointed. "You're really determined to waste my time with denials, evasions, indignation? Let's skip all that."

The hooded blue eyes met Orton's. Vincent said, "Bobby Soxer."

Orton had long ago made up his mind that if anyone ever said those two words to him, he would not react. His only chance would be to pretend he'd never heard them before. But now they hit like a blow. He cried out and fell back. Vincent watched him coldly. Orton ran at the door of the garage. Hammered it with his fists and shouted for help.

Vincent let him go on until he had to stop and gasp for breath. Then he said, "Maybe you noticed, this isn't a neighborly neighborhood. The houses on either side are empty. The people across the street are inside with the air-conditioning running. No one can hear you."

Orton swung round to face the slender white-clad figure. "You're not an ONI agent. Or if you ever were, you've gone into business for yourself."

"The main point, as far as you're concerned, is that I'm not bound by any legal constraints."

Orton ran at the man, arms out, reaching for his throat. Vincent ducked and punched. All the wind knocked out of him, Orton collapsed to the concrete floor, gasping. His eyes were closed, but he felt Vincent lifting him up. Easily. As if he weighed nothing. He opened his eyes, to see his forearm being put between the jaws of a vise. Before he could lift it out, Vincent's fingers spun the handle. Blocks of steel trapped Orton's wrist. He looked up at the wall, the gleaming pliers and drills and saws. He screamed and struggled.

Vincent just watched him until the paroxysm of terror passed.

Coughing, Orton said, "You're going to kill me."

"Yes. But I can offer you a painless death. Well, almost painless. In return for the answer to one question. Where is the bomb?"

"I don't know. Russia somewhere. Probably doesn't exist anymore. Please, let me go!"

"No," said Vincent calmly. "Too late for that lie. You already told me, your father never served Communist Russia. Captain Mel Orton and his fellow agents, Captain Bart Lester and Lieutenant Commander Morgan Walker, disobeyed their orders from the Kremlin."

"You know about Lester and Walker."

"Yes. I know enough to tell if you try to lie to me. So give me the truth. What happened at Hunter's Point Naval Base in August 1945?"

"My father was an idealist. So were the others. They were horrified by the bombing of Hiroshima and Nagasaki. Tens of thousands of civilians incinerated, men, women, and children. And here was the third bomb, Bobby Soxer, that they were to send across the sea. The date was already chosen, the target already selected. They didn't know Japan was going to surrender. They wanted to deny the bomb to the Americans—*and* the Russians."

"What did they do with the bomb?"

Orton had been staring at his trapped hand, wriggling desperately, hopelessly. But talking about his father, telling somebody for the first time of Mel Orton's courage and humanity, affected him strangely. He was not as frightened. He was even able to meet Vincent's merciless eyes. "They dumped it. Bobby Soxer is now rusty junk at the bottom of San Francisco Bay."

"You're lying."

Orton continued to hold his gaze. "What do you plan on doing with the bomb, asshole?"

"Defiance is not going to get you anywhere. You've made the wrong choice. A painless death is far preferable to what's going to happen to you now. Fortunately, I will give you plenty of time to change your mind."

He reached across the workbench. Deliberated a moment, and chose a pair of pliers.

Orton closed his eyes again. Retreated deep into himself. His father had been brave enough to prevent Bobby Soxer from being used. Now it was his turn to do the same.

40

St. Louis County Police headquarters, a low, sprawling brick building, was baking in the midday heat. The only parking space Laker could find was at the edge of its vast lot, and he stopped halfway to the building to mop his brow and take off his suit jacket. As he reached the door, it opened. A burly African American man came out. He, too, had his suit jacket folded over his arm. There was a holstered pistol on his belt.

Laker took a guess. "Detective Ackerman?"

"Yeah, but I'm in a hurry. They can take care of you at the desk."

He tried to sidestep, but Laker got in front of him again. "Your errand have anything to do with the Orton homicide?"

"What if it does?"

"I'd like to ride along."

Ackerman had heavy eyelids, both upper and lower, that gave him the look of a lizard. Half-asleep until it struck. "The public information officer will help you. Now please get out of my way, sir."

"I'm not a reporter," Laker said, and showed his creds.

Ackerman forgot he was in a hurry. He took Laker's NSA identification card in his hand and read it from top to bottom. Compared the photo to Laker. Handing it back, he said, "Don't see something like this every day. Okay. Come on."

They walked across the hot asphalt to Ackerman's unmarked car. The interior was stifling. Ackerman turned on the engine and got the air-conditioning going full blast.

"Why is your agency interested in Orton?" he asked as they drove off the lot.

Laker'd expected the question, but hadn't made up his mind how to answer it. The truth was that Ava, working with a pile of moldering old files at the Pentagon, supplemented by an array of websites, had identified Capt. Melville Orton as operations manager at Hunter's Point in August 1945. Earlier, he'd been stationed at Pearl Harbor during the time Hirochi Ryo was recruiting agents. That was enough to make him worth checking out. He was dead and so were his children, except for a son named Theodore, who lived in St. Louis. Arriving at Lambert–St. Louis Airport, Laker had picked up the *Post-Dispatch.* On the front page, he'd found a story about the grisly murder of Theo Orton, and known immediately that the Shapeshifter was still one step ahead of him.

Ackerman was waiting. Laker said, "My boss will call your boss."

"I just *love* working with the feds," muttered Ackerman, blinking his lizard eyes.

"I don't blame you for being pissed off. You had bad

luck, catching this case. The media interest is pretty intense. I read the *Post* story."

"They didn't get all the details of the victim's injuries. But somebody is bound to leak crime scene photos. Then we'll have a full-blown media frenzy. Psycho killer on the loose. Coming soon, discovery of another mutilated victim."

Laker nodded sympathetically. "And the politicians will be on your back, demanding results. Any leads so far?"

Ackerman slowed and turned off the highway into a subdivision. The streets were in poor repair. The modest houses had seen better days. "Orton was a retired machinist. Lived a quiet life. Finances in order. No criminal record. No indications of drug use. He didn't deserve to die like that. I don't know who would. "

"And the crime scene?"

Ackerman made a left turn, stopped, and pointed out Laker's window. "That's it."

It was a ranch house, probably built in the '50s, with peeling paint, a leaning mailbox, and a brown lawn. Yellow tape barred the garage door. Ackerman said, "The renter paid in cash. Added some extra so he wouldn't have to show ID. Around here that would ordinarily mean he wanted to use the place as a meth lab. The landlord has allowed that sort of thing in the past. We leaned on him, and he gave us a full description of the renter. Caucasian, 35 to 40, long dirty-blond hair, five-nine, 220, tattoos on both forearms."

Ackerman took his foot off the brake pedal and the car eased forward. "We're wondering if the renter and the killer are the same guy. Don't suppose you could unofficially give me a hint? While we're waiting for your boss to call my boss?"

"Probably the same guy. He seems to work alone. But I wouldn't set too much store by that description."

Ackerman gave him a sharp look. "You have a better one?"

"No."

Through the heavy eyelids, Ackerman squinted at him. "You shittin' me, Laker?"

"I'm not withholding any information on your perp, Ackerman. We just don't have any."

Ackerman sighed. "You want to hear about the vic's injuries?"

Laker didn't. But he said, "Go ahead."

"Twelve teeth and all fingernails extracted. Six fingers cut off. Shoulders dislocated. Third-degree burns on face and genitals. All done pre-mortem."

"Jesus. When the media get hold of all that—"

Ackerman nodded. "Psycho killer. The public will be plenty scared. Imagine doing all that to a fellow human being, for no reason."

The public would be even more scared if they knew there *was* a reason, Laker thought.

They turned another corner. A patrol unit was parked next to a roll-out trash cart on the curb. The cop was sitting behind the wheel, engine on and air-conditioning running.

He got out and put on his cap as Ackerman pulled up beside him. He was a young white man with an unlined brow and pockmarks of acne on his cheeks.

"What've you got, Bledsoe?" Ackerman said, getting out of the car.

"I got a major break in the case, sir."

"Don't start writing your commendation yet. We're two full blocks from the crime scene. Just give me the story."

Bledsoe pointed to the house across the street. "The guy who lives there flagged me down. Said his neighbor"—Bledsoe pointed at the house they were standing in front of—"is a lazy son of a bitch who forgets to roll his cart back after the garbage truck goes by. I said it was too soon to cite him, but the guy said that wasn't why he flagged me down. He said his kid got curious and lifted the lid. And he's been screaming ever since."

"Let's have a look." Ackerman had been pulling on latex gloves as he listened. He stepped up to the rollout cart. Flies were swarming around the lid. There was a smell that wasn't just the usual sickly sweet smell of garbage rotting in the sun. It got powerful enough that Laker started breathing through his mouth when Ackerman lifted the lid. He reached in and pulled out a white garment, soaked with red stains. Blood.

Laker moved closer. It was a short-sleeved shirt, with bars on the collar and ribbons and a badge above the left pocket. Ackerman said, "This is a navy uniform, isn't it?"

"Yes," Laker said. "Tropical White Long, they call it. Collar bars of a lieutenant s.g. "

Ackerman was examining the badge, of a globe with a sword through it. "What's this thing?"

"It's the shield of the Office of Naval Intelligence."

Raising his heavy eyelids, Ackerman looked at Laker. "Well now," he said. "I'm getting a glimmer of why you feds are interested in this case. We're going to have to see if these bloodstains match the ones at the crime scene.

My guess is they will, meaning the perp dumped his shirt here as he left the area. And when your boss calls my boss, we're going to have a lot of questions for him."

"The St. Louis cops are going to give you a hard time," Laker said.

"Don't worry about it," Mason replied. "I've had a lot of experience stonewalling local cops."

Laker was back at Lambert–St. Louis Airport, in a small windowless office in the international arrivals area. The TSA had agreed to let him use their secure line.

"The call I'm really not looking forward to," Mason went on, "is the one I'm going to have to make to Admiral Grantham at ONI. There was always the possibility the Shapeshifter was going to turn out to be a rogue agent from one of our brother spy shops. It was the possibility I liked the least."

"I have my doubts."

"You mean, if the Shapeshifter was ONI, he wouldn't have been so careless with that shirt?"

"So far he hasn't been sloppy."

"I hope you're right. But it has to be checked out. And Grantham will cooperate, once he's through yelling at me."

"How's Ava?"

"She took Orton's death hard. Said if only she'd worked faster, you would have gotten to him before the Shapeshifter. I told her, look on the bright side. His death confirms you had the right guy."

"Did that console her?"

Mason grunted. "Kid's going to have to grow a thicker skin, she wants to survive at the NSA. But she's back at work on the organizational charts and duty rosters. Orton couldn't have been working alone. She's trying to figure out who else at Hunter's Point was in Ryo's network."

"So maybe this time I can get to him before the Shapeshifter? I don't know. She may be wasting her time."

"Maybe Orton gave the Shapeshifter all the information he needed? That what you mean?"

Laker hesitated. He thought about the bloodstained shirt, Ackerman's description of what had been done to the corpse. "Orton resisted. For a long time. He must've been a helluva brave man. But we have to assume that everything he knew, the Shapeshifter got out of him."

"Let's hope it wasn't enough. Let's hope he has to move on to the next name on Tillie's list. Give us another shot at him."

"That would be good for us. Not so hot for the next guy on the list."

41

The swarthy man was watching soccer from Germany on the big-screen TV over the bar, but he went along smilingly when Dick Lester said he wanted to switch to the Marlins game. So they got to talking, sitting side by side on their barstools. Lester liked to make friends with strangers in bars. It was better than drinking alone, sure. But for practical reasons, too. At the end of the evening, he'd need somebody to drive him home. His license had been pulled after his third DUI arrest.

For a soccer fan, this guy seemed all right. He said his name was Ferdi Serym and he was from Turkey. Lester had never met a Turk before, far as he knew. The guy's black hair looked like he'd just come in from the rain, shiny and lank. He had dark brown eyes, and a long, swooping nose that made Lester think of the beak of a bird of prey. His skin was olive, with an uneven beard, heavy on the upper lip, thin and scraggly on the cheeks. He smiled a lot; his crooked teeth didn't make him self-conscious. He was wearing a T-shirt, shorts, and sandals, which was what everybody except a few lawyers was wearing in Sarasota on an even-hotter-than-usual August day.

It was nice and cool in the bar, one of Lester's favorites. There was a big window looking out on rows of palm trees and parked cars, but he liked to go to the back, where it was dark. Best thing about the bar was that his wife Ashley didn't know about it yet. When he was in a bar that was on Ashley's list, he could never relax. She sometimes sent the chauffeur in the Mercedes to search the bars, find him, and bring him home. Occasionally he wished he'd married the kind of woman who could only call the bartender and plead. Of course, Ashley's money did smooth his path through life. He had to admit that.

Ferdi didn't seem to know much about baseball, but he listened patiently to Lester. When it was his turn, he said he was at FSU studying engineering. Irrigation systems, to be exact. He wanted to help the farmers in eastern Turkey, where it was dry. Lester couldn't follow that part very well. He was relieved when Ferdi got up to go to the john.

Lester waved to the bartender and pointed to his empty glass. When the bartender came over with a refill, he looked like he had something to say. He had a high, rumpled brow and heavy, dark-framed glasses and looked like a high-school principal. Lester could never remember his name.

"Mr. Lester, I think you ought to be careful with this guy."

"Who, Ferdi? He's okay."

"Never seen him in here before. And he's an Arab." The bartender put an elbow on the bar and leaned closer.

"Before you got here, he was watching the soccer game and got babbling to another rag-head. I understood one word—*shah*."

"Shah?" Lester didn't recognize the word. "You mean, *sheikh*?"

"Whatever. You know, what the Arab terrorists call their leaders."

"He's a Turk, not an Arab."

"Whatever. He looks like an Islamic extremist to me."

Lester squinted at the bartender, trying to figure out if he was serious. "I think he's an Islamic moderate. He drinks. You must have noticed."

"I've noticed you're on your fourth and he's still on his first. Watch it."

Lester waved the guy away and started on the fourth drink. When Ferdi came back, he drained his glass and ordered another. Lester was reassured; the guy was okay. By the time Lester was on his fifth drink, he was ready to take up his favorite subject.

"Ferdi, you ever heard of Brigadier General Bartholomew B. Lester?"

"Someone in your family?" Ferdi asked in his strangely accented, rather whiny voice.

"Just answer the question."

"No, I'm sorry."

Lester slapped the bar triumphantly. Harder than he'd intended to. His palm stung.

"When I was growing up—and going bad, the way dad saw it—he used to tell me that the name of Bart Lester is known and respected everywhere. And I've spent my life proving him wrong. Seeking out places where nobody gives a rat's ass about Bart Lester."

"Well done," said Ferdi, lifting his glass.

He put it down without drinking from it. Lester remembered what the bartender had said about Ferdi pacing himself. Then he forgot it.

"What did General Bart do to become so eminent?" Ferdi asked.

"Fought in Korea. He'd been in The Big One, too, but—"

"The Big One?"

"World War II. They kept him mostly stateside. He hated that. When another war came along he was delighted. He fought like hell in Korea. Won every medal there was. Served in Vietnam, too. He was a general by that time and could have avoided it, but Bart Lester always answered the call of duty. He was all army, all the time."

"I sense that you do not admire him."

"He was crap as a father. And husband. And the funny thing was, no sooner would he screw up one family than he'd start another. Went through four wives, each with a set of kids. And he liked to start fresh, you know? Act like the previous sets of kids didn't even exist. And he always had an excuse for not calling you back or answering your email. The U.S. Army needed him."

Lester finished his drink. "You know that saying, patriotism is the last refuge of the scoundrel? Well, it was the first refuge of my father."

He looked at Ferdi. People generally laughed at this line, but the Turk didn't. He looked kind of sad. After that, they didn't talk much more. Went back to watching the ballgame. Lester ordered another drink. He was in the angry phase now. He wanted to drink his way past it, into the who-gives-a-shit phase. No use being angry at General Bart Lester, who'd been resting in Arlington for twenty-two years.

So Dick Lester sipped, and gazed at the energetic figures on the big screen. Gently, slowly, like a fade-out in an old movie, darkness and unconsciousness closed in.

He awoke just as slowly and gently. He was conscious first of a gentle rocking. Then the smell of salt water, the feel of a breeze against his cheek. He opened his eyes on the blackness of sea and sky, divided by the lights of Sarasota on the horizon. Looking around, he found that he was sitting in the backward-facing chair at the stern of his own cabin cruiser. The fighting chair, as it was called by pseudo-Hemingway assholes who imagined engaging with sailfish. To Lester it was the drinking chair. He'd spent many happy afternoons here with a few buddies and coolers of beer.

It was all very nice, until he started to wonder how he'd gotten here. That was when he became conscious of the pressure across his chest, looked down to see thick straps across his chest and waist. He could move only his limbs. He tried rocking the chair, but it was bolted to the deck.

He flinched as a dark shape passed in front of him. It was Ferdi. He sat on the transom, facing Lester.

"How did I get here?" Lester asked hoarsely. His throat was dry and his head felt awful, but he was used to that.

"You gave me the keys to the marina gate and your boat, after I helped you out of the bar."

"What are we doing here?"

"I don't think your father was so bad," Ferdi said, in his strangely accented voice, as if they were merely continuing their conversation from the bar. "He was a dutiful and respected soldier. His family was out of sight, out of mind. His fault was the typical American one. Taking it for granted you are right, turning your eyes away from the evil you do."

Ferdi leaned closer. "Consider the way your countrymen reacted in 1979, when we overthrew the Shah and took your diplomats hostage. How could we do such a vile deed, you protested. You conveniently forgot that you had deposed our ruler and put the Shah in his place, and supported him while he oppressed us so cruelly."

"The *Shah*," said Lester. "You're Iranian."

"Your self-righteous, cruel treatment of my country has continued," Ferdi went on. "You made us suffer for years with your trade sanctions, finally forcing the weak factions in our government to sign a treaty blocking our nuclear program. There are other factions in our government that think you owe us a nuclear bomb."

He straightened up, gazed into Lester's eyes. He said, "Bobby Soxer."

"Bobby who?"

For a fleeting moment, Lester experienced an unusual emotion. He felt good about himself. Years ago he'd made up his mind that if anyone ever said those words to him, he would play dumb. It'd be his only chance. And he'd pulled it off. No hesitation, no betraying the surprise and fear he felt.

Had it worked? He stared at the shadowy face of the Iranian against the bobbing horizon line of lights, looking for signs of confusion or doubt. He saw neither.

"Captain Bart Lester, U. S. Army," Ferdi said. "Captain Mel Orton, U.S. Navy. And Lieutenant Commander Morgan Walker, U.S. Navy. The men who pulled off the biggest theft in history. No one ever knew, until now."

"How—" Lester began, but could go no further. Fear closed up his throat.

"How did I find out? A long story, and I don't have time for it. I'm going to ask you some questions. I warn you, I know enough that I'll be able to tell if you're lying."

A plane passed over. Lester heard its engines, looked up at the tiny lights moving against the field of stars. Yearned to be on it. To be anywhere but here.

"Lester, Orton, Walker," the Iranian went on. "All for one, and one for all. After they made their brave decision to deny the bomb to their Soviet spymasters, what did they do then?"

Lester swallowed. He said, "They put it on a cart, ran it down to the end of the pier, dumped it in the water."

The Iranian shook his head "I told you it was pointless to lie. They had no need to do anything so crude, so risky. They were logistics officers, with the vast transportation resources of the U.S. military at their command. For them, the simplest, safest way to steal the bomb was to ship it somewhere else. Change the labels on the crate, shift it to a new location in the warehouse, write up the orders to send it away."

The Iranian got up. Lester shrank in the chair as he approached, fearing a blow. But the Iranian bent over him and made a few quick movements, binding his left wrist tight to the arm of the chair with a bungee cord.

"What—what are you gonna do to me?" Lester choked out.

The Iranian returned to his seat on the transom. "Nothing. If you become more cooperative. Where did Bobby Soxer go?"

"I don't know. You gotta believe me. I have no idea."

"Good. The truth. Your father and his comrades were honorable men who had made a principled decision. They lavished on each other all the admiration they would never get from the world. All for one, and one for all. They hoped their sons would be—how you say?—chips off the old block. Just in case they weren't, and we know that you are not, they tried to *make* them that way."

"How do you know all this?" Lester asked. "Who told you? It had to be Orton or Walker."

"It was Orton. Mr. Walker and I have not yet had the pleasure. But Orton was not at his best by the time we got to this part. So you tell me. Describe the arrangement."

"There is a code to the bomb's location. Each of us has one piece of it. That way, we would all have to agree. None of us could find the bomb on his own."

"And you could not agree?"

"Hell, no! Orton wanted the bomb to stay hidden. To protect his father's precious reputation. I wanted the opposite. Deliver the goddam thing to the *New York Times*, expose my asshole dad who spent his life posing as Mr. Spit-and-Polish. And Walker? He was only interested in money. He wanted to sell the bomb to the highest bidder."

"So Bobby Soxer remains in whatever hiding place your fathers contrived for it. Good. Now all I need is your piece of the code."

"Won't do you any good. Orton didn't give you his. I know that stiff-backed son of a bitch. He—"

"You want to know how I persuaded him? A demonstration can be arranged."

The mild voice terrified Lester. He was close to blubbering. But he swallowed hard and tried to compose himself. He had one last chance to get out of this alive. "Look—I'll give you my piece of the code. Just take me back to shore and I'll tell you."

The Iranian got up. He disappeared from Lester's view. Suddenly he reappeared on his left side. He had a pair of long-handled loppers for limbing trees. The short, sharp blades straddled Lester's little finger.

"No!" he cried out.

"The code."

Lester gazed at his immobilized hand. The finger between the gleaming edges of the blades. He said, "J29"

"That's all?"

"J29. That's all. Really. *Please*."

The blades closed. The finger fell to the deck as blood spurted. Lester could not believe it until the pain hit. He screamed.

"Tell me the code."

The blades were now straddling his ring finger. Lester cried out, "J29. That's it. I swear I didn't lie."

The clippers withdrew. "I thought you didn't. But I had to make sure. Sorry."

Lester sat whimpering in his chair. Blood was pouring from the stump of his finger. He closed his eyes.

"Here, this will help," the Iranian said. He pressed something smooth and cylindrical into Lester's free hand. A bottle. Lester brought it to his lips, felt the burn of the vodka going down his throat. The pain dimmed a little.

When he opened his eyes, the Iranian was gone. He was belowdecks. Lester heard metallic bangs. He was hammering on something. In a moment he returned.

"You opened the sea-cocks," Lester said.

"Yes. Based on the volume of water pouring in, I estimate the decks will be awash in half an hour."

"Untie me. Please!"

The Iranian laughed, for the first time. A low, delighted chuckle. "You idiot. I didn't tie you up. The chair has a harness, for when you're fighting a big fish. I suppose you've never used it. All you have to do is unbuckle it."

Lester scrabbled at the straps until he found the buckle and released it. Now it was easy to unhook the bungee cord. His whole arm was throbbing with pain. He tried to stand, couldn't keep his balance, sank into the chair.

"That's right, just stay there," the Iranian said. "It would be a long swim back to shore. A mile, easily. And there's a strong riptide you'd have to fight. Just stay there and finish the bottle. Drowning is an easy death if you don't fight it. Just open your mouth and swallow. You've had plenty of practice at that."

The Iranian had been stripping as he spoke, down to his shorts. He had a lean, muscular body. When he was finished talking, he turned and dove over the side. Lester could just make him out in the moonlight, arms and feet lashing the water as he headed for shore.

The boat was growing more stable as its hull filled with water. Lester looked at the distant band of lights. Too far off. Nothing there worth reaching. He took another drink.

42

"We're too late, aren't we?" Ava said.

She was sitting beside Laker as he drove along the causeway from the airport. Seagulls cavorted overhead, and blue water on either side of the road sparkled in the morning sun. He'd put on a short-sleeved shirt for the trip to Sarasota, and the hairs of his forearms were bristling in the cold wind from the car's air conditioner.

"I wouldn't say that," he replied. "Lester's body has not been found. In fact, the cops say they wouldn't even have declared him a missing person yet, if it wasn't for the fact that he was last seen drunk and in the company of a suspicious character—suspicious according to the bartender's report. There may be nothing to this."

"Lester's boat is missing from its dock at the marina, remember."

"Any minute he could return, with a sunburn and a hangover."

"No," said Ava. "It's too much of a coincidence.

Bart Lester worked directly under Mel Orton at Hunter's Point. Now his son disappears, just a couple of days after Theo Orton was murdered."

"The cops said it all depends on the bartender's report. They said see what you make of him."

Ava slumped in her seat, refusing to be comforted. "I should have been quicker. I spotted General Lester as somebody we should check out right away. Then I got bogged down. He's long dead, and he left twelve children by three marriages, and they were all hard to locate and contact. If Dick Lester's been murdered, it's my fault."

"If he's been murdered, it's the Shapeshifter's fault, Ava."

The bar where the missing man had last been seen was on a quiet, palm tree-lined street a couple of blocks from the beach. Its large windows had heavy green drapes on thick brass rails. The inside was dim even in mid-morning. No patrons had arrived yet. A game show was playing on the big TV over the bar. The bartender was cutting lemons into wedges. He seemed to take the job very seriously. Or maybe it was his lined forehead and old-fashioned spectacles that gave him a somber air.

"Mr. Grasso?" Laker said. "Detective Matuchin sent us over."

"Yes. He told me to expect you." Grasso seemed pleased that they'd come. He reached over the highly polished bar to take Laker's NSA identification. He studied it for a while before handing it back. "Agent Laker," he said.

"Mr. Laker will be fine."

"Can I see hers, too?"

Ava stepped up to the bar. Clumped up, really, because she still had the surgical boot on her right foot, broken in the fall down the dumbwaiter shaft. She handed over her ID. Again, Grasso doted over it, like a boy with a vintage Stan Musial baseball card. The guy seemed to be quite a cop fan. Even a fed fan.

"You kicked up quite a fuss, Mr. Grasso," Laker said.

Grasso beamed. "Just doing my duty as a citizen, Agent Laker. Like the posters say: When you see something, say something. And I didn't wait till it was too late. I warned Dick Lester about that guy right away."

"Start from the beginning. Who came in first?"

"The Turk. Or that's what he told Dick he was. To me he looked like an Arab. He didn't say much to me. Ordered a beer, asked if he could watch football. I said he'd have to wait for Labor Day. Guy didn't get the joke, so I knew right then he hadn't been in America long. I let him switch to a soccer game. After a while another camel jockey came in. They didn't seem to know each other, but they got to babbling about the soccer game. I caught one word."

"What language were they speaking?" Ava asked.

"Arabic for sure, Agent North."

"It couldn't have been Farsi?"

Grasso looked at her blankly

Ava said, "There seems to be some confusion in your report about that one word you recognized."

"I thought he said 'Shah,' Agent North. But Dick said it must've been 'Sheikh.' That's what the terrorists call their leaders, right?"

"But Dick didn't share your suspicions."

"Right, Agent Laker. Dick wasn't picky about his

drinking companions. He's a very affable guy. From his second drink to his eighth, anyway. After that he gets ornery. Anyway, when he came in, the so-called Turk was alone. I thought right then, he's been waiting for Dick. So I kept an eye on them."

"What did they talk about?" Laker asked.

"Baseball, at first. Then Dick started running down his father, as usual. He thinks that instead of serving his country, his father should have been home, *parenting* him, as they say these days. Well, you don't have to be Dr. Phil to see what the real problem was. Dick knew he didn't amount to much in life, compared to General Bart Lester."

"When did you decide to call the police?"

"The minute they left, Agent Laker. Dick was out on his feet. Barely able to put one foot in front of the other. He was leaning on the Arab as they went out the door. I thought, I don't like the look of this. And picked up the phone. You think I was overreacting?"

"No," Laker said. "You did the right thing."

Grasso's somber face became even more grave. "Then you think Dick's in trouble, Agent Laker?"

"Frankly, Mr. Grasso, I think all Dick's troubles are over."

Back in the car, Ava was silent while Laker got the engine and air conditioner going and pulled out into the street. Then she said, "The Shah. Which indicates that the so-called Ferdi Serym was not a Turk. Not an Arab, either. He was an Iranian."

"That's what it indicates, all right."

"Laker, suppose the Shapeshifter really is an Iranian agent?"

"Mason is still checking out the possibility that he's an ONI agent gone rogue."

"I never did buy that theory. But an Iranian makes sense. Nobody knows what's really going on in Teheran. The moderates signed a treaty that slows their nuclear development program. But the hardliners would love to get hold of a bomb. And use it against Israel."

"The Shapeshifter isn't going to suddenly get sloppy at this point. If he really was an Iranian agent, he never would've mentioned the Shah."

"He's just trying to throw us off, you mean."

"He has to figure that we're on his trail. That we're smart enough to make the connections between the murders of Orton and Lester and the fact that their fathers were stationed at Hunter's Point."

"For all the good it does us. We keep showing up too late. If only we could get ahead of the bastard."

"Who's next on your list, Ava?"

"For all we know, the Shapeshifter has all the information he needs to find the bomb. He doesn't need to go looking for any more descendants of Hunter's Point officers."

"If that's true, we've hit a dead end. So let's assume it's not."

"Lucky Laker." She was looking over at him. "You really believe your luck will hold, don't you?

"When I have no other choice."

They had reached the freeway entrance. Laker took the turn and accelerated up the ramp.

"We're heading back to the airport?" Ava asked.

"Yes."

"Then where?"

"You tell me. Who's next on your list?"

"Laker, I have nothing worthy of being called a list. Dozens of Hunter's Point officers have children still living. A couple of them are still alive themselves. There's no logical way to determine who could have been an accomplice of—"

"Once you had Orton, you figured out Lester. Now you have the two of them. Who's next?"

"All I have is a best guess. Based on the lines and boxes on the Hunter's Point organizational chart. And the fact that before the war this man was assigned to a cruiser based at Pearl Harbor, where he could have been recruited by Hirochi Ryo. Maybe."

"The name?"

"Lieutenant Commander Morgan Walker. He has one child still living, Harry Walker."

"Living where?"

"Cleveland."

"Then that's where we're going." Laker glanced at his watch. "If your guess is right, we're only twelve to fifteen hours behind the Shapeshifter. Let's hope that's good enough for us."

"Let's hope it's good enough for Harry Walker," Ava said.

43

At House Supply, a big-box store in a mega-mall near I-480 in the Cleveland suburbs, Harry Walker was working the evening shift, doing greeter duty. He was a wiry old guy, more hair on his forearms than his head, eyebrows like inverted Vs and a goatee he'd dyed to its original black. It was a face like a child's drawing of the Devil, and smiling didn't make Walker look any more benevolent. He probably wasn't cut out to be a greeter.

The floor manager Mr. Berkholder—Walker *loved* having to call a man thirty years his junior Mister—had told him he'd have to make the greeter concept, which was new to House Supply, work. It was up to him and his fellow geezers to keep the do-it-yourselfers from being intimidated as they entered the vast, impersonal store. Make it seem as friendly as the little hardware stores House Supply had driven out of business. The greeters would also serve as good PR for the caring corporation that gave jobs to retirees who couldn't make ends meet on their pensions.

That covered Walker. He'd made a career of being downsized just before he vested. Now he was scraping along on Social Security only. The pittance he earned here made a big difference in his life. Enabled him to put gas in the car, take his grandson to an occasional Browns game. He had to make it work, as *Mr.* Berkholder said.

So he stood in front of the doors saying, "Welcome to House Supply!" Most shoppers didn't get the concept. They looked right through him and walked on by. Others ducked their heads and muttered they didn't need any help. The ones who did want help were a real pain. They'd ask him where some exotic tool was and he'd have no idea. One old guy silently placed a strange, oily mechanism in his hands and gave him an imploring look, expecting him to fix it on the spot.

Eventually Walker'd had enough. He moved over to the side and leaned on a shopping cart. When the doors opened he called out "Welcome to House Supply!" Nobody figured he was talking to them.

When he looked back on his life, as he had too much leisure to do, he always concluded things had started to go wrong when he dropped out of Ohio State. His dad said that was all right, Ohio State had too many defense contracts, just as well not be involved with them when they were doing evil.

Morgan Walker was against all forms of violence, even bawling out his son for partying and skipping class. He'd been a career Navy man, but World War II made him do a one-eighty. He spent the rest of his life working to ban the bomb. Harry'd grown up in a chaotic house, full of envelopes to stuff and lists of congressmen to be called. There were always strangers sleeping on the couch, in town for a protest march. Morgan regularly spent nights in jail, having been arrested for civil disobedience.

Long before he was old enough to grasp the complexities of nuclear disarmament, Harry had known instinctively that his dad just didn't understand what life was about. Namely, money. Let Jane Fonda and Vanessa Redgrave do the demonstrating. His dad ought to be supporting the family. But between the absences and the arrests, Morgan Walker had a hard time holding on to a job. Any job.

Life had played the same practical joke on Harry that it'd played on other baby boomers. He spent his youth pointing out his father's mistakes. And his adulthood repeating them. Too many mornings he turned off the alarm and got in late. Too many times he argued with co-workers. Harry couldn't hold a job, either. Only difference was, he didn't have a Cause.

He put his hands in two of the many pockets of his carpenter's apron in House Supply orange. Gazed idly out the glass doors into the parking lot. The sun was low in the western sky, but the lot was still full. He couldn't see any empty spaces, except the handicapped ones just across from the door.

A sleek red car with rear fenders like a supermodel's hips pivoted nimbly and slid into one of those spaces, right under the "Handicapped only, $50 fine" sign. It was a Ferrari, the new 458 Italia model. A young guy hoisted himself out of the driver's seat and headed for House Supply. No sign of a disability. Blond hair, expensively cut, sunglasses, a tan linen suit, white shirt, no tie. Walker was thinking of calling the cops. See if a $50 parking ticket would make any impression on this beauty. He reached for his cell phone. Then it came to him.

This might be the guy he was waiting for.

His hand came out of his pocket and he moved back to his position in front of the doors. They slid open and Mr. Ferrari walked in.

"Welcome to House Supply," Walker said.

The guy hadn't taken off his sunglasses. He approached Walker with a smile. Perfectly even teeth, white against his suntan. He read Walker's name tag.

"Harry Walker. Just the man I want to see."

"Yeah? Who are you?"

"Brent Armitage."

He put out his hand. Walker looked down at it. "I just greet verbally. Hugs and handshakes are against the rules."

"Sorry." The hand dropped. "I'd like to talk to you about a matter of mutual interest. Let me take you to dinner."

"My break's not for another hour. And it's only twenty minutes."

Armitage was still smiling. "I understand the constraints. Why don't we take a stroll, as if you're escorting me to the section where I can find the item I've asked for?" He had a stilted way of talking and a faint accent, German or something. "Would that be allowed?"

"Sure."

He turned and they set off down one of the wide, busy aisles, lined with merchandise up to far above the level of their heads. House Supply looked more like a warehouse than a store.

"So?" Walker said. "State your business."

"It's highly confidential. Can we go somewhere a bit more secluded?" Armitage asked.

"Secluded? Sure. I know just the place."

Laker had a thing for cars. He didn't talk about them much, which Ava appreciated, but she knew he was restoring a '64 Mustang. And she'd seen his eyes light up when the guy at the Hertz counter at Cleveland-Hopkins Airport said he had a Camaro convertible available. Now they were barreling down I-480, Ava slumping in her seat and holding the brim of her hat down with both hands. He'd been driving fast since they'd left Harry Walker's apartment building, where his neighbor informed them of where he worked.

Shouting above the wind-roar, she said, "You seem to think Walker working as a greeter at House Supply makes him more likely to be our man."

"At least we know he was alive and well at 2 pm, when he left for work."

Ava glanced at Laker's golfing jacket. It was a warm evening, no reason for him to be wearing it. Unless it was to cover the Beretta M9 in its shoulder holster. She decided not to ask.

The lumber department was located in a far corner of the enormous store. Noisy when the power-saw was cutting boards to measure, it was quiet now. They walked down empty aisles between stacks of cordwood, shelved sheets of plywood tall as a man. There was the dry, pleasant smell of sawdust.

"Secluded enough for you?" Walker asked, as he gestured for Armitage to go past him into a side aisle.

"Yes."

Walker didn't follow. He waited until Armitage was a few steps away. His hand came out of the apron. There was a gun in it, a .22 target pistol. Armitage turned and saw it. He went as still as a deer, when you come upon it in the woods, coiling all its muscles for a leap. Walker raised the pistol until it was pointed at Armitage's head. He saw the man relax. Arms hanging at his sides, both feet flat on the floor. It wasn't the first time he'd had a gun pointed at him, Walker instinctively knew, and he didn't think he was out of options.

"You can put that away," he said calmly. "I'm only a businessman with a proposition for you."

"Oh, I know who you are. What you did, anyway. I watch the news. I know about Orton and Lester."

He expected a reaction, but the tanned, handsome face remained expressionless.

"I'm afraid I don't," Armitage said. "Perhaps you could tell me about them?"

"No. Tell me about yourself. Who the hell are you?"

"Armitage is my real name. I'm from Geneva."

"New York?"

"Switzerland."

"And what do you do, Armitage?"

"As I said, I'm a businessman. I buy and sell."

"What kind of merchandise."

"I'm the man you want to go to, before you go to war."

"Arms dealer," said Walker. He was still pointing the gun at him, the blade sight lined up on his nose.

"Yes. And between us, we can put on the international market the most valuable property ever to be offered."

"For sale to the highest bidder?"

"I believe those are the terms you've had in mind? For quite a long time."

"So you got that out of Orton or Lester?"

"I know everything about . . ." He hesitated, then the smile reappeared. "About Bobby Soxer. Except for one bit of numeric code, which you can provide me with."

"You're moving too fast, pal. I'm still thinking about ordering you to assume the position while I call the cops and tell them I have a murderer to turn over to them."

"You must enjoy working at House Supply."

Walker didn't have a reply to that. He found that the blade sight was wavering. He put up his left hand to brace his gun hand.

"I wish you'd put that away," said Armitage. "We're going to be partners. Let's go have that dinner and talk it all over. We don't want to miss our reservation, which was hard to get. You know Lola Bistro?"

"Heard of it." Never dreamed of being able to afford it, he thought. Armitage raised his arm and checked his watch, a big Rolex. The glint off the gold distracted Walker. Too late he said, "Keep your hands at your sides."

Instead Armitage folded his arms. "Harry, I don't think you're going to shoot me."

The barrel was wavering. Walker took aim again. Said, "Dick Lester walked out of a bar with you and hasn't been seen again. I'm pretty sure he won't be."

"I'm well aware that I'm not dealing with Dick

Lester now. Come on, Harry, forget Lester and Orton. They were losers. Obsessed with their fathers. Stuck in the past. You're the one who's always known the right thing to do with Bobby Soxer. And I'm the one to help you. Let's get going."

Walker lowered the pistol. He said, "You first."

Armitage smiled and walked by him. They headed toward the entrance. Over his shoulder Armitage said, "Remember to put the gun away, Harry. We don't want to alarm the customers. Only don't put it back in that ridiculous orange apron. You're about to take that off. For good."

Walker flicked the pistol on safe and slipped it into his trouser pocket.

The automatic doors slid open and Ava, hobbling in her surgical boot, followed Laker into the bright, deliciously cool interior of the store.

"Welcome to House Supply," said a man who could not be Walker. In fact, he didn't look like the usual senior-citizen greeter at all. He was a young man with a short haircut and tiny round glasses. He had a necktie, a shirt pocket lined with pens, and a cell phone holstered to his belt. His name badge said, "Berkholder."

"We're looking for Harry Walker," Laker said.

The smooth young face sprouted clefts and wrinkles of annoyance. "You just missed the old bastard. And he won't be coming back."

"What happened?" Laker asked.

The wrinkles shifted, as anxiety replaced annoyance. "Sorry, sir. I'm not supposed to use that kind of language in front of a customer. It's just that I'm kind of pissed off—sorry, didn't mean to say that, either."

"It's okay, we won't complain to management. Just tell us what happened."

"I came down here and Walker wasn't at his post. So I went looking for him. Met him coming up the aisle. He took off his apron and gave it to me—no, threw it at me. Said something I won't repeat. Then he and the other guy walked out the door and got in a red Ferrari."

"Other guy?"

"Blond guy, in sunglasses and a suit. Don't know who he was."

"And this was how long ago?"

"Five, ten minutes. No more."

"Thanks."

Pivoting on his heel, Laker set off at a trot. Ava limped after him. Outside the sun had set but it was still light. The neon signs of the stores were just beginning to show their brightness. They returned to the Camaro. Laker backed out of the space, shifted and stamped the accelerator. With engine roaring they took off, weaving among slowly moving cars toward the exit. Reaching the main road he swung the wheel into a tire-squealing left turn.

"Shouldn't you turn right?" Ava said. "That's the way to the interstate. More likely they went that way."

"We just came that way. They would've had to pass us."

"But we weren't looking for them."

"I'd have noticed a red Ferrari."

Laker switched his headlights on high beams, ignoring the annoyed flashes from oncoming drivers. Development tailed off on the far side of the mall, with only a few gas stations and fast-food franchises separated by stretches of woods. Laker slowed as he passed each one, looking for the Ferrari.

They came to a Jimmy Dean's, sign dark, windows boarded up, no cars in the lot. Laker hit the brakes, swung into the entrance. Now she saw what he'd seen, and gasped. A man was lying in the drive-through lane. He was motionless. A smear of blood on the asphalt behind him indicated he'd crawled from the back of the building, trying to get to the road. He hadn't made it.

"Stay here."

Laker was out of the car, leaving the door open. In a crouch he moved quickly past the man. The Beretta was in his hand. He looked around the side of the building. Then he straightened up and holstered the gun, nodding to Ava that it was safe to get out of the car. She hobbled to the man's side and went awkwardly down on one knee. He was a bald, skinny old guy: Walker. She called to Laker, "He's alive."

The man's breathing was loud and uneven. Laker knelt beside her and they turned him over. His skin was dusky, his lips blue. He opened his eyes, attempted to speak but couldn't. On the right side, his shirt was soaked with blood from a bullet wound.

"We have to stop the bleeding," Ava said.

"The bleeding's not as bad as it looks. He's not hemorrhaging. He's asphyxiating."

"But Laker, he's breathing."

Walker's mouth was wide open and his whole torso was quaking with the effort to take in breath.

"His lungs aren't working. Air's building up in the chest cavity and the lungs are collapsing. Have you got a pen?"

"A what?"

"A pen."

She reached in a pocket and handed him a Bic. Laker tore open Walker's shirt, exposing the quaking flesh over his ribs and the small hole made by the bullet. Holding the pen in his fingertips, Laker took aim and deftly plunged it into the hole. Walker grunted.

Ava pulled out her cell phone and began to touch keys.

"Don't dial 911," Laker said.

She looked at him, puzzled.

"He's going to an Outfit safe house, not to the police."

"But he needs a doctor."

"He'll get one. For the moment he's out of danger."

She could hardly believe it, but the next couple of minutes proved Laker right. Walker's breathing became steadily less labored. Some color returned to his face. He swallowed and gasped, "Water."

Ava went to the car and bent to retrieve a bottle of Dasani from under her seat. When she returned, Laker had Walker propped against the wall of the building. The Bic jutting from between his ribs made her cringe. He took the bottle in his left hand and drank, taking several long swallows before he began to cough. When he gave the bottle back, the water was tinged pink. He looked at her, then at Laker.

"You cops?"

"Close enough. We're after the man who shot you."

"Son of a bitch. He fooled me. Said we were partners. But all he wanted was the code. "

"What code?" Ava asked.

Walker didn't seem to hear her. "Soon as he got that, he shot me and pushed me out of the car."

"You'll be okay. Just rest." Laker took out his cell phone.

"Am I goin' to a hospital?"

"Close enough," Laker said again.

44

"The Shapeshifter finally made a mistake," Laker said.

"I'll say. He should've made sure Walker was dead." Mason sounded indignant. He hated it when agents were careless. Even enemy agents.

Laker was at the TSA office in Cleveland-Hopkins Airport, where he'd obtained use of the secure phone line by flashing his Homeland Security creds.

"There were three pieces of the code. Walker explained it to us. He gave us his piece," Laker went on. "So far we have no idea what it means. It's a fourteen-digit number. Ava's working on it."

"But the Shapeshifter has it, too." Mason said. "And he has the two other pieces of the code."

"Yes. We have to assume the Shapeshifter now has all the information he needs to locate the bomb."

"Shit. Where's Walker now?"

"In a Medevac helicopter. On the way to our safe house, the Pennsylvania one. He was cooperative at first. That'll stop, once he realizes the kind of charges and prison time he's facing. I don't think we'll get any more out of him."

"For now we'll keep the bastard under wraps. Anybody who wants to talk about the right of habeas corpus can kiss my ass."

"Walker told us the Shapeshifter said he was an arms dealer based in Geneva, named Brent Armitage, who wanted to sell the bomb on the international market. That could have been calculated to appeal to Walker, but it could be true. Anyway, it's worth checking out."

"I wish it were true."

Laker was confused. "Say again, boss."

"I wish his plan was to sell to the highest bidder. But it's not."

"Wait—you mean you know who the Shapeshifter is?"

"There have been developments."

"You know what he's going to do with the bomb? How?"

"We've sent a plane for you, Laker. It'll be on the ground in twenty-eight minutes. Make sure you and Ava are ready to board."

An aide came on the line to explain to Laker where to find the plane. Laker had to make him repeat it. His brain was teeming with speculations about the Shapeshifter. And Mason's tone of voice, even more than what he said, had rattled him.

He hung up the phone and left the room. In the narrow, windowless corridor, Ava was sitting on a plastic chair, tapping keys on her iPhone with both thumbs. The leg with the boot was extended in front of her.

"I've been a numbskull, Laker. I've spent the last half-hour doing fancy stochastic tricks with the code, trying to break it. A complete waste of time."

In that case, Laker thought, he wouldn't ask what "stochastic" meant.

"Then it hit me. What I should have realized as soon as I saw it was fourteen digits."

She looked up at him, saw he was still clueless. "It's obvious when you group the digits by putting dashes in." She held up a slip of paper, on which she had done so.

"My skull must be number than yours."

"It's an ISBN. International Standard Book Number. I just put it into amazon.com. We'll have the title in a sec."

Ava raised her phone and watched the little screen. Her face fell. "Shit. No result. I must have been wrong."

"Never mind now, Ava. We have to meet our plane. We're going back to Washington."

The plane, a USAF Gulfstream C-37A, landed at Andrews AFB shortly before midnight. An SUV was waiting on the runway to take them to Mason's house in McLean, Virginia.

Mason held on tight to the handrail as he led them down to his basement. He was looking better, though. The bandages were off, the surgical staples removed. There was now only the intricate tracery of healing incisions on his forehead and cheek. A black patch covered his left eye. Laker asked if the doctors thought he would recover the sight in that eye. Mason shrugged and said he'd always wanted to look like a pirate. He was out of pajamas and robe, into pants and shirt.

A computer with an oversize monitor was set up on the poker table in Mason's man cave. A technician was tapping on the keypad. Mason said that he was setting up a secure Skype connection. When he was finished, he nodded to them, went upstairs, and shut the door. They were alone.

Mason said, "Ava, this is going to be kind of hard for you to take."

Her eyes widened. She didn't say anything.

"The man who murdered Tillie was her grandson."

Ava shut her eyes tight in disbelief. "You mean my *brother*? One of my *cousins*? That's crazy!"

"A cousin, yes. But one you never knew about. Sit down."

Three chairs had been lined up facing the monitor. The screen showed a desk with an American flag on a pole behind it. Portraits of the President and Secretary of State on the wall. Laker said, "Where is this?"

"Our embassy in Tokyo."

He heard voices and noises offscreen. Then a woman appeared. As she sat down behind the desk, he recognized the stout figure and untidy gray hair of Joanie.

"Joanie!" he said. "I thought you were in Honolulu."

"She's been busy," Mason said. Turning to the screen, he said, "Joanie, I want you to go over it all again for Laker and Ava. From the beginning. But first I want to apologize for my stupidity. I kept you at the reception desk for too long, rebuffing ordinary citizens who wandered into the Outfit. When you return, you'll have a position better suited to your abilities."

Joanie gave her grandmotherly smile, crinkling the corners of her hazel eyes. "Thank you, sir."

"Last time we heard from you," Laker said, "the Episcopal archbishop's office was stalling you. They'd taken custody of the records of the orphanage where Tillie's daughter had been placed in 1942 when it closed."

"Right. The archbishop's assistant was a stickler."

"But you found a way to get around him."

"Hung around the office and made friends with the secretaries. Bosses have no idea what really goes on in an office."

"I'll bear that in mind," said Mason dryly. "Tell Laker and Ava what you found out."

"Tillie's daughter Kiyoshi—"

"Kiyoshi," Ava echoed.

"Yes. There was a mix of races at the orphanage, as in Honolulu itself. They named children based on how they looked, and Kiyoshi apparently took after her father. She lived in the orphanage for only a few months. She was adopted by a Japanese immigrant couple named Tashiro. Once I had that name, the records search was straightforward. After the war, thc Tashiros moved back to Japan. In 1970, Kiyoshi married a man named Chosuke Mishima, a worker on the Honda assembly line. In 1972, they had a son, whom they named Akiro."

"The Shapeshifter?" Laker said.

"Yes."

Laker glanced down at his lap. His hands had balled into fists. He opened them, flexed the fingers. Akiro Mishima. Now the adversary had a name and an age.

He was a just a little older than Laker. "How about a recent photo, Joanie?"

"She'll get to that," Mason growled. "Stick to chronological order, Joanie."

"I lucked onto a juvie court file that provided a lot of information on Mishima. At eleven, he assaulted an Okinawan schoolmate. Beat him up quite badly, apparently just for not being Japanese enough. The court-appointed psychologist did a sympathetic report. He said Mishima had endured a lot of bullying from schoolmates for being of mixed race. He has East Asian features, but blue eyes."

Laker glanced at Ava. She murmured, "His grandmother's eyes."

"Mishima knew it, too," Joanie continued. "Knew that his mother had been abandoned by *her* mother, who was a Westerner. The psychologist said that his way of coping was to turn into a Japanese superpatriot. He hated the West."

"Was the report enough to keep Mishima out of juvie jail, whatever the Japanese call it?" Laker asked.

"No. He was behind bars for years. But he seemed to rehabilitate himself. He got into Tokyo University, where he earned top grades. His IQ was off the charts, apparently. But there were more violent incidents. Mishima was expelled. He joined the Ground Self-Defense Force."

"The what?" Ava asked.

"It's what the Japanese call their army. So everybody will know that they don't do offense. Again, he did well. Got into the elite Special Forces Group. Rose in the ranks. But somewhere along the line, he was recruited by a secret society of officers. Patriotic hardliners who thought the Japanese armed forces were too dominated by America and too anti-militaristic, and that they'd done more than enough apologizing to their neighbors for World War II atrocities."

"I'm guessing they did not remain secret," Laker said.

"Right, Tom. They went public in a big way. Did you get the video I emailed, sir?"

"Yes. I've watched it five times," said Mason grimly. "Hang on while I show it to Laker and Ava."

His hands went to the keyboard. Joanie disappeared from the screen, replaced by an inset video window with the BBC logo. "This incident took place August 6, 2009, at Hiroshima. It caused a lot of commotion in Japan, but didn't get much coverage in Western media, except for the BBC."

Mason clicked the dart and the video began. It showed the skeletal Genbaku Dome, the Cenotaph, children's monument, and other buildings of the Peace Memorial Park. Paper lanterns drifted in the river. Multicolored origami figures were displayed in gardens. The Peace Bells were rung. A narrator was speaking in Japanese. English subtitles said that this was the annual commemoration ceremony, when the Japanese mourned the dead and prayed for world peace. Its main focus was the moment of silence at 8:15 A.M., the time the bomb was dropped.

The video showed hundreds of people stopping what they doing, folding their hands, bowing their heads. The image blurred as the camera was whipped around. Its operator had seen something. The camera steadied and zoomed in.

It focused on men in front of the blasted brick wall and empty windows of the Genbaku Dome. The men unfurled a colorful poster. It showed a single gigantic flower. The subtitle said it was an oleander, the symbol of Hiroshima. One of the men set down a box and another jumped on top of it. He was wearing a full-dress military uniform, complete except for the cap. In his hand was a long bladed dagger.

"Is this Mishima?" Laker asked.

"Yes," Mason said.

The camera zoomed in again as Mishima began to speak, and Laker leaned forward to look into the real face of the Shapeshifter. The piercing blue eyes he recognized. He'd looked into them before, in Dupont Circle, an instant before Mishima threw the punch that knocked him cold. Mishima's thick black hair was close-cropped and bound in a *hachimaki,* a white headband with Japanese letters painted onto it. He had high cheekbones, a long aquiline nose, a wide mouth with a heavy underlip. It was a distinctive and memorable face. Laker was amazed at the Shapeshifter's skill in altering everything about it.

Mishima had a cordless microphone. In a deep, resonant voice, he began to harangue the crowd, waving the dagger in his other hand. The subtitles said, "Japanese, the Americans said we must turn away from violence. After what they did to us. Hypocrites! They said we must be ashamed of our past. But only violence can take away our shame. The fault is not with us but with the Americans. We have been wronged, and we must take revenge."

That was as far as he got. A roar went up from the crowd. The image shook as the cameraman was jostled. People were rushing at Mishima. Ordinary people, not police. Many hands grabbed at him. The microphone and dagger fell to the ground. Mishima was dragged down from his makeshift platform. He disappeared from view as more people surrounded him. Some were holding up their cell phones to take pictures. Uniformed police were arriving now, wading into the crowd.

Mason stopped the video. Joanie reappeared. "Wrap it up for us, Joanie, please."

"The dagger was a *wakizashi*, or samurai short sword. Mishima was planning to commit *seppuku* after his speech. Instead he was court-martialed and spent three years in prison. The Japanese were outraged. They saw what he'd done as desecration of the dead."

"And then?" Laker asked.

"It gets murky. The Tokyo Police think he became an enforcer for the Yakuza, misusing his Special Forces skills. He was a suspect in several homicides. But this was when he started using disguises, and the cops found it impossible to track him. Six months ago, he vanished completely."

"Okay, Joanic. Catch the first plane home. We need you." Mason broke the connection, and the monitor went blank. Slumping in his chair, he rubbed his scarred brow.

From the door at the top of the stairs came a knock. A voice said, "Sir, can I come down?"

"Not now, Harpring," Mason called back. He looked at Laker, then Ava.

She spoke first. "Obviously Mishima was obsessed with his parentage. He must have dug into it. Somehow he found out that his grandfather was a traitor to

Japan, and his grandmother was an American spy. We can imagine the effect it had on him."

Laker said, "His quest for revenge became personal. He wanted to prove his loyalty to his homeland. Strike back at his grandmother and her country."

"Anybody have any doubts about what he's going to do when he gets hold of Bobby Soxer?" Mason asked.

"No," Laker said. "He's going to turn our bomb against us."

There was another knock on the door.

"Harpring, just wait," Mason called.

"Sir, I think you'll want to see this," said the muffled voice from behind the door.

"Come on down, then."

Footfalls descended the stairs. Laker turned to see Harpring, a thin young staffer with marmalade-colored hair and a freckled face, approaching with a parcel in hand. He grinned excitedly at Ava. "You were right, Ms. North."

Ava's face was pallid, her eyes clouded with shock at all she'd heard. She said, "What are you talking about?'

"The code. It *was* an ISBN. But the book's so old and obscure, Amazon doesn't carry it. The Library of Congress had a copy, though." He set the parcel on the table.

Mason gazed at it balefully. "Thanks, Harpring. Go away."

Harpring looked crestfallen as he turned away. He'd thought he had a breakthrough that would please them. They waited in silence for the door at the top of the stairs to close. Laker was feeling the same bleak premonition as Mason. This was not going to be good news. It was Ava who reached for the parcel and unwrapped it.

The book was a road atlas, titled *Praeger's 1979 5-Boro Atlas New York City.* She opened it at random, looked at a map of South Brooklyn. She said, "The other codes, the ones Orton and Lester had, are a page number and a grid reference, I suppose."

"I'm sure you're right," Laker said. "They'll lead Mishima to the bomb's hiding place."

"The man's luck is holding," Mason said. "Transporting the bomb would be a real problem. But he won't have to do that."

Ava looked at him. "You mean, New York is the target?"

Mason nodded. He was staring at the map, but it wasn't streets and parks that he was seeing. "Eighty thousand people died at Hiroshima," he said. "Seventy thousand at Nagasaki. Mishima will get his revenge. He'll more than even the score."

45

Akiro Mishima arrived in New York as himself. Almost.

He was portraying Tadamichi Esaki, a senior executive from Tokyo, meaning that his own face needed only minor modification. He'd added years and pounds, a little gray at the temples, a bit of flesh under the jaw. The usual tinted contact lenses. To establish his wealth, he had a pair of eyeglasses with fashionable, squared-off frames from Prada, as well as a blue suit, well-tailored to minimize his paunch, white shirt, peach silk tie from Ferragamo.

As he followed the bellman carrying his suitcase, he was pleased to see other men who looked very much like him in the lobby of the Hotel Katabano. The boutique hotel on Park Avenue attracted wealthy Japanese who wanted to enjoy the luxuries of home. Which was what Mishima had in mind.

At the desk he exchanged bows and greetings in his native tongue with the polite staff. They were eager to comply with his requests. Yes, despite the late hour, the *sento,* or bathhouse, was still open. It was equipped with the *denki buro* he preferred. The masseur was off-duty but would be summoned. Yes, he was trained in *shiatsu.* Yes, a full breakfast would be brought to his room early tomorrow: miso soup, *tamagoyaki*, *nori*, and a variety of *kobachi.*

The bellman showed him to his suite on the top floor. It was traditionally furnished with wood floors, *tatami* mats, and *shoji* paper screens. Mishima expressed satisfaction and refused the bellman's offer to unpack for him. Once he was alone, he sat in a *zaisu* and folded his legs. His briefcase rested on the table in front of him. He opened it, and took out a well-worn copy of *Praeger's 1979 5-Boro Atlas New York City.*

P17 was the code number he'd extracted with such difficulty from Theo Orton. As he flipped to page 17, he frowned. Each grid square of the maps covered several blocks. A large area to search. He hadn't anticipated difficulties at this final stage. When he reached page 17, he found that most of the map was blue, indicating the waters of upper New York Bay. Along one edge of the paper was a wedge of Manhattan, on the other a longer slice of the Brooklyn waterfront. In the middle was Governors Island.

The grid reference Dick Lester had provided was J29. The only part of the rectangle that wasn't blue was Governors Island. Mishima was relieved. The island was small. The search wouldn't take long. Now he remembered that in World War II, the island had served as headquarters for the U.S. First Army, of which Capt. Bart Lester was an officer. No doubt the connection had served to facilitate Lester's arrangement of a secure hiding place for the bomb.

Mishima closed the atlas and put it away. Making his plans for tomorrow, he gazed thoughtfully out the window, not noticing the magnificent view of the glittering midtown skyline against the night sky until the floodlit spire of the Empire State Building abruptly went dark.

Having read a great deal about New York, he knew that the floodlights went out at 2 am. It was thc carly morning of August 4.

They didn't get home until the middle of the night. Laker's loft was hot and stuffy. He offered to turn on the central air, but Ava said it would cool the place down more quickly to open the windows. She walked the perimeter of the huge place, heaving up the balky old wooden sashes. It was an unseasonably cool night, and the air that blew in was delightfully fresh and moist. A light rain was falling, which reminded her of her visit here. Less than a month ago, but it felt like years.

Laker was rolling up the hides of the teepee he used as a bedroom. Ventilation, plains Indian-style. Between the wooden spars she could see that he had a wide and comfortable-looking bed in there.

"You want the shower first?" he asked.

"I want the bathtub, with you in it."

She took his hand and pulled him into the one corner of the loft that had walls. The bathroom was equipped with a shower cabinet, but she preferred the big, old-fashioned claw-footed tub. She put in the plug and twisted the faucet handles. By the time she unstrapped her surgical boot, Laker was half-naked. She helped him finish the job, then stood back to admire.

"You haven't put on many pounds since you were a running back at Notre Dame."

"Tried not to."

"Added a few scars, though." Frowning, she ran her hand along a seam that ran across his hip. "A nasty one. How did you get it?"

"That's classified. Stop talking and get naked."

"Yes, sir."

In a minute she was lying back in the big tub, with Laker pressed against the whole length of her, the water slowly rising around them, his hands in her hair, his lips kissing her eyelids, her brow and cheeks, her mouth. Then he shifted lower, hands caressing her breasts, lips and tongue her nipples. After a while, a long while, he gave her another order.

"Sit on the edge of the tub."

"Yes, sir." She hoisted her bare, dripping body out of the water. "But why?"

"Because I can't hold my breath when my tongue is out," answered Laker, as his head went down between her thighs.

They made love a second time in the teepee, and afterward Ava tumbled into a deep sleep. She awakened a couple of hours later, to the dim light of predawn. Stepping out of the teepee and pulling on a robe, she saw Laker in the living area, talking on his cell phone. He was speaking softly, but it'd been enough to wake her. Limping without her surgical boot, she made her way to where he was sitting on the sofa. He was fully dressed in a lightweight tan suit. On the coffee table in front of him was a color photo of a purple flower. It looked familiar, but she couldn't remember where she'd seen it.

Laker ended his call and smiled at her. "Good morning. Shuttle leaves in an hour. We'll get coffee at the airport."

"Okay, I'll dress." But curiosity held her. "What's this?"

"Reproduction of a painting called *Oleander,* by Seiki Kuroda."

Now she remembered. "The poster Mishima and his friends put up, before he spoke at Hiroshima."

"Right. The oleander was the first flower to bloom after the bombing in 1945. It's the official flower of Hiroshima. Most of Kuroda's works are in Japanese museums, but this one, his masterpiece, is in the Whitney."

"In downtown Manhattan?"

"Yes."

Ava considered the implications. Didn't like them. She sat down in the chair across from Laker. He glanced at his watch. "The car will be here—"

"Never mind. Explain this to me."

"Joanie emailed the transcript of the interview with Mishima, after his arrest. He talked a lot about this painting, how significant it was to him of Japanese resurgence. He'll go to the Whitney to see it."

"Before he destroys it along with the rest of the city."

"Only he's not going to, because I'm going to be waiting for him at the Whitney."

She looked at him and waited. But that was all.

"You mean that's your plan?" she said. "Your *entire* plan. You actually got Mason to approve it?"

Laker turned his good ear. "Do you have a better idea?"

"There's something you maybe haven't thought of, you and Mason. It occurred to me while we were watching the video of the Peace Festival last night—"

"It's occurred to us."

She went on as if he hadn't spoken. "August 6 was the day Hiroshima was destroyed. Mishima's revenge will be sweeter if he sets off the bomb on August 6. Today is August 4."

"That's what Mason and I figure."

"We've got to sound the alarm. Deploy every resource we've got."

"You mean have the NYPD issue an All-Points Bulletin for Mishima? Give them that old video? Ava, the one thing we can be sure about is that he doesn't look like that now."

"We have to find the bomb, then."

"Search all five boroughs? In two days?"

"Evacuate the city."

"And cause a panic. Not to mention alerting Mishima. Any of your ideas would alert him." He shifted forward in his seat, meeting her gaze. His tone was grave and urgent. "That would lose us our advantage. Right now, Mishima has no idea that we know who he is and where he is. Finally we're a step ahead of him. We set a trap and he'll walk into it."

She sighed and looked away. "You're very convincing."

"But you're not convinced."

"No. But I can see how you talked Mason into this. Your confidence. Your reputation. Lucky Laker." She shook her head. "*Arrogant* Laker is more like it."

"Ava, we don't have a lot of options. This is the best one."

"We can't risk everything on it. There must be something else we can do."

"What?"

"I don't know."

A car horn sounded in the street. Laker glanced at his watch and got up. He said, "Sounds like you're not going with me."

"You don't need me to sit on a chair in a museum and keep an eye on a painting. I'm staying here."

"Ava—"

"I know, you can have four muscle-bound men here in a few minutes to drag me to some safe house in Maryland for the duration. Please don't. I promise I won't call the NYPD or the mayor or the *Times*."

"What will you do, then?"

"Oh, what I usually do. Go to a library. See what I can find in a book."

The horn honked again. Laker picked up his suitcase. "I have to go. Please call me."

Ava nodded as he turned away. It didn't occur to her until he was gone that they hadn't kissed good-bye.

46

During the Revolution, the Americans had bombarded British ships from an earthwork on Governors Island. After the war, they'd built a massive sandstone and granite fortification on the spot, called Fort Jay, to guard the approaches to New York Harbor. But no enemy ship had ever gotten within range of its guns. The island, having been passed around the Army, Navy, and Coast Guard for a couple of centuries, had recently become a public park.

Mishima had ridden over on a ferry packed with pleasure seekers on a sunny summer morning. It had taken the rest of the day to locate Bobby Soxer's hiding place. But he'd felt reassured rather than frustrated. Captain Bart Lester and his colleagues had done their work well. The hiding place was secure, and he was confident he'd find the device in good condition. Getting to it was going to take preparation. Equipment would have to be obtained, a ruse conceived and executed.

But there was ample time, and no one to hinder him.

This moment was to be savored. He paused before Fort Jay's main gate to admire the sculpture atop it, an American eagle with wings spread, perched atop a cannon, backed by unfurled banners. Then he strolled in the opposite direction from the ferry slip, exploring the rest of the island.

The surroundings became less martial. He walked along a green shaded by tall trees and bordered by an old stone church and plain, spacious houses of brick and wood. They'd been built for officers in the early nineteenth century. Some were being converted to the headquarters of arts organizations, he noted. That might be useful to know.

He wandered on to the island's north shore. The water came into view, and the Statue of Liberty. Turning, he saw the looming skyscrapers of the financial district, so close yet remote on the other side of the water. Here was a refuge from the raucous city. He passed a field where people were playing softball. Others were picnicking or dozing in hammocks. Stepping aside as a group of laughing cyclists peddled by, Mishima reflected that war was a thing of the past for Americans. They still had to send their soldiers to fight in distant lands, and their media told them they were vulnerable to terrorists, but in their homeland they felt safe. How short their memories were. He picked out the tallest and most silvery of the skyscrapers: the Freedom Tower. Only a few years had passed since it'd replaced the fallen World Trade Center.

He joined the crowd for the ferry ride back to Manhattan. Sated with pleasure, they chatted easily among themselves. Mishima was dressed like the rest of them, untucked shirt, shorts, sandals, Mets cap, sunglasses.

He hadn't bothered with the dark contact lenses today. In windy conditions they were irritating. Anyway soon he would be finished with hiding the color of his eyes.

Only a few minutes later, he emerged from the Manhattan terminal into a world of concrete and steel. He hailed a taxi. Traffic was heavy, the ride long. It was a relief to enter the cool, tastefully furnished lobby of Hotel Katabano. The desk clerk bowed as he approached. "Good evening, sir."

Mishima glanced at his watch. It was a minute past five. He appreciated the punctiliousness of the salutation. "I wonder if you could do something for me."

"Of course."

"I would like to have flowers delivered to my room."

"Yes sir. An assortment?"

"No. All oleander."

The clerk was entering the information on a keyboard. "Do you have a preferred color, sir?"

"Purple."

If you gazed at it for long enough, you forgot you were looking at a flower. The artist had painted a single oleander bloom, on a huge scale. The canvas was as tall as Laker, as wide as his spread arms. It was just a circle of five petals, each one a subtly different shape, rendered in multiple shades of purple.

"You must really like Seiki Kuroda."

A guard had paused beside the bench he was sitting on. She was a young Latina with a long braid down her back. Considering what a trendy place the Whitney was, the guards' uniforms were stodgy: black suit, white shirt, black tie.

"Huh?"

"You've been here a long time."

"Oh. Yes. It's the first Kuroda I've ever seen. Maybe it's the flower itself that attracts me."

She nodded. "They're beautiful. But don't plant 'em in your garden."

"No?"

"Oleander's poisonous. Every bit of it, flower, leaves, stems. Never touch it."

"Thanks for the warning."

"But you're safe enough looking at a painting."

Smiling, she walked away. Turned after a few paces. "Oh, closing time is in fifteen minutes."

He nodded. An entire day wasted, Ava would say. He wondered where she was. What she was doing. If she was going to call.

47

Rush hour on the morning of August 5, and Capitol Hill was bustling. Ava was sitting at a tiny table in an overpriced coffee shop. Behind her, the espresso machine hissed and panted. Across the street stood the headquarters of the Gray Outfit. It looked much like the old townhouses on either side of it, now that the bay window Akiro Mishima had smashed had been replaced, as well as the marigolds and zinnias in the front garden he'd trampled. You could almost believe it was, as the placard next to the front door said, the office of the National Alliance of Auto Parts Distributors.

The door of the coffee shop opened and a pale, blond, flat-chested young woman came in. She was the person Ava'd been waiting for. She looked like she needed coffee this morning. As if she hadn't slept well. Weariness and worry put years on her youthful face. As she waited for the barista to make her latte, she was drumming her fingers nervously on the counter.

Planting her surgical boot, Ava rose and stepped up behind her. "Rafella Söhn?"

The woman jumped, twisted round to look over her shoulder. She seemed reassured to see it was another woman, not much older than herself. Kinder perhaps to put an end to her dawning relief, Ava thought. Her first fearful reaction had been the right one.

"I'm Ava North."

Rafella's reaction was instantaneous. She tried to flee. But she only took a step before two men sitting at one of the cafe's sidewalk tables sprang up and blocked the door, watching her with flat eyes.

"What you've feared is happening," Ava said. "At least the wait is over."

Rafella's eyes rolled up in her head and she stumbled. Ava took her arm and helped her into one of the rickety chairs at her table. She called out to the barista to forget the coffee order. She had a glass of cold water ready on the table to offer to Rafella, who took it in both hands and sipped carefully. She was shaking, but she managed to look Ava in the eye.

"I don't know what you're talking about. I want to see your ID before we go any further."

"You know who I am and why I'm here. What you're really thinking about is, where did I go wrong? What was the fatal slip-up? The answer is, you took out a book by Gerald Styron called *The Second Bomb*. You didn't request it at work, you borrowed it from your local library. That was smart. It held me up for a couple of hours."

"I still don't know what you're talking about. Is it illegal to read books by revisionist historians?"

"No. What's illegal is passing secret information to enemy agents. It's called treason."

She forced a bark of laughter. "If you had any real

evidence against me, I'd be in handcuffs and on the way to the federal courthouse by now."

"Your day in court will be delayed. You're going to a Gray Outfit safe house in the country, where you will be interrogated by the people you've betrayed. After Sam Mason has a few words with you."

Rafella looked like she was going to faint again.

"If you answer my questions, it will go easier on you. You may also help to save many lives. I think that matters to you. That's why I'm giving you the chance."

Rafella bowed her head and covered her face with her hands. After a minute's silence she said, "Who is he, really?"

"His name is Akiro Mishima."

"Is he a terrorist?"

"He's something worse."

Rafella dropped her hands. "I was such a fool. I had no idea what kind of man he was until too late."

"You're not alone in being fooled."

"He approached me as Ikio Ozawa, a historian from Tokyo University. I did check him out online, but he'd prepared a false trail for me. He knew that when I was in college I'd gone to demonstrations supporting President Obama's drive to reduce nuclear arsenals. Said that showed my idealism and he needed my help. He seemed sort of shy and clumsy. A foreigner. An academic. If he'd been different, tried to seduce me, it would've aroused my suspicions."

"He's clever. He reads people and prepares a script and role for himself accordingly."

"He told me about the work of this man Styron. He was a physics professor, an expert on technical aspects of the World War II nuclear bombs. His book asks the question, Wasn't destroying Hiroshima enough? Why did Nagasaki have to be flattened, too? His answer was that it was a horrible experiment by the U.S. military establishment. Little Boy, the bomb dropped on Hiroshima, was a uranium gun-type weapon. But the scientists at Los Alamos had developed another type, a plutonium-implosion design they thought was superior. Fat Man was that type. The Americans dropped it on Nagasaki just to see how it worked. They were horrible racists, Ozawa—I mean Mishima—said. The 'Japs' weren't even human beings to them."

"Styron couldn't prove those charges," Ava said. "His work was discredited and his university fired him."

"Mishima said Styron was right, he just hadn't been able to find the evidence. That was why he needed my help. He wanted something very small from me. To locate Styron. After his disgrace, he dropped out of sight."

"Yes," Ava said. "The rumor was he'd gone off the grid, become some kind of survivalist."

"It seemed harmless enough, what Mishima wanted me to do. And not risky. I just had to put in a routine request to all federal and state agencies for information, saying it had come from an officer of the Gray Outfit."

"But that wasn't the end."

"No, of course not. Once I broke the regulations, he had a hold on me. The scholarly disguise was dropped. He wouldn't say who he really was, but I knew he was an enemy agent. He didn't value me as anything but an intel asset. He'd expose me if I didn't do as he said. And what he wanted, of course, was information about Mason and Laker. And you. The raid on the building—was it Mishima himself who broke in, who killed those men?"

"Yes."

"He didn't tell me that was coming. I was as shocked as everyone. But once it happened, I knew I was partly to blame. I was so terrified. I hated him. And myself. But I kept doing what he said."

Rafella straightened her hunched shoulders. Took a deep breath. "What you said before—you're right. I'm glad the wait to be caught is over. The future can't be worse than the past for me."

Ava didn't say anything. She hoped that was true but doubted it. She said, "I'll tell Mason you've been cooperative. I have one more question. Where is Styron?"

Rafella smiled bitterly. "Mishima was never interested in Styron. That was a ploy, to put me in his power."

"It was. But he really did want to find Styron. Do you remember the address?"

"It's not an address. You go north from the village of Hamilton, Vermont, on Route HH. Go eleven miles and there's a road on your right. It doesn't have a name, and after a while it's hardly even a road. But when you come to a house, it's Styron's."

"Thank you." Ava rose. It was the signal the two men had been waiting for. They came into the shop and stood on either side of Rafella's chair. She rose shakily. The man on her right took her elbow and led her away. The other paused to ask, "You coming, Ms. North?"

"Not just now."

She opened her purse and took out bills to pay her check. She'd promised Laker that she would do nothing that might alarm Mishima. Which meant that she'd have to go see Gerald Styron herself.

48

Midway through the second day of his vigil at the Whitney, Laker had developed a pattern that he repeated with only slight variations.

He walked to the window and gazed out at the Hudson River and the skyscrapers on the New Jersey side. Then he crossed to a sculpture that looked like a ten-foot-tall blue saxophone. Next he strolled into the adjoining room and circled a twice-life-size figure of a smiling towheaded boy, made of some kind of shiny plastic. Across from it was a pile of television monitors reaching to the ceiling, where he lingered for another few minutes. Finally he headed back to his starting point, passing a low platform in the middle of the room, on which stood a cluster of man-sized wooden blocks sprouting loops of cable. To himself he called them the gas pumps.

From the corner of his eye, he was able to see Kuroda's *Oleander* the whole time. But walking slowly and pausing among other visitors who were doing the same thing, he was inconspicuous. Mishima wouldn't notice him.

If Mishima ever showed up.

Laker dismissed the thought. He'd made the plan and Mason'd okayed it. Second thoughts were useless and, worse, distracting. They led to memories of Ava's criticisms yesterday morning, and speculations about where she was now. Pointless. He had to concentrate. Appraise each person who approached the Kuroda. Any one of them might be Mishima.

Standing at the window, Laker watched without turning his head as the latest candidate slowly crossed the room toward the huge purple canvas. It was a kid, a Midwestern tourist trying to look like a downtown aesthete, in gaudy sneakers, tight black jeans, a T-shirt that bared tattooed arms, a dumb little porkpie hat atop a pile of blond hair.

Only the hooded blue eyes gave Akiro Mishima away.

The moment he was sure, Laker stopped looking at him. Mishima was preternaturally alert. He would feel a gaze directed at him for too long. Laker slowly turned away. His fingers were vibrating with the urge to draw the Beretta from its holster and shoot.

But there were people moving between them, more people behind Mishima. Laker would have to get closer. He strolled in the opposite direction from Mishima, pretending to look at paintings. Continued until he was between the room's entrance and Mishima. Only then did he turn and begin his approach.

Back to him, Mishima was slowly approaching the Kuroda painting. He seemed fascinated by it, almost in a trance of concentration, but even so Laker didn't risk staring at him. He looked past him to the giant oleander, taking only an occasional glance at the figure in the porkpie hat to gauge distance. He was closing in. He had no intention of trying to take Mishima alive. The man was a master of unarmed combat. Laker couldn't risk his getting away. As soon as he was close enough he'd draw the Beretta and put a bullet in the back of Mishima's head. Two more paces. His right hand slipped beneath his jacket.

"Oh hi there, you're back again."

The Latina guard from yesterday was passing him with a smile. At the sound of the voice so close behind him, Mishima looked over his shoulder. Recognizing Laker, he was paralyzed with disbelief. In half a second he'd recover. No time to draw and level the Beretta. Laker lunged.

They hit the floor with Laker on top. But Mishima used his momentum against him, grabbed his shirt, and kept on rolling. Coming up on top he clouted Laker with his forearm, a clumsy but powerful blow that allowed him to tear himself free from Laker's grip. In an instant he was on his feet and moving.

Propping himself up on an elbow, Laker saw the Latina guard, standing in the way of the hurtling figure, spreading her arms to stop him. Laker started to shout a warning to her. Too late. Mishima's right arm shot out and up, his fist catching her under the chin. The force of the blow lifted her off her feet.

Laker scrambled upright. The gas pumps were in Mishima's path and he barreled straight through them, knocking them over like bowling pins. Laker followed. He was dimly aware of the chaos in the room, people staring at him or Mishima, crying out, backing away or crouching. Passing the guard he glanced down. She was lying still, her head turned at an unnatural angle.

Mishima was exiting the next room as he entered it. He was sprinting down the corridor. A few more strides and he'd vanish down the stairs. Laker had to risk a shot. He stopped, drew the Beretta, and fired.

The nine-millimeter slug blew the chubby plastic cheek off the sculpture of the smiling boy. Twenty paces beyond it, Mishima was reaching the stairs. By the time Laker leveled his weapon again, Mishima was descending them, only the top half of his body visible. Too small a target. Laker went after him. People were screaming, dropping to the floor, shrinking back against the walls of the corridor. As he passed, Laker noticed that some of them had their phones out. Calling 911 to report an active shooter in the Whitney. The police response would be swift and massive.

And the shooter they'd describe would be Laker.

He reached the stairs and ran down them. Couldn't see Mishima. Stopping to take that shot had cost him distance. At the bottom of the steps he was in the crowded entrance lobby. People in line at the ticket counter were looking around with anxious expressions. They'd heard the tumult from the floor above and didn't know what was going on. Laker caught sight of Mishima as he pushed open one of the glass doors and ran out into the street.

Laker followed. Under the hot afternoon sun the sidewalks were uncrowded. He saw Mishima on the left, running toward the intersection. A blue-and-white police car with roof lights flashing plunged to a halt in front of him. Mishima stopped, pivoted, ran to a stairway that led up from the sidewalk. By the time Laker reached it, the two uniforms were out of their car, drawing their pistols.

"Stop! Drop the weapon!" the nearer one yelled at him.

"Federal agent!" Laker yelled back as he mounted the steps. He didn't think that would do him much good. Hoped they'd at least hesitate before shooting him in the back.

Scrambling to the top of the steps he found himself on the High Line. The elevated railroad converted to a long skinny park was crowded as usual on a summer afternoon. Laker tucked his pistol into the front of his pants and pulled his jacket over it. He plunged into the crowd, bending his knees a little and lowering his head to minimize his height. Hoped the cops behind him would not be able to spot him among the people strolling, taking pictures of the river views, examining the flowers planted in the old rail tracks, buying souvenirs or drinks from vendors.

Somewhere ahead of him, Mishima, too, would be blending into the crowd. Laker scanned the sea of bobbing heads, hoping to spot a porkpie hat atop a haystack of blond hair. But by now Mishima would've discarded the hat and wig. Improvised some other disguise.

Sirens were screaming all around him. He edged closer to the railing and looked down into the street. More police cars were going by, light-bars rippling. Some of them would be heading for the next stairway to the High Line. They'd box him in. Laker couldn't allow them to catch him. They'd take him to an interrogation room. They wouldn't believe his story until they checked out his ID and talked to Sam Mason. And then? A federal-state-city clusterfuck. Useless attempts to locate the bomb, to catch Mishima. Arguments. Leaks. Public panic.

The only chance was for him to stay free.

Laker wove his way through the strolling crowd, keeping his head down. He had to get off the High Line. He couldn't jump, the drop to the street was too long. So the only way out was up. Tall apartment buildings crowded in close to the High Line. He scanned their flanks of glass, steel, and concrete. Finally saw what he was looking for.

A row of balconies ran up the building on his left. The lowest one was in reach. Barely. He dodged and wove through the crowd toward it. Hopped up on the railing. Crouched and sprang.

Each hand caught one of the metal uprights that held up the balcony's railing. He was stretched out full length, feet dangling. Something hit his right foot. It was the Beretta, which had slipped out of his waistband. He looked down as it fell to the street thirty feet below. Behind him people were shouting. Somebody bellowed, "Police!" and he knew guns were pointing at his back. He could only hope they'd hesitate a little longer.

Hand over hand he climbed the vertical bars. As soon as his toes reached the concrete slab of the balcony he threw himself forward over the railing. No shots yet.

He got his feet under him and raised his head.

The balcony wasn't empty. A young woman in a

bikini was sitting up in a lawn chair, pressing a towel to her chest and staring at him with wide, frightened eyes.

Laker raised a calming hand. "All I want is to get out of here."

She pointed through the sliding glass doors. He ran into the apartment, spotted the front door. On a coat tree beside it hung a rain jacket. He grabbed it as he unlocked the door and went out to a corridor. There were elevators but he didn't bother with them. Pushed through a door to the stairs and hurtled down three flights. As he crossed the lobby he pulled on the jacket. It was much too small, but at least it had a hood. He pulled it over his head and went out to the sidewalk.

He turned in the opposite direction from the High Line and walked away, not too fast. People would be at its railing looking down. He waited for shouts but didn't hear them. When he came to an intersection he rounded the corner of a building and rested his back against the wall, taking deep breaths. He'd gotten away.

But so had Akiro Mishima.

49

It was dark by the time Mishima reached Gerald Styron's house in Vermont. He took the final turn in the hilly road and emerged from the woods. The motion detectors picked up his car and the floodlights went on.

After Styron's book had been exposed as a fraud and his university fired him, he'd responded with a final broadside against a corrupt and doomed society, and turned his back on it. In Mishima's estimation, Styron had never been anything but a crackpot, and his disgrace had pushed him over the edge. But he was a brilliant physicist, and his technical knowledge of early nuclear devices was solid.

The house was a boxy concrete bunker. Its few windows were high off the ground and heavily reinforced. Coils of barbed wire and cemented-in fragments of broken glass guarded its roofline. Solar panels surrounded the observation platform where Styron was standing with his rifle in hand. Knowing Styron wouldn't recognize his rental, Mishima tapped the pre-arranged signal, three shorts and two longs on his horn.

He parked near the garden patch—all vegetables, no flowers—and approached the house. He could hear the generator that supplied Styron's electricity grinding away. They were miles from the road and the nearest house. Styron appeared in the doorway, without his rifle, wearing one of the ugly denim jumpsuits he had adopted when he became a hermit. He was a skinny, bald man with a gray beard. His habitual scowl was even more unwelcoming than the rifle.

"I'm sorry I'm late," Mishima said.

Styron folded his arms and looked down on Mishima. He was tall enough to look down on most people and enjoyed doing so. "The radio was talking about a ruckus at the Whitney. You?"

"An unexpected run-in with Thomas Laker. What did the news say? Have they arrested him? Identified him?"

"Neither. He's still at large."

"It doesn't matter. He's a spent force. We can disregard him."

Styron chuckled. Only one topic amused Styron, as far as Mishima knew, and that was human folly. Preferably the folly of the person he was talking to. This annoyed Mishima, as did the way Styron was standing in his narrow doorway, blocking Mishima's entrance. "Maybe you're a little too cocky, pal," Styron said.

"What do you mean?"

"Our plan—meaning *your* plan—has a little hitch."

"No. There's no hitch. Laker did not raise the alarm. He wanted me to walk into his trap. He staked everything on his ability to defeat me, one-on-one. And he failed. He has nothing left now."

Styron's contemptuous look hadn't changed. He said, "I have someone I want you to meet."

He turned and led Mishima into the dim, sparsely furnished interior. A figure was lying on the banquette against the wall. Styron turned on a light, and Mishima saw that it was Ava North. Her wrists and ankles were bound with duct tape. The dark red hair was loose and disordered. The gag that covered the lower part of her face was bloodstained. Above it, her left cheek was bruised and swollen. But her dark eyes gazed steadily at Mishima.

"She showed up this afternoon," Styron said. "Of course my motion detectors picked her up and my cameras showed me who she was. So I got ready. Put the Sig Sauer in my pocket and went out to work in the garden. When she questioned me I played dumb. Said I had no knowledge or interest in events in Washington or New York, not since the bastards took my professorship away. My *tenured* professorship, which they couldn't have done if America still believed in academic freedom or any of its other supposedly cherished ideals—"

"Stick to the point, Styron."

"So I just leaned on my hoe and let her ask questions."

"How did she get here?"

Styron's smile broadened. Mishima realized that his voice had betrayed how shaken he was to see Ava North here. "How do you think, pal? She found your source in Washington. Rafella Söhn. Turned her."

"No," said Mishima.

"Everything Rafella knew, she got out of her. How you used my book to approach and recruit her. How she located me for you. And Ava North figured out some things Rafella never did. Like why you need me. To arm the bomb. I would've shit my pants and told her everything, if I was the kind of guy who panics. Fortunately for you I'm not. I waited for my moment and hit her with the hoe. By the time she recovered she was looking down the barrel of my Sig."

"Ungag her."

Despite his scornful manner, Styron obeyed when Mishima gave an order. He cradled Ava's head and unwound the gag. Ava said nothing. Just gazed steadily, coldly, at Mishima.

He approached to stand over her. "It was you I was really up against," he said. "All the way back to Hawaii, I've sensed your mind working against me. Laker was easier to defeat than you."

"You underestimate Laker," she said. "He isn't done yet."

Beside Mishima, Styron gulped. Under his beard, his throat was scrawny. Mishima could see his Adam' s apple go up and down. For all his bragging of a moment ago, he was scared of the helpless woman lying on the banquette. His nerves were going to be a problem, Mishima realized. But for the moment he wasn't interested in Styron. He bent over Ava.

"What are you thinking, cousin?" he asked.

"I'm wondering, how did it feel, murdering your grandmother? Was it any different from all the other people you've killed?"

"No. It's hardly my fault that we never got to know each other."

"She had to abandon your mother. She had no choice—"

"Not even when the spymasters asked her to turn whore? Try to get a man to betray his country? What a joke on the Americans, that he'd been a traitor to Japan all along."

"That's how you came to be. The joke is on you."

Mishima flinched. "No! I chose my identity. I am Japanese. And I chose my mission. Revenge."

"You won't complete it. Laker is waiting for you in the city."

"What's he going to do?" Styron said. Mishima could hear the quaver in his voice. "What else does he know?"

Ava was silent.

Styron stalked across the little room, past his small stove and dining table, to the workbench in the corner. He did all repairs himself, so it was well-equipped. Drills, saws, screwdrivers, pliers hung from the wall in glittering array. Vises were clamped to the bench. "Get the truth out of her!" Styron shouted. "You know how to do it."

"She's bluffing. Laker's no threat to us."

Styron returned to Mishima, facing him squarely. "I'm not going to walk into a trap! We get everything she knows out of her before we head for the city."

"Back off, Styron."

He fell back a step. "Find out what she knows. Or I'm not going. And what are you gonna do without me?"

"You're reacting just the way she wants you to."

"What the fuck are you talking about?"

"She's a temptress. Like her grandmother. Only much braver. She's inviting us to torture her." He bent over Ava, ran the tip of his finger over her forehead and down her nose. She didn't flinch.

He straightened up and spoke to Styron. "She's been trained by the NSA. She will stall us and trick us. Give us scenarios so plausible we'll have to check them out. It took hours to get the truth out of Theo Orton. It'll take days to get it out of her. And the truth is that she knows nothing. Laker knows nothing."

"We gotta make sure," Styron said. "Strip her. Tie her to the bench and—"

"I *am* sure. Shut up," Mishima said, and Styron did.

Mishima bent over Ava again, gently cradled her head, and wound the gag around it. He said to her, "You would have died like a samurai committing hara-kiri. Ritual self-disembowelment. Suffering to show your loyalty. A glorious death. I'm sorry I must deny it to you. But I will give you a fitting death. You will go with us to the city. You will be blasted and burned to nothing along with millions of your countrymen."

He straightened and turned to Styron. Waved him to the table across the room. Styron sat down, still grumbling. "There's no goddam reason why we have to explode the bomb tomorrow except you say it's got to be August 6."

"There will be no change of plans, which means that we'll leave in a few hours. And I want to get a little sleep first, so—"

"Sleep! Are you joking?"

"It's probably too late for you to learn self-control, Styron," Mishima said dryly. "But I value your expertise. What do you have to tell me?"

"You'll recall from my book that Little Boy, the Hiroshima bomb, was a gun-type fission weapon. A crude design. Fat Man, the Nagasaki bomb, was an implosion type with a plutonium core, the same as Gadget, the bomb tested at Trinity. It was a better design. Bobby Soxer will be the same."

Styron bent to pick up a large, heavy box from the floor and heaved it onto the table. "Which means that we can set it off the same way they set off Gadget."

Mishima opened the box and looked in. He saw loop on loop of black insulated cable. "What is it?

"I had a hell of a time getting hold of this thing. Had to find a seller who would take cash and not demand ID. It's an exploding bridgewire detonator. We connect each lead to a high-explosive column. They go off simultaneously, which compresses the plutonium core and sets off the chain reaction. To make them do that we supply them with a terrific jolt of electricity from a large and powerful battery."

"Just as Oppenheimer's men did at Trinity?"

"Yes. With one difference. They sent the detonation signal to the battery by throwing the switch in their bunker a mile away from the blast site. It traveled over a long cable. Not feasible for us. So we'll have to use a clock timer."

Mishima frowned. "Complicated."

"This is a fucking nuclear bomb, pal. You can't light the fuse and walk away."

"How long does the timer run?"

"Five hours."

"We're going to leave it for five hours? No. Far too long."

"Barely long enough. We have to get off Governors

Island. Then we have to get off Brooklyn, which in case you didn't know, is also on an island. I want to be on the mainland when all hell breaks loose. So I can *walk* back here if I have to."

"We can't leave the bomb undefended for that long."

"Nobody's gonna find it. This is non-negotiable, Mishima. I'm the only one who knows how to rig the bomb to detonate, and that's the way I'm doing it."

"Then I must accept."

Mishima bowed his head. Westerners liked it when a Japanese did that, he'd noticed. But he was thinking that tomorrow, when the bomb would be under their hands, would be a different story. He'd bend Styron to his will. There'd be no five-hour wait.

50

The dawn of August 6 came to Manhattan in the usual way, the sun rising from the Atlantic, lighting first the spires of the Empire State Building, the Chrysler Building, and the other skyscrapers so that they glittered against the blue sky. At street level, darkness lingered on a little longer.

An NYPD patrol car driving along near-empty Twelfth Avenue slowed and pulled to the curb. On one of the benches facing the Hudson River, a homeless man was lying asleep. The driver's side door opened and a middle-aged cop, his light-blue uniform shirt bulging over his gut, slowly climbed out. You could tell rousting homeless people wasn't his favorite duty. But the guy on the bench raised his head and saw the cop coming. He made a placating wave and rose stiffly from the bench to limp away. The cop went back to his car.

Head down and shoulders hunched, Laker walked on. He wore a greasy Yankees cap and had a tattered blanket draped over his shoulders. He'd found them in dumpsters. Joggers and dog walkers passed him. Nobody glanced twice at the homeless guy.

He'd seen, on televisions in hotel lobbies and store windows and coffee shops, surveillance video from the Whitney, showing himself and Mishima. The Latina guard was dead. Witnesses were confused about who'd hit her, the man with a gun or the other one. Both should be considered dangerous. The search for them was ongoing.

Laker wondered if Mason knew what had happened. Probably. But there was nothing he could do. It was now too late even to consider evacuating the city, or launching a search for the bomb. Mason would continue to rely on Laker.

Who had staked it all on his hunch that Mishima would pay a visit to the oleander painting. And he had. The plan had worked flawlessly, except that at the crucial moment Laker had failed. Mishima had beaten him again.

The battery of his cell phone had gone dead. Last time he'd been able to check, there'd been no message from Ava. He'd heard nothing from her since they'd parted in Washington two days ago. She might have nothing to report. Might still be mad at him.

Lucky Laker, she'd said. Arrogant Laker.

No question the second description was accurate. He'd proven it. But how about the first?

When you have nothing else, press your luck. It was Laker's old rule. He'd followed it at Pearl Harbor, when his search for Tillie's past hit a dead end, and he wandered the base until he stumbled on the historian's office. Now he turned away from the river and headed east into the city on West 28th Street. He discarded the blanket but kept the cap. He walked slowly toward the rising sun, head up, eyes open for a clue, an idea, anything.

Old row houses gave way to tall office buildings as he neared midtown. Cars and pedestrians multiplied and the noise level ratcheted up steadily as the city woke up and went to work. He passed a line of small palm trees in pots. Soon he was following other pedestrians single-file down a narrow aisle between green banks of shrubs and trees. Merchants sat on folding chairs on the sidewalk outside their stores, keeping an eye on their potted zinnias and marigolds. So many that they attracted a rare Manhattan butterfly. Some of the merchants were negotiating with the florists whose vans were parked on the street. He'd wandered into New York's wholesale flower market.

Laker paused before a sort of frozen fireworks display, dozens of yellow starbursts of gladioli. He frowned. An idea was fluttering around him, just out of reach. Like the butterfly. He shut his eyes to the colors, closed his ears to the noise. Waited for it to settle.

Suppose it wasn't just Koruda's painting that fascinated Mishima? Suppose he was obsessed with the flower itself—the oleander, symbol of Hiroshima's death and rebirth?

Laker pulled out his phone, remembering only then that it had lost its charge. He tossed it in a trash can. He dug in his other pockets as he walked along. Thank God you could still find pay phones on the streets of midtown. He had some quarters. He would turn to his credit card when they ran out. There were lots of florists in Manhattan.

* * *

Ava had begun the long journey shivering, before dawn in Vermont. At the end of it, she was stifling in the heat of the car's almost airless trunk. Mishima had redone her bonds, gagging her, tying her wrists and ankles before they started. He hadn't bothered to remove the surgical boot, just tied the cords over it. She'd hoped she could get her foot free, but hours of wriggling hadn't worked. Flexing her wrists, trying to stretch the cords, she'd managed only to flay her skin till it bled.

She assumed they were at the end of the journey. The car had been motionless for a long time, its engine off. She could smell salty air, hear seagulls crying. There were noises of machinery. But the only voices she heard were Styron's and Mishima's. The trunk lid lifted. Blinking in the light, she looked up at Mishima. "Sorry for your discomfort," he said. The angular face was grave. He wasn't mocking her. "The final stage of the journey will be more pleasant."

Grasping her by the shoulders he hauled her into a sitting position. Then, without any sign of strain, he lifted her bodily out of the trunk and draped her over his shoulder. She struggled to lift her head and look around. There was no one near. She saw cranes and warehouses and the detritus of an industrial waterfront. She recognized it. He was carrying her down a pier in Erie Basin, Brooklyn. He bent at the knee to set her down on her feet. Styron was waiting to help manhandle her aboard a boat, an open twenty-foot vessel that smelled of well-oiled machinery. Its engine was idling. Styron and Mishima were dressed as workmen: boots, yellow vests, hard hats.

They laid her down on a bench and Mishima threw a loop of rope over her, deftly tying her down. The bench was vibrating as the engine idled. Craning her neck, she saw a jackhammer, tool kits, a battery smelling sharply of acid, a lot of other equipment she didn't recognize.

Mishima cast off lines as Styron stepped into a small open pilothouse and put his hands on the wheel. The bench shook under her as the engine's thrumming got noisier. They were under way. Lifting her head as much as the ropes allowed, Ava saw that they were heading north, toward the skyscrapers of Manhattan.

When he entered the suite atop the hotel, the first thing Laker saw was the large basket of purple oleander. He'd expected it. The seventeenth florist he'd called had said that he had a standing order for a delivery every day to Mr. T. Esaki at the Hotel Katabano. Today's had already gone out.

Ms. Sato, the assistant manager, followed Laker in and closed the door, pocketing her passkey. He'd taken the chance of presenting his NSA creds at the desk, and the staff had cooperated. They were a bit concerned about Mr. Esaki, who hadn't been seen since lunchtime the day before.

Laker prowled the rooms of the suite, unsure what he was looking for. It was simply but luxuriously furnished. The big windows commanded views of the midtown skyline. It was very neat. Mr. Esaki, described as a portly, middle-aged man who spoke poor English, had left few traces.

In the bathroom, an expensive briefcase stood on

the floor. Laker placed it on the counter and opened it. Ms. Sato, looking over his shoulder, took in her breath in surprise: sunglasses and spectacles with various types of frames, wisps of false mustache and beard, full wigs.

"I don't understand," she said. "Mr. Esaki is an electronics executive, not an actor."

Laker picked up a small plastic case and opened it. In little wells of storage solution floated dark contact lenses. That wiped away the last traces of doubt. Mr. Esaki was Akiro Mishima.

He went into the dining room, where Mishima seemed to have set up an office, with a laptop on the table, a notepad, a couple of manila envelopes. The top page of the notepad was blank. He canted it toward the light, but there were no indentations of writing from the page above. He checked the wastebasket. It had been emptied. He opened the envelope and slid out the *Praeger 5-Boro Atlas of New York City.* Riffled through it, but found no marks or notes.

That left the laptop. He booted it up. Opened the browser and went to the history. The latest website visited was a city government URL. He clicked on it. The page was headed:

CITY OF NEW YORK
Department of Citywide Services
Construction Permits Office

Laker memorized the room number and address.

"Do you have any idea where Esaki-san has gone?" asked the concerned Ms. Sato.

"Maybe," Laker said.

* * *

Ava lay in the darkness of a large metal trunk, head bent and legs doubled up. It was being rolled on a dolly. She could hear the squeaky wheels. That was the only sound. Mishima and Styron weren't talking. The silence gave way to distant music and laughter. She knew that she was on Governors Island. Styron had been steering the boat toward a pier when Mishima opened the trunk, heaved out long, heavy loops of black insulated cable, and manhandled her into it.

The merry sounds ceased abruptly. She thought they'd wheeled her into a building and closed the door. The box was lifted; she heard the men grunting as they carried it a short distance and set it down. For a while she listened to footfalls, to heavy objects being dropped near her. The men were talking now, but she couldn't make out what they were saying.

Catches snicked open and the lid lifted. Mishima bent and lifted her up and out of the box. His long, chiseled face, normally so severe, was softened by an expression of quiet joy. Her limbs straightened, tingling as the blood rushed back into them. She looked around at a dim, windowless room. A basement, probably. She couldn't tell how large it was. There was a cinder-block wall in front of her. On the floor sat the generator, jackhammer, and other equipment the men had brought.

Styron approached the wall with hammer and chisel. He began to make a gouge in it at waist level.

Mishima propped her against a support beam. He unbound her wrists. Ava tried to fight, to push him back, but he was too strong. He pulled her arms behind her and tied her wrists on the other side of the girder.

He came back to stand in front of her and removed her gag. “Scream if you wish. No one can hear you.”

She didn’t doubt him.

He stepped back, dropping the gag on the floor. “We are in the basement of a warehouse in the Fort Jay complex,” he said. “For you, the last place on earth.”

Styron picked up a rope and tossed one end over one of the girders that supported the low ceiling. He fashioned a crude noose. “We’re gonna make a hell of a racket.”

“That’s all right. We are entirely legal.” Mishima turned back to Ava. “The warehouse is being transformed into an arts complex. As your mighty, peace-loving nation continues to beat its swords into ploughshares.” He had been taking a piece of paper out of his pocket, as he spoke. Unfolding it he gave it to Styron. “Our permit. Post it on the door. And one of these.” He handed over a big, brightly colored poster that said, CONSTRUCTION ZONE DO NOT ENTER.

Styron didn’t obey at once. She’d noticed that he bridled whenever Mishima gave him an order. “You sure we’re in the right place?”

Mishima picked his way through the equipment to the wall. “Old floor plans show a room beyond this one. In recent ones it disappears. Because Captain Bart Lester, working through his connections in the U.S. First Army, made sure of a hiding place where the bomb would be kept safe.” He placed his palm on the cinder blocks, turned to grin at Ava. “It’s been a long hunt for you and me, cousin. Now only this wall separates us from our goal.”

She twisted her head to the right as far as it would go. She could see Styron climbing a short flight of concrete steps. Mishima threw the switch of the generator and it began to whir and chug. Work lights aimed at the wall came on, and in their backwash she could see Styron opening a metal door at the top of the stairs.

Mishima had put on ear protectors and goggles. He went down on one knee and used both arms to heft the jackhammer. He inserted it through the noose, which he then tightened so that the jackhammer was horizontal. Carefully, he guided the beveled, sharp-pointed tip into the gouge Styron had made in the wall. Mishima pressed the switch and the howling, slamming din began.

The Department of Citywide Services was halfway up the Manhattan Municipal Building. That was enough height to give Laker a fine view to look at as he paced. This was the office whose website Mishima had been looking at, and Laker was waiting for the staff to find the clerk Mishima had dealt with when he came in two days before. The Verrazano Narrows Bridge was faint and spindly in the distance, Staten Island a gray-brown blur. Orange ferries crawled like beetles across the blue waters of the harbor, passing between the Statue of Liberty and Governors Island.

He turned back to the room. A formidable bureaucratic barrier of dark oak and wrought iron separated the public from its servants. It had a row of eight windows, of which seven had lines in front of them. The end window was empty. Laker was about to resume pacing when a clerk appeared at the window and beckoned him. The clerk was a stocky African American man with glasses, white shirt and tie, and dreadlocks. He smiled at Laker. "Hey man, they said you wanted to see the guy who waited on Mr. Esaki?"

Laker nodded. Mishima would have applied for the permit sometime before Laker surprised him at the Whitney, when he was feeling free and clear. Laker'd guessed he had used the same identity documents as at his hotel.

The clerk's fingers were flying over a computer keyboard. "I'll bring him up in a sec. They said you're from the NSA?"

"Yes."

"Wow. So what did this Esaki guy do?"

Laker sighed. Every once in a while, in New York, you came across somebody who *wasn't* in a hurry, and it was always at the worst possible time. He said, "He's just a person of interest. You found him yet?"

With deliberation, the clerk adjusted his glasses and scanned the screen. "Here we go. Tadamichi Esaki, vice president of the Hadeo Children's Theatre Foundation. We had to rush that one through. He wanted to begin work the day after tomorrow—today, I mean."

"Where?"

"That permit was a real pain, you know?"

"Okay, but where's the work being done?"

"All Mr. Esaki wanted to do was knock down one non-load-bearing wall. He had the required floor plans, engineers' reports and permissions, and supposedly the whole island has been given to the city, but since it used to be federal property—"

Laker put up one hand, palm up. "Tell me right now. Where?"

The clerk looked miffed, but answered promptly.

"Storage Facility B, basement, Fort Jay, Governors Island."

The jackhammer hung in its noose, silent. Its work was done. The men were now battering a jagged hole in the wall with sledgehammers. At the moment, Styron was leaning on his hammer, resting. Mishima kept swinging away. His bare forearms were slick with sweat and his shirt was soaked through. He was panting. Ava sensed that his calm, triumphant mood had changed. So close to the goal, his nerves were getting to him.

The room was filled with dust. Ava was coughing, and her head still rang with the clamor of the jackhammer. But she had been using her time while the men hadn't been paying any attention to her. Her ankles were tied together, but Mishima hadn't bothered to tie them to the beam. She'd been wriggling her right foot in the surgical boot, making slow progress in freeing it.

The hammering ceased. Ava held still. Mishima stepped through the hole in the wall. Styron, coughing and blinking, approached her. But it was only to pick up the halogen lamp on its stand. He stepped through the hole and set it down. Under the glaring light, he and Mishima were only shadowy forms in the swirling dust. Wood cracked and splintered. They were tearing open the crate in which the bomb had traveled so long ago.

Gradually the dust settled, and Bobby Soxer came into view. About ten feet long and five feet wide, it was black and bulbous, with a squared-off tail assembly. Its metal skin gleamed under the bright light. Styron circled the bomb, muttering to himself as he examined it. Mishima stood back, chest heaving, wiping his brow with his sleeve.

Ava resumed her efforts. At last her foot slid out of the boot. She looked at the chisel Styron had dropped on the floor when he was through with it. She hoped it was in reach.

Another glance at Mishima and Styron. They were only interested in the bomb. She stretched out her right leg as far as it could go. Pointed her toes. The chisel was inches beyond them. She strained until her groin and ankle muscles ached, but her toes couldn't touch the chisel.

She withdrew her leg, tucked her foot halfway into the boot. She could only wait and hope for another opportunity.

The pilot cut the engine of the ferry and it glided between the wooden pilings of its slip. Ahead was the dock and the red-painted iron viewing tower with GOVERNORS ISLAND painted on it. Beyond, low brick buildings and a green hill topped by tall trees. Laker, standing at the barrier in the bow, could hear the wind blowing through their leaves.

A happy crowd, eager to land, gathered around him, talking excitedly. A man and a boy with a baseball and gloves. A couple wheeling bicycles. A family of four laden with picnic basket, ice chests, blanket. A young woman pushed her baby carriage into the space next to Laker and smiled at him from under the floppy brim of her sun hat.

He couldn't smile back. Had to resist a crazy urge to

tell her, to tell everyone, *don't get off this boat.* Ride back to Manhattan and keep on going west, fast as you can. But it wouldn't do any good. He clamped his lips shut and looked straight ahead.

There was an unbearable moment when it seemed to him that the shore wasn't getting any closer. That the ferry had stopped moving. The crewman trying to unlatch the bow gates with clumsy fingers wasn't making any progress. The man walking down the pier to open its gate was moving his arms and legs but not getting any nearer to it.

The spell was broken. The engines came to life, thrumming in reverse. The bow met the dock. The gates swung back. Laker was the first ashore. As he ran up the hill he heard laughter behind him. Somebody called out, "Hey, what's the rush?"

Styron had pulled the halogen lamp closer and was hunching over the bomb. Its bulbous form now sprouted loops of heavy black cable.

Mishima stood watching. He'd had nothing to do for the last few minutes but stand there, yet he couldn't get his breath. His chest was still heaving, agitation growing with each passing moment. He said, "What the hell's taking so long?"

"Demolition has to be simultaneous in each of the thirty-two high-explosive columns," Styron said without looking up from his work. "To compress the core uniformly. If it isn't, the plutonium will just leak out. Like the jelly out of a donut when you bite into it. You want your big bang, pal, you'll let me do this right."

"You can do it right faster."

Now Styron did look up. "What's your hurry? There's no rush till we set the timer."

Ava North said, "There'll be no timer, Styron."

He straightened with a whiplash movement. *"What?"*

"Shut up!" Mishima started toward her. It'd been a mistake to take off her gag. He was going to put it back.

Styron caught his arm. "Go ahead, lady."

"You heard what he said last night. Five hours is too long. He's decided not to leave the bomb at all. So you won't, either."

Styron looked at Mishima, who snatched his arm free and backed away.

"He's obsessed with suicide," Ava went on. "He had the dagger ready, nine years ago at Hiroshima. After he made his little speech he was going to slit his belly open, if the crowd and the cops hadn't stopped him. You heard what he said to me last night. He promised me a fitting death. You think he'll give himself anything less?"

Styron was still looking at Mishima. "You lied to me."

Mishima hadn't wanted it to go this way, but he was prepared. Reaching under his vest, he drew his Glock Ninc.

"I don't owe the truth to a man like you," he said. "A disgraced man. An enemy of your own country. What do you have to live for, all alone in the woods?"

"I think there's not much point in us talking," Styron said. "Cause there's this gulf between us. You're crazy and I'm not. No way I'm gonna stand right next to the bomb and flick the switch. Not gonna happen, pal."

Mishima flicked off the safety and leveled the weapon at Styron. "Get back to work."

Styron turned and walked toward the stairs. He passed Ava without a glance.

"Come back!" Mishima shouted. "One more step and I'll shoot."

Styron paused at the foot of the steps. He said, "You haven't left yourself much room for threats, Mishima. Maybe I prefer a bullet."

He turned and grasped the banister. Mishima fired.

Styron screamed and collapsed. Blood spurted from his thigh.

"No!" Mishima cried out. He ran to the fallen man, bent over him. He'd aimed at the back of Styron's knee, meaning only to immobilize him. Then drag him back to complete the arming of the bomb. But he'd missed. The bullet had hit the femoral artery. Styron's lifeblood was pouring away. Mishima lifted his head to look in his face. His eyes were open, but already he was losing consciousness.

The door at the top of the steps swung open.

Laker.

Mishima backed away, raising the Glock. Laker froze at the top of the steps. His hands were empty. No gun. Mishima held his breath, lined up the sights on Laker's heart. He wasn't going to miss again.

A sudden impact and the gun went spinning into the darkness. Astonished, Mishima looked at Ava North. Somehow she'd gotten her foot free. She'd kicked his hand.

He turned back to Laker. The man was fast. Already he was down the stairs, only two paces away. Crouching, raising his hands, he closed in. "Nowhere to run this time, Mishima," he said. "Let's finish it."

Mishima had beaten him before. But now he looked

in Laker's eyes and saw that the man expected to win. Mishima backed away. His arms were tired from swinging the sledgehammer. No, he admitted to himself. It wasn't just his arms that were tired. He'd been defeated. He wanted only to escape.

One last chance.

He feinted left, as if he was going to try to get around Laker to the steps. Laker shifted to block him. Mishima pivoted and ran the other way, toward the jackhammer hanging from the rope. He pulled it back, flicking the switch. The motor roared to pounding life and the beveled tip became a blur. He pointed it at Ava and let it go. Saw her eyes widen, her mouth open to scream as it swung toward her.

Laker dove, arms straight out, open palms striking the side of the jackhammer. Still pounding, it swung away. Laker fell full-length on the floor. Mishima's maneuver had worked. The way to the stairs was clear. He could escape. But Laker lay on the floor, helpless for the moment. Mishima had only to grasp the head of the enemy who'd defeated him and twist, breaking his neck. He couldn't resist. He stepped toward Laker.

A bolt of agony struck him in the spine. He'd forgotten the jackhammer. It'd swung back, and the sharp tip was pounding through his guts. He looked down to see blood spraying from his abdomen as the tip emerged. Mishima tried to stay alive and aware. The last duty of the samurai committing hara-kiri was to suffer and atone for his failure.

It was no good. Blackness engulfed him.

EPILOGUE

"Laker? Your wood stripper doesn't taste too bad today," Ava said.

She was standing at the old safe he used as a liquor cabinet, holding a glass filled with Speyside Cardhu.

"I told you the taste would grow on you," Laker said. He was at the long dining table he used as a workbench, the pieces of a carburetor for a 1964 Mustang spread before him.

"It's not that. It still burns all the way down. But on a chilly day, it burns good."

It was Labor Day, and ordinarily Washington would have been baking hot. But today skies were gray and a wind from the north was bringing autumn weather a bit early. The many windows of the loft were open, and the city below was almost eerily quiet. It seemed that Laker and Ava were the only Washingtonians spending the holiday at home.

"So what are we going to do this afternoon?" she asked. "I don't mind if you watch football."

He shook his head. "Never did take to the pro game."

She walked over to look at the carburetor. "Then can I meet the Mustang?"

"It's not fit to be seen yet. Too many holes in the bodywork."

"So what are we going to do?"

"We could strike your tent."

She laughed and turned to looked across the room at the pup tent. She'd put it up the first time she came to stay with Laker. "Does this mean I've got a standing invitation to your teepee?"

"Whenever you like."

She kissed him and sat at the table beside him, her hand on the nape of his neck. "Can I ask you something I've been wondering about?"

He turned his good ear.

"What happened to Bobby Soxer?" she said.

"It no longer exists. It was disassembled *in situ* by an expert from the Nuclear Regulatory Commission. The bits and pieces were crated and taken away, the expert sworn to secrecy."

"So no one will ever know."

"If Sam Mason gets his way."

"The Third Commandment of Washington," said Ava. "Let sleeping dogs lie."

"After 'Don't rock the boat' and 'Cover your ass.' "

She continued to fondle his neck as she leaned close to him. "That standing invitation to the teepee. Can I take you up on that, like, now?"

ACKNOWLEDGMENTS

A big thank-you to David Linzee and Marilyn Davis for their invaluable assistance. And as always, thanks to Dominick Abel and Michaela Hamilton.

Don't miss the next exciting thriller
featuring Thomas Laker

THE HAVANA GAME

Coming soon from Pinnacle Books,
an imprint of Kensington Publishing Corp.

Turn the page to read an intriguing sample chapter . . .

1

Don't look at anybody.

His trainers had told him that. All of them. He'd been trained by both sides in this war, and considering they were enemies, it was funny how similar the training was. Especially the dictum *When you're operational, don't look at anybody.*

The danger was that they would look back. Make eye contact with some stranger, and he might remember you. And when he was asked, be able to describe you.

So he kept his eyes on the square of worn linoleum floor, smeared with slush and mud, between his boots. He'd memorized the route, counted the stops, and knew that there was one more stop before his. It wasn't necessary for him to look up at signs.

The tram was crowded. It was one of the narrow, old-fashioned cars they used in the city center to please the tourists. He was one of the standees, holding onto a loop of worn leather, allowing his body to sway as the tram turned left or right, slowed down or speeded up.

He didn't have to look at his fellow passengers to know they were all white. Which meant he was conspicuous. In a country of white people, he was olive-skinned and black-haired. Lucky for him the weather was so cold. He could keep his cap pulled down on his forehead, his scarf wrapped around his mouth and cheeks. His face was almost as well covered as that of a woman wearing a burqa. Only the eyes showed, and he was keeping them fixed on the floor.

A small object wobbled and rolled into his field of view. Bumped into his left boot and lay there. Yellow ring and pink bulb: a baby's pacifier. He suppressed the impulse to look up. No need to do anything about this. In a moment, an arm would appear, as the mother bent to retrieve the pacifier. He would not look at her.

Seconds went by. The pacifier just lay there against his boot. Without raising his head, he peeked out from under his cap brim. Four paces to his left, a baby was sitting on a woman's knee, a pretty woman with bright blue eyes and cheeks flushed from the warmth of the car. She was wearing a knit cap with a yellow ball on top. The baby was fretting, waving his fat little arms around, but the mother hadn't noticed that he'd lost his pacifier. She was talking with the man beside her. Possibly the baby's grandfather. He had a full white beard, round steel spectacles, and a jolly smile. He looked like Santa Claus. A lot of the old men in this country did.

Someone was looking at him. He could feel the gaze, as palpable as an icy draft. Forgetting his training, he raised his head and looked.

It was a middle-aged woman in a head scarf squinting at him, thin lips pursed in disapproval. She'd noticed the pacifier and was wondering why he didn't return it. Maybe thinking he was going to pocket it. She was going to remember him. She'd be telling her friends, "There was one of *those* people in the tram, and you know, they'll steal *any*thing."

Maybe she was about to point him out to the other passengers. Or address him, loudly demanding that he return the pacifier. Then the whole car would notice him and remember.

Letting go of the strap, he bent and picked up the warm, sticky pacifier. Holding it with the tips of his fingers to show he had no designs on it, he made his way up the crowded aisle. The child's mother and Santa Claus were laughing and talking and did not notice him, even when he was standing over them. He extended his arm, offering the pacifier.

The mother's cheeks flushed even pinker and she covered her mouth in embarrassment. Santa Claus took the pacifier and made a show as if he was about to put the grimy bulb back in the baby's mouth. The mother batted it away in mock horror. Both of them looked up at him, laughing, inviting him to share the joke.

He nodded and turned away, moving carefully on the tilting floor. He felt sick to his stomach. That was another reason you tried not to look at anybody. One they didn't dwell on in training. If you started seeing the targets as people, it was harder to carry out the operation.

The tram shuddered to a stop. His stop. The doors folded open and he stepped out onto the platform, into the cold wind. This was the broad avenue that ringed the ancient center of the city. Spires and domes looked black against the dark-gray sky. It was almost nightfall.

The platform was a bright and aromatic island. It was a large, busy one, because this was where the city and suburban lines crossed. It had a roof, with electric heaters hanging from the beams, their coils glowing orange. On long counters, merchants had laid out treats: roasted chestnuts, pastries filled with meat, sausages, smoked herring, fruit, and candy. Funny how the cold air made the smells especially delicious.

On his earlier visit he'd noticed the anti-terrorism precautions. The trash receptacles were just steel rings from which clear plastic bags hung. He couldn't read the notices, but knew they warned people to watch for abandoned parcels. CCTV cameras were perched under the eaves of the roof.

Nothing to hamper him.

He walked around the counter where two women were selling hot chocolate. They had a line of customers and didn't notice as he paused beside the stack of cardboard boxes containing marshmallows. Counting down to the sixth box, he slid it halfway out, inserted one finger in the cutout from the cardboard flap, and flicked a toggle switch. Then he slipped the box back in place and walked away. It had taken only a couple of seconds.

Descending the steps to the snowy street, he took from his coat pocket a rectangular plastic object, which he held to his ear. Anyone giving him a second glance would assume it was a cell phone. It wasn't.

He wished that flicking that toggle switch had set a timer counting down. That would have meant it was all out of his control now. He might even be caught in the blast himself. He'd be thinking only about getting away from here quickly.

But the switch had only armed the detonator. The cell phone was really the transmitter he would use to set off the bomb. The planners had told him it had to be done that way, for maximum effect.

No need to look at his watch. He could hear the other tram approaching. The city had excellent public transportation; the trams always ran on time. He glanced over his shoulder. The suburban tram was pulling in. It was newer and sleeker than the one that ran around the city center. The city tram was still sitting on the opposite track, doors open. The controllers always held it so that passengers could switch lines.

He was passing an old church. Ducking behind one of its pillars, he took the detonator away from his ear and rested his finger lightly on the button. On the platform, the doors of the suburban tram slid open. Passengers poured out. People were stepping out of the old tram, too. They'd been enjoying its warmth until the last moment before they had to change. The platform was thronged with people.

Now.

But as he was about to press down, a yellow dot caught his eye: the ball of wool atop the cap of the mother. Holding her baby in one arm, she used the other hand to raise the lapel of her coat to shield his face from the wind. The old man limped behind her, a shopping back in each hand.

He lifted his finger from the detonator. In a few seconds they would be aboard the new tram. The doors would close. Steel and safety glass would protect them. If he just gave them a couple of seconds.

He fought off the wave of weakness. Turning his back, he pressed the button.

A brilliant flash made the snow sparkle. The pillar at his back shielded him from the shock wave, but the roar of the explosion hurt like ice picks thrust into his ears. He was deafened, but only for a moment. Sooner than he wanted to, he could hear the screams.